Paradise Point

A mid-life Romance

A Novel

Cynthia A. King

ISBN: 979-8-89324-069-6

Table of Contents

Dedication

To Pierre, who, much like this book, is a complete work of fiction

Part One

Chapter 1

Aimee took her eye—and hand—off her grocery cart for just a second. She had to wedge her shoulder to hold open the broken trunk latch of her old Honda while she loaded her items, but she needed two hands to lift the case of bottled water. She turned away for just a second, but it was long enough for her groceries to roll away, only stopping by coming to rest against the most exotic car in the lot.

"Oh!" she said as she put her hand over her mouth. *Dang, I always did have champagne taste,* Aimee thought, and ran over and grabbed her cart. She saw what might definitely be considered damage, perhaps only a paint chip or a whisper of a ding, but because the car was a sleek, black Tesla, it drew plenty of attention. People tended to give it a good once over, prompting the comment, "Wait a minute, is that a dent?"

Aimee looked at the make and swore under her breath. "A fucking Tesla? What kind of asshole drives a Tesla to the grocery store?"

She retrieved her groceries, loaded her car, and put the cart away. Aimee dug through her handbag, looked for a black marker, and waited for the owner of the Tesla, her arms crossed over her chest and a frown on her face.

"Excuse me? Do you need some help?" a male voice said from behind. She turned as a man in khaki shorts and a well-worn navy blue tee shirt approached. He wore Birkenstocks. He looked nice. Pleasant. Good-looking, even. He had hairy legs. The blue tee matched his blue eyes. He was a few inches taller than her and in no hurry as he strolled over.

"Sorry. I'm waiting for the douche bag that drives this car." She pointed at the Tesla.

"Why?"

"My cart got away from me and sorta left a mark."

"Where?" He looked at the spot. "Oh no. And you didn't take off?"

"No, but I thought about it. I could fix it in like two seconds," Aimee said and held up the marker, "but karma and all. I still would like to know what asshole drives a Tesla to the grocery store."

"Here," he said and stuck out his hand. "Let me see that marker."

"No."

Before Aimee had a chance to blink, he grabbed it out of her hand.

"Hey! That's mine!" she said and tried to grab it back. He held it over her head; his height gave him the advantage, and he put it out of her reach. Aimee lunged for it again, this time hooking his arm.

"Give me back my pen!" she said, wrestling with his arm, trying to bring his hand closer. He didn't yield and watched her struggle, but the determined look on her face said she wasn't playing. He only meant to tease her, but she didn't seem to get the joke, so Mitch relaxed his arm, allowing Aimee to snatch the Sharpie away from him.

"What is wrong with you?" Aimee said sharply and put the marker in her pocket.

"What is wrong with me? What is wrong with you, fighting with some stranger over a two dollar pen? I thought you were going to slug me if I didn't let go."

"I was if you didn't give it back."

"I can't imagine what you'd do over a Bic pen."

"Nothing, but if it was my Mont Blanc, I would've slit your throat." Aimee smiled at the visual.

"You're crazy," he told her. "Let's start over. How would that fix this?" He gestured at the dent.

Aimee gave him a look, took the marker out of her pocket, and pointed to the tiny ding in the finish. "See, it's small enough that the light bounces off and calls your eye to it. The black ink would darken it enough to absorb the light, and your eye won't notice it."

He grabbed the marker and tested her theory before she could grab it back. He looked at it and said, "You're right," and passed back the marker.

"Quick, before the guy comes."

"How do you know it's a guy?"

"Because a woman would drive her Range Rover." She pointed at the car. "This probably belongs to some short guy with a little dick."

"Define short."

Aimee looked at him and narrowed her eyes. "You've got to be kidding me. *You're* the driver. The douche bag. The asshole. The pencil dick midget. You know, you could have stopped me at any point."

He smiled, a nice wide smile with white teeth. "Why? You were just getting started. My name is Mitchell Raleigh. I am the driver, but it's not my car. It got repo'd, and I'm driving it to Albany. It's nice to meet you, Ms., Mrs.?"

"I'm not sure I want to tell my real name."

"Then give me a fake one."

"It's Aimee. Aimee Dunsmore." She paused. "Maybe. It's maybe Aimee Dunsmore."

"Nice to meet you, Ms. Maybe Aimee Dunsmore. I think I saw a coffee shop across the street. Let's walk over, have a cup of coffee, and take care of this, but you're buying. That sounds like your real name," he said as they waited for the light to change. "Unless you have a prepared alias, you whip out whenever you get in trouble."

"It is, and I do, but I forget to use it."

"Do you get in trouble often?"

"Usually, I cause trouble. One stupid, innocent, everyday thing happens, and trouble follows. Like this." Aimee pointed back to the Tesla. "People must lose control of their carts every day; this is a grocery store, for crying out loud. But they catch theirs, or they roll harmlessly away. I, on the other hand, managed to nick the most expensive car in the place. It will probably cost more money to fix than I make in a month."

"Yet you stayed to make it right."

"Not really. I stayed to avoid karmic retribution. Maybe I did this and took off in a past life, so I have to stay now to avoid paying for it in the future. I don't know. I felt bad about leaving, that's all."

Mitch held his arm out, his palm facing her, waiting for the traffic to clear before she stepped off the curb. Aimee wondered whether it was because he was a gentleman and cared for her safety or he thought she was a lunatic and would run into traffic. *A gesture of a man with children,* Aimee decided. He dropped his arm when it was safe to cross, and they walked over to the coffee shop.

Aimee gave him an appraising look. Initially, she thought he looked decent enough, but now she'd say he was handsome. He was about six feet tall, with shaggy brown hair and a few more grays than he was happy about. He had dark blue eyes trimmed with dark lashes and a friendly smile. Mitchell Raleigh had good teeth. What convinced her to say yes was his nose. He had a strong bridge, and the tip still held its shape.

He looked like some older hipster dude, and he told her she had to buy him coffee. He called her Ms. Dunsmore. Aimee figured he must not be hitting on her, or else he'd offer to buy the coffee. Mitchell Raleigh was just some guy paid to repo cars.

They crossed the parking lot to The Cafe Nirvana; the logo painted on the door was a coffee cup with steam in the shape of a lotus blossom. Taped underneath was a handmade sign that said 'Restrooms for Customers Only.' He held open the door for her and asked, "Is there a Buddhist temple nearby?"

Aimee looked at him, trying to see if she overlooked the fact he was a weirdo. "Why would you ask that?"

"First, your talk of karma. Second, the name Nirvana."

She relaxed. His question didn't seem too odd in light of the context. "I don't think so. My sense of karma is more like what goes around, comes around, and I think the name means it's really good coffee. Heavenly, even."

It was nice and cool inside, not too busy, so they quickly found a table. He sat down and gave Aimee his order. It wasn't for some complicated drink, just black coffee. She went over to the counter and ordered the same but with extra cream and sugar. She came back empty-handed.

"Where's my coffee?" he asked.

"Don't worry about it. He'll bring it over when it's ready," Aimee said as she took the seat across from him.

Mitchell looked at Aimee and smiled. It was his turn to study her face. She looked back at him, her gaze steady and clear. She had brown eyes, the shape and color of almonds with gold speckles. They seemed to light up from the inside. Her full upper lip looked right at home when she smirked. Her hair was dark brown and hung like a curtain on both sides of her face. He liked her broad smile and the slight cleft in her chin. She was tan and looked healthy, not like those women who baked themselves basted in baby oil in their youth only to pay for it now with wrinkles and liver spots.

Aimee Dunsmore looked like she was tan from being outside doing something like gardening. Her skin was remarkably unmarked, with no freckles or an abundance of moles. No unsightly skin tags or age spots. It was smooth and rippled as the muscles underneath expanded and contracted, not a bit droopy or crepey. Mitchell realized she was watching him look at her and reached for something to say.

"So, Aimee, do you want to keep this off the books or through insurance?" She opened her mouth to reply, but Steve came over with their drinks and a plate of small cookies. He thanked Steve and looked at his steaming drink. He looked at her steam as well.

"Might be a while 'til they're cool enough to drink."

"Well, here," she said and took a wallet out of her small bag. It hung across her body, the strap cut between her breasts. He blinked to break his gaze so he wouldn't stare at the exact place where he inexplicably wanted to rest his face.

"Let's take care of this now and get it over with," she sighed and pushed the papers over. He looked at her and pushed them back.

"Listen, I don't need all that. Just give me your name and number. If it goes that far, I'll let you know." Aimee took the marker and wrote down her number on a napkin. He pulled the napkin and marker back. Both disappeared under the table.

"Hey! That's my marker! Give it back!" Aimee said.

"No. I might need it later to touch up the paint." Mitch sipped his coffee. "It's cool enough to drink now."

"Thanks." She took a sip. "So that's what you do? Repo cars?"

"Among other things."

Aimee laughed at him. He tried to act cool and mysterious but failed.

"What's that supposed to mean? Are you an international spy with Interpol trying to bust a luxury car ring? You're a car thief dealing in high-end cars? Run a chop shop? Part of a drug cartel? You're some kind of secret agent with the Feds?" she said with a smirk. Mitchell smiled.

"This aging hipster look is just one of your many disguises?" Aimee said.

He frowned. "What do you mean, 'aging hipster'?"

Aimee smiled at her direct hit to his ego. "Nothing. I kind of like it, with your shaggy hair and sunglass tan lines. You must spend a lot of time on the water. Do you repossess boats, too?"

"Okay, that's enough of that," Mitch said. "It is a repo. I didn't repo it; I'm just moving it from A to B. As far as any mark on the finish, it has been repossessed. One could argue the prior owner did it."

"That's true. You won't need my Sharpie," she said and stuck out her hand. Mitchell pulled it out of his pocket and gave it back to her.

"Here. Keep it. I have your number now. I don't need it anymore."

It was her turn to frown. Aimee took a sip of coffee. "A fat lot of good that will do you. You don't live here, so it seems rather pointless."

"I'll just keep it in my little black book under 'prospects' should I ever move here."

Aimee couldn't help poking him further. "You really are an aging hipster emphasis on aging. Most people under fifty have never even heard of a little black book."

Mitchell laughed. "You're no spring chicken yourself, Aimee if you know what one is, too."

"Thank God," she said. "I was worried you were going to hit on me. Any guy who calls a woman old obviously can't expect to score with her."

"I figured you'd be a good fit for my grandfather."

"Is he local?"

"Unfortunately, no. He's only allowed out of the home for day trips."

"Oh well." She finished her coffee. "My loss."

"Not really. He has dementia and would forget about you the minute you left the room." He drank the rest of his cup. "I, on the other hand, could never forget you. Ready?" They cleared the table, and he threw out the trash. "Let's go."

They walked back to their cars.

"Do you have any plans for later today?" Mitchell asked her. "Feel like taking a ride to Albany?"

So he *was* hitting on her. "No, thank you. I have a deadline I have to meet. Nice to meet you, Mitchell Raleigh, but I do need to go now."

"The pleasure was all mine, maybe Aimee Dunsmore," he said as he walked her to her car. "Until we meet again."

"Yeah. Sure. But I really have to go."

Mitch had sworn off women since the divorce, and this sudden urge to make a play for her came out of nowhere. He felt a connection he couldn't explain like they had known each other in an earlier life, but he missed his opportunity, and fate would not let him miss it this time. The universe was pushing him toward her for some unknown reason. She was slowly pulling him into her orbit. Karma indeed.

"Goodbye," he said as he walked back to his car. He got in and rolled the window down, prepared to drive by and give her a wave. He waved, she waved back, and through the open window, he heard a male voice yell,

"Aimee! Hold up! I want to talk to you!"

Mitchell had pulled past her. He had to check the rearview mirror to look at the guy who called Aimee, but he was too far away to get a good look. Now, his curiosity was piqued on two fronts; by Aimee and her lack of a ring and the guy who could be his competition.

Chapter 2

"Oh, hi, Billy. What's up?"

"Who's your new boyfriend?"

Aimee looked at him and shook her head. She looked at that familiar face, as familiar as her own. A classmate since second grade, his last name was Dolan, sentencing her to a lifetime of him by her side when called alphabetically. He sat next to her in most classes and stood next to her in assemblies.

Billy reminded her of a hummingbird with ADHD. He was always swinging his head to move the hair out of his eyes, but over the years, there was less and less to move. He had good teeth thanks to thousands of dollars of orthodontics, and his skin has cleared up since high school. He grew into his looks and later grew out of them. He was divorced and moved back to live with his parents.

"He's not my boyfriend. Why, what's it to you?"

"Nothing. I wondered where I could buy a Tesla." He sounded envious.

"I couldn't tell you. I only talked to him because my cart dinged his car."

"Was he pissed?"

"Not really. He's just passing through. Besides, shouldn't you move out of your parents' house before you buy a ride like that?" Aimee laughed.

"Yeah, that child support's a killer." Billy smiled and flicked what was left of his hair out of his eyes. "I used to be so cool. Now I drive a minivan."

"Oh well. Good to see you, Billy. I've got a deadline I need to meet, so I've got to go. See you around," Aimee said as she got in her car and headed for home. She arrived, brought the groceries in and put them away. Aimee gave neither

Mitchell nor Billy a passing thought and got ready to work. Aimee went into the small den she used as an office. It used to be her Dad's, but he let her have it when he retired. She powered up her computer and went to work. Aimee did have a deadline.

Aimee got up the following day, and her mind wandered to the past as she sat in the same kitchen chair she sat in since she was a little kid. The only difference was she drank coffee now instead of chocolate milk. She got lost in her thoughts of the past, how this place used to be a home, a hub of noise and activity, only now so quiet you could hear the clock tick and the furnace kick on. Even though she lived through so much and enjoyed all kinds of adventures, to think it started all those years ago with her first job after college at Paradise Point.

Chapter 3

Aimee's mom died entirely by surprise due to a ruptured blood vessel in her brain. Her dad came home from work and found her collapsed on the kitchen floor. It threw the whole family into shock. Nobody ever thought about Marie Dunsmore not being there.

Aimee was the youngest of four. Her brother Eddie was the oldest, then Carrie, her brother Sam, and Aimee, the littlest sister. She was a junior in college when her mom died. Her brother graduated the year before; he was back at home looking at career options. Sam stayed there to keep their dad company while he searched. Sam found a job that required him to travel, but he was in and out, so their dad wasn't home alone too often. Aimee came home after she graduated, which allowed Sam to accept a promotion and relocate to Washington, DC.

Aimee didn't mind returning home; she needed to do some career evaluating of her own. Her degree in creative writing qualified her for nothing. She thought about getting her MFA, but that would only qualify her for a better class of nothing.

Aimee considered moving to NYC, but the publishing world was getting tighter and tighter; the age of digital media changed the landscape of the printed word, and she couldn't quite make herself sign on for so much with so little return.

She freelanced articles and substitute taught, leaning towards getting her teaching certificate. Aimee didn't want to teach, though; she didn't like the kids. She thought the kids were rude and disrespectful. They all wanted to be rappers, anyway.

Aimee's dad started dating; he met a woman named Sally through a friend. She was the exact opposite of her mother. Where her mother was smart and quiet, Sally was loud and vivacious. A tall, bleached blonde with an outrageous manicure who watched reality shows like 'The Bachelor' or 'Wheel of Fortune.' Marie Dunsmore never watched TV. Sally owned her own hair salon and did very well.

They were both sides of the same coin: a woman who would tend to Joe's needs, and he'd love her and care for her, and the woman who took a chance on him many years ago and gave him such a wonderful home and family. He'd love her forever, but Marie Dunsmore was in his past. Sally fit seamlessly into their lives.

The children were adults now, so changes could be made absent the guilt or betrayal that sometimes occurs when a person has moved on. There was no need for the support his kids had gone out of their way to provide, but Aimee had nowhere else to go, so she stayed. She debated her options when her old college roommate called with an offer that would set her down the career path she was on today.

***

Her roommate's father was a lawyer in the entertainment industry and needed a ghostwriter. A much-loved movie star who had become a recluse the past twenty-five years was coming out of retirement, starring as the matriarch of this multigenerational family saga. Its release date is set to coincide with Dolores Reardon's ninetieth birthday. Some P.R. Hack thought some presence in print would maximize her return on all fronts. It morphed into a memoir.

She requested a young girl who would function as her ghostwriter or a transcriptionist to take every memory Dolores could recall and stitch it all together in part tell-all/ part farewell. Her involvement was to remain anonymous.

“My dad asked me if I knew of anyone, and I thought of you,” Carson said.

Now that’s a name that belongs up in lights, Carson Withers, Aimee thought. “I’m still unknown. The only other person who knows who I exist is the mailman, but he thinks he thinks my name is ‘Occupant.’”

“Find a lawyer,” Carson told her. “My dad’s FedExing you a contract. They need a quick turnaround time. They want you to stay at her compound for the summer and turn whatever she shares into a book by September. She’s got this enormous place in the Hamptons. I think it’s called ‘Paradise Place’ or something like that. There are worse places to stay.”

***

Before Aimee knew it, she was living in Dolores Reardon’s pool house. It was set up with the latest technology, a desktop computer and a dot matrix printer to help her with a quick turnaround time.

The first time she met Ms. Reardon, she was scared. Aimee wasn’t sure if she was what the actress wanted. Sure, she was young, unknown, and unpublished, but what if their personalities clash? Aimee figured she was a star years before she was born; the movie star was probably used to fixers and sycophants. Aimee decided just to shut up and let her reminisce, record it, and type it up for review the next day. She figured she’d know the best approach after their first meeting. Aimee was to meet her at three p.m. in the ‘salon.’

Aimee thought she was already in over her head because she wasn’t sure what was meant precisely by ‘salon.’ The housekeeper, Rita, came promptly at 2:55 to usher her into the main house. They entered through a side door to access the living quarters. Aimee was shown into a small sitting room, small being a relative term because the house was huge. Aimee placed her recorder and a small notebook on the table next to the oversized chair she sank into and waited for Ms. Reardon.

She appeared precisely at three p.m. She was casually dressed for a movie star, with silky pants and a flowing blouse. A brightly colored scarf was draped over her shoulders. *What did I expect? Her to lounge around in a ball gown?* Aimee thought. She was taller than Aimee expected. Even if she walked slowly, it was sure-footed. Her face was the same one she was born with, showing the years; her skin wrinkled and sagged, but her eyes were clear, and the distinctive green color she was known for was as bright as ever. Aimee stood up to introduce herself. Dolores had a short, sharp, blonde bob. Her hair moved with her head.

"Hello, Ms. Reardon. I'm Aimee Dunsmore, the writer the book company hired to help you gather your thoughts together for your book."

"Aimee. How lovely." She reached out and took Aimee's hand with both of hers. "It's so nice to meet you. I'm Dolores Reardon, but you can call me Dodo. Take a seat, and let's chat."

A Hollywood legend who goes by Dodo? This assignment is looking better and better, Aimee thought.

"Nice to meet you, Dodo. Why don't you tell me a little bit about what you think your book should say to the average reader? There is a whole shelf of books by famous people. Why should the reader pick yours?"

"That's an excellent question. Why choose my story?" Dodo mused.

"The main purpose is to celebrate your comeback and ninetieth birthday."

"Oh, pooh. My comeback. I never went anywhere. And my birthday? Sometimes, it's a curse to live this long. Let's have a cocktail and discuss this over a drink. What would you like?"

"Oh, I'll just have a glass of white wine. Chardonnay is fine." Aimee didn't drink, as a rule, but she was taking her cues from Dolores. Rita appeared out of nowhere with an Old Fashioned for Dodo and a glass of wine, perfectly chilled, for Aimee.

"Well," said Dodo, "if you were looking at that wall of books, why would you choose mine?"

Well played, thought Aimee. "Now, that is an excellent question. If I were looking at that wall, I'd see your name. Everyone knows your name, but so little about you. Pretty soon, all it will be is a clue in the Sunday Times Crossword Puzzle if we don't get you back in the public consciousness.

"If I picked up your book, I'd be looking for some juicy details. I don't think your humble beginnings would be a draw. Most people have humble beginnings. The public's fascination with celebrities should be your hook. Think about it. Old Hollywood Glam, in contrast to all these pseudo-celebrities who think their lives are so valuable, buys space in the tabloids and hires photographers to follow them around.

"I think what people want to know is not all this tabloid stuff; they want the truth about celebrities. You're famous for having five husbands, but why those men? What did they bring to the table that made you say yes? I think we should turn the recorder on, and you tell your stories—just your memories about how it was in the business. There's that famous story about how you were discovered. You worked in the shoe department at Bloomingdales and sold some Hollywood bigwig's wife a pair of shoes. The next day, she brought her husband in to meet you, and the rest is history.

"If the truth is better, tell it. If not, let it alone. Over your career, you have worked with a lot of famous people. I'm sure you have lots of memories regarding the treatment of women back in the day. The treatment of minorities. Like Jimmy Cagney was a practicing Satan worshipper, not really, but you know what I mean. Little tidbits like that.

“You recently finished a role in what’s supposed to be the mega-blockbuster of the year. You were also the star of one fifty years ago, *The Road to Forgiveness*, maybe some comparisons between the two and how the business has changed. Let’s make it more of a memoir rather than an autobiography. If you have any pictures you’d like to include, the story of why it’s important enough to have in the book should be in there, too.

“What I’d like to do is spend time recording your memories, type them up, and read them out loud. If you like the sound of it, we keep it. If not, pitch it out. After we do this for a while, we can decide how to lay the book out. Chronologically, or chapters, or by sections. If we did a section on parties, the first page should be a photo of you in full glamour mode. If you have scrapbooks, we could mine those for memories.”

Dolores looked at Aimee and sipped her drink. “I like you. I like how you want to tell my stories. Let’s do this: start at two, have a cocktail at three, and keep going until I get tired or hungry. That way, you have all morning to type up the previous day. Not only do I have scrapbooks, but my mother also saved everything; I have journals I wrote during every film. I saved them to use now; I thought I might want to write my autobiography someday. Now, I think I’ll let you do it. Let’s start tomorrow. I hope you’re comfortable in the pool house. Swim as much as you like, and feel free to walk the beach. Just let someone know if you’ll be alone.”

***

Chapter 4

The two of them bonded over the experience. They formatted it by decades. Each chapter was introduced with a photo hand-picked by Dodo. It ended with a collage of scrapbook clippings culled from her mother's collection. Katherine, the editor, was all over Aimee and wanted daily updates. Aimee said no. The impressive length and breadth of the project were what sold it; sending it in little bites diluted it.

Aimee was able to send her the first three chapters and polaroids of the corresponding photos. Katherine immediately wanted to pull her from the project and replace her with a more seasoned writer. Dodo laughed when she heard that.

"Give me that phone. I'll call that woman and deep-six the whole project. You are exactly who I need to do it the way I want. You just let me be. If I didn't feel like talking, you didn't make me, but you knew when you started looking at all those pictures, I'd start explaining them. I talked even when I didn't know it.

"It feels like a celebration of my life, not just my career. We may have to throw a party when we're finished, invite all those hotshots out here and show them all your hard work."

"I think that's a great idea. The last chapter should be all about the charity work you've been doing since you disappeared. You are instrumental in preserving the ecology of this stretch of beach. You created the Forever Wild Paradise Point Dune Preservation Association to keep it from developers. You were a tree hugger before it was popular. Rumors about poor health confined to a hospital bed, my ass," Aimee said.

In the third week of August, the publishing house was sending out a photography specialist to curate the images, and Katherine was coming, too. She couldn't stand the way Aimee was integral to its success. Little miss, nobody pulled it off in spectacular fashion.

"As long as they're gone by three p.m." Dodo laughed.

"I think she wants to decide on the cover photo. Little does she know we have that settled, too." They both liked a picture that had never been published before, from when she won her first Oscar. She was standing there in a stunning silk Grecian column dress, holding the Oscar over her head in one hand with a triumphant smile on her beautiful face.

"I look like the Statue of Liberty." Dolores laughed.

"You look like a winner. The best revenge is living well."

"I am a winner. As you age, some things you recall, as a matter of fact, while some get lost in the sheer volume of experiences one has. Putting together this book has allowed me to relive my life, the joys as well as the tears. We didn't hold back any juicy gossip, either. I forgot about the time I got so mad I pulled off Joan Crawford's wig at the *Rancheros* premier."

"Yes. Thank goodness your mother saved some article about it from a movie magazine."

"I've decided to dedicate this to my mother. She was my biggest fan. I'm also calling it *A Well Lived Life, a memoir by Dolores Reardon as told to Aimee Dunsmore.*"

"I'm not sure that's going to fly. I'm supposed to be a ghostwriter. Anonymous."

"I know that's what I said I wanted," Dodo said. "I didn't want someone with a preconceived idea about who I was and drive the book towards their vision. I didn't have a vision. I thought it was going to be some marketing piece to go along with the movie. What we created, though, is something that can stand on its own. We created the history of me. My stories of the good old days of old

Hollywood. Stories about my old friends and enemies, how I've managed to stay relevant all this time."

"Um, Dodo, I don't think that last statement is correct. Most people think you're dead or severely incapacitated. There are people my age that probably have never even heard of you."

"I don't know if you know this, but I'm considered a Gay Icon because of my early work with several AIDS/HIV charities," Dodo shared. "I lost quite a few friends who were in the closet, afraid to reveal their diagnosis. I supported them right to the end and even paid for a couple of funerals. I helped humanize the AIDS crisis. I raised money and funded research to take it from a death sentence to a manageable disease. The Gay community has been part of my most loyal fanbase."

"We mentioned it in the book but didn't go into depth about it. I had no idea how important you were in the early days. We mainly focused on your environmental causes and conservation."

"I'm sorry we didn't go in-depth, but that's not why I did it. I assumed most people knew about it; there have been so many medical advancements. What I did was so long ago." Dolores shrugged.

"If it weren't for what you did all those years ago, there wouldn't be the medical advances they use today." Aimee pointed out.

"There's nothing Hollywood loves more than a good comeback story. Being reintroduced to the world as the grande dame of Hollywood that's what's putting all this together: the book, the movie, and my career. I can't wait to see Meryl's face when I win the Oscar."

"Dodo, you are in a supporting role. This whole project was to use you and capitalize on your reputation to 'put asses in the seats.' Be grateful they don't want to exploit you. They want to honor you."

"Oh, pooh. Hollywood is all about illusion. They want movies to make money nowadays. It always was about money. Actors delude themselves; they think they are 'Artistes.' I can put asses in the seats, as you say, but I don't have the responsibility of carrying the film. The big-name stars of the project have that job.

"Thank you, Aimee. I am going to be ninety. People don't live forever, and when I die, I'm sure there will be some posthumous documentary about me. At least I've made my statement now. Anything to the contrary, I don't give a shit about. It's Me, About Me, by Me." Dolores held her arms wide apart.

"Maybe that should be the book title."

"It's my swan song. I'll be going out on top."

"Well, don't go anywhere soon. Now comes the hard part. Promoting it all. Do we launch it before the movie, so you can do the press and create a buzz about the movie, or after, when people see you and want to know more?"

"Before. This is about my life. That other thing is just a movie."

"I'm not sure we have any control over the launch anyway. Why don't we have a cocktail party, like an inside launch, for the publishers and anybody else who worked on the book? You should have it here. People will start talking about how beautiful this place is and figure no wonder she's been MIA. She's not a recluse; she lives in paradise. Once you're here, who needs the outside world?"

"That's a wonderful idea. Let's have a mock-up or trial run, but I want to celebrate. When the book people come in August, make sure I remember to mention it."

"Do I get a plus one?" Aimee asked.

"Darling Aimee, I have no idea what that is," said Dolores.

"A date."

"You can bring anyone you want. I've dominated you all summer. I didn't even think you might have someone special in the city. I didn't realize you were sacrificing your personal life to work on this."

"Nothing quite so romantic. I don't know anybody in the city; I live about five hours north of there. There's nobody special at home."

"Well, who is it? I didn't know you went out socializing. I retire rather early, so you do have plenty of time to get out and meet people. You're so young and pretty. I'm not surprised you found somebody special."

"Wait a minute. I don't go out and socialize. I've walked into town a few times to go shopping, but that's it. I mostly swim here and walk the beach at sunset."

"Again, I ask, who is it?"

"The FedEx guy. His name is Connor. I've talked to him a couple of times because of all this shipping back and forth. I get the door if Rita's busy. I've met him a few times while walking the beach at sunset. He seems like a nice guy. He's always going to these big, fancy places for work, but I don't think he's ever been invited inside one. I think he'd enjoy it."

"He must like you; all the beaches around here are private. He's trespassing." Dolores pointed out.

"Oh. I think most of these places are vacation homes, unoccupied most of the time. He would know which ones are vacant and access the beach that way. You are the only full-time resident I've seen."

"Then you must invite him. He's been a part of this book, too."

"I guess he has, hasn't he? How would all the back-and-forth communication get done if not for him delivering it?"

***

Chapter 5

Aimee liked to walk the beach in the early evening; she loved to time it so she could sit on the deck stairs and watch the sun drop below the horizon. Sometimes, Mother Nature got out her paintbrush and treated her to blazing colors. Other times, she used a lighter touch and softer palette and washed the clouds in indescribable colors like baby doll pink or unicorn purple.

Afterward, she walked up the Dune Association-approved deck walkway to Dodo's large expansive green lawn. She walked past her little cottage and into the French doors of the main house's kitchen. Just like the refrigerator of her parent's house, she stuck her head and whined, "There's never anything to eat in this house,' only this time, she was overwhelmed with the choice of it all. Aimee usually got an ice cream sandwich and headed back to the pool house to bang out whatever she had left to do, watch TV, and read. By the time the TV timer went off, she was usually asleep.

***

The following day, she was looking for a package. Aimee called out, "Rita? Rita? Have you seen a package?" She was by the front door when she heard knocking. "Rita? I'll get the door." She opened the door; it was the FedEx guy.

"Hello," Aimee said. He was wearing shorts that stopped above his knee; she thought he had cute calves. He wore a logo snapback cap. When he smiled, he had dimples and a strong chin.

"Hello. I have a package for Aimee Dunsmore."

"That would be me," she said and reached for the box. "Thank you."

He handed it to her but didn't release his hands. "Where are you always walking to? I drive a lot, so it's not uncommon to see people walking around, but I see you more often. Where are you going, Aimee Dunsmore?"

"Why should I tell you? I don't even know your name."

He held out his ID badge and dangled it in front of her. Connor Edmond, it read.

He let go of the box to get his badge, and she grabbed the box and held onto it.

"Hello, Connor Edmond. I'm not going anywhere when I walk. It's mostly to move around after typing all morning. At night, it's mostly to catch the sunset."

"Nice to meet you, Aimee. Maybe I'll see you out and about."

"Maybe." She said as she smiled through the door at him. Aimee turned and walked down the hall to the kitchen.

Rita knew it was wrong to eavesdrop but didn't want to interrupt. She smiled at Connor. Whenever she answered the door to him, he was always looking over her shoulder deeper into the house in the hopes of catching sight of Aimee. Today, he had the good fortune to meet her.

***

Aimee went out for nightly strolls and found him cutting between houses to join her. Every once in a while, he'd reach for her hand, and she let him hold it.

Connor was a few years younger than her; he was in his last year of college studying to be a mechanical engineer. Connor thanked her for all the work. It was a summer job, and Aimee's project kept him busy. He went to NYU but grew up out here. Where to everyone else, it was paradise; to the locals, it was hell.

The population almost tripled in the summer, crowding the restaurants and sidewalks. The traffic was so heavy it took an hour to go ten minutes in the off-season. They needed the economic boost to the town's bottom line, so they endured the crush. Connor wanted to leave and not come back. It was freezing cold with a cutting wind most of the time in the winter. He was not done in the city and planned to stay there or go somewhere else after he graduated.

"Look," Aimee said, holding up their entwined fingers, "I'm not interested in a one-night stand or even a summertime stand. I'm here to do a job, and then I leave. You really shouldn't waste your time. Find some cute girl you went to high school with and have a meaningless affair; she'll seek you out at the reunion to try to pick up where you left off."

"Will you kiss me? Hey, don't look at me. You're the one who brought it up. Will you kiss me?" He waited for her answer.

"Do you have herpes?" Aimee asked him.

"Absolutely not!" he said with an indignation he couldn't fake.

"Okay, sure. Maybe later."

"Okay. Let's walk."

Aimee pulled on his hands, and they walked to the deck stairs. They sat close to each other on the steps. The sun went down, and he kissed her. Connor sighed. "I wish circumstances allowed us more time to see if this would develop into anything."

"That would be nice. We seem to get along quite well."

"Who knows about the future? All I care about is right now," he sighed and kissed her again. And again.

It was her turn to sigh. Aimee kissed him back. "Who knows?"

It was getting dark, and she walked him up to the road, cutting through Dodo's yard. "Let's do this again tomorrow night. I leave next week." He kissed her and started walking towards town. Aimee headed back and came in through the front door.

"I see you, Rita. Have a good night," she said into the darkened front room.

***

Aimee walked through to the pool house. Everything was finishing up. The book. Connor. Her stay. Time to get used to being back in a small town living a small-town life. Aimee wondered how she could do it after spending time here. It wasn't the lap of luxury where she spent the summer; it was the vastness of it all. The sky. The ocean. Even Dodo. Her life had been lived, well, larger than life. *I could live to be her age and still not have half the experiences,* Aimee thought.

She also considered the vastness of Dodo's loneliness; her only contact was with business associates or Rita and Mr. Jimmy. She was ninety years old, with nobody to show for it. No family ever called. She never had any natural children, and her stepchildren never showed any signs of caring.

Aimee was sure as soon as Dodo's health failed and she was on death's doorstep, they'd show up like vultures fighting over carrion. She hoped Dolores could hold out until her moment of triumph. She deserved it.

The following day, there was a knock on the front door. It was Connor.

"Good morning," Rita greeted him.

"Good morning, Rita. I have something for Aimee Dunsmore. Is she here? I'd like to deliver this personally."

"I think you might need to go around to the pool house, but she could be in the kitchen. Let me check."

Rita walked into the kitchen. Aimee was in the kitchen making a cup of coffee. "Someone's at the door for you."

"Thanks, Rita," Aimee said, with a big smile on her face. She headed to the door while Rita followed discreetly behind her. Rita went into the dining room and cut over to the living area. She pretended to dust; her real purpose was to listen to the conversation happening at the front door.

"Oh, hi, Connor. How are you today?" Aimee said and leaned against the door frame.

"Hi there, Aimee. This is for you." He handed her the envelope. "I just wanted to double-check you're going for a walk tonight. I won't be around anymore. Today's my last day. I'm leaving this weekend. I wanted to walk the beach with you one last time and watch the sunset."

"Yeah, sure. I'd like that. I'll meet you down the beach later." She took his delivery and shut the door, a smile on her face. She went back to her cup of coffee. She liked to sit at the kitchen table of the main house, drink her coffee and read in the morning. The kitchen of the main house was large and full of windows. She could make coffee and have it in the pool house, but it didn't catch the morning sun like the kitchen of the main house. Rita followed her.

"The man at the door is very nice, Miss Aimee. I think he likes you."

Aimee blushed. "Yes, I think he does. It's been a really low-key summer thing. We just walk the beach and talk. He's leaving to go back to school."

"You know, Miss Aimee, Mrs. Reardon has been alone for many years. This past summer has been so good for her; to have you here brings life to this place. I know she made that movie, but that was work. Hearing you open and close doors and the doorbell ring brought life back to her. Making that book let her live her life all over again. She loved that, and she just adores you."

"I wondered about her being so isolated. For a woman who was so far ahead of her time, to fade away wasn't right. She was here and made her mark. People should know about the real her. To live alone out here makes no sense. Dodo should be out there and give other women the courage to live the life they want.

"I'll make sure she enjoys her last hurrah as much as I can. The book will give her a chance to be in the spotlight, and she won't have to share it with anybody else. Solo, center stage. Right where she belongs. And Rita, I know you're old school and all, but you don't have to call me 'Miss.'"

"It's easier that way. I don't worry about mixing up the order of things; if I have to start worrying about which one is which, I'd have to retire. Not really. She hasn't had this many visitors, ever—maybe the film people. Miss Dodo enjoyed herself. She was looking forward to making a movie. The volume of people involved overwhelmed Dodo. She did her scenes and couldn't wait to return to the serenity of her house. She told me that. You came and stayed all summer. She had a ball reliving her life for your book. Having someone to share it with one last time made her happy."

"I know, Rita. She's not even close to being done. Her ninetieth birthday is in January. The book launch and the tour. The movie premiere, and press."

"She should hire you and have you help her. Be her escort. You know her well enough to tell her things like, 'You need to take a nap if you want to stay up later.' You worked on the book. She can always talk about that."

"I'd love to, but there's the movie. They'll probably do something cheesy, like have that kid from the film be her date. I'm sure it's all planned out to a tee. Maybe I'll give her lawyer a call and make the offer.

"We need a caterer for the book people," Aimee told Rita. "Dodo wants to open her house for all the world to see, so she's throwing a cocktail party for the editors and others involved. I can ask Connor if he knows anyone local. I'll be all done and have to go back home."

"Oh, no. You can't leave," Rita said.

"I finished my job. I'll help her promote the book, but that's a ways off. It's time to go."

She met Connor down the beach, and they talked about where they'd be next summer. A surprise was waiting for them when they returned to Dodo's walkway. A bottle of wine in an ice bucket and two wine glasses. They toasted to the golden sunset and to the gold speckles in her eyes. Connor was leaving tomorrow but coming back next Saturday to be her date for the party. Aimee even invited her father and Sally.

They walked up the deck to the yard, Connor with the silver tray.

"I'm kinda tipsy, so you'll have to put that on the kitchen countertop and walk me to my door." He did as he was told and walked her the fifty feet to her door. He kissed her, faithful and fierce. She kissed him back, and she felt a shiver run through him.

"Oh, man," he said. "Did you feel that?"

"Yes." She breathed. She kissed him until it happened again.

"That's you?" he said against her lips.

"Uh-huh."

"Oh, man. I can't wait until next week, " he said as he shivered again.

***

Connor was able to refer her to a friend, an event planner who handled all the details for the book party. All she had to do was find something to wear. She was talking to Dodo about dress shops in town when Dodo suggested Aimee try her closet.

"I don't think so. People grow a lot bigger these days."

"Perhaps, but the one I have in mind was always a little too big." She called Rita and sent her to get the dress. She came back with a dry cleaning bag covering a shapeless, silky, black dress. "Go try it on," Dodo insisted. Aimee went into the bathroom and took the bag off. She wasn't sure which side was the front. One side had a deep cowl. That had to be back. Her whole back would be exposed. The front had a smaller cowl at the neck. She couldn't wear a bra. She came out, and Dolores pronounced her in that dress, which would get people thinking she was the movie star.

"I've never seen a transformation quite like yours. That dress hugs your figure. Mostly I see you in gym clothes and T-shirts. I knew you had great legs. Those I could see, but the rest of you is a surprise. I don't think those book people will even know it's you."

"I'm not sure it's my style, Dodo. I can't wear a bra, and it's so low in the back my underwear will show. I might look like a movie star, but the first time I move, it's going to just slip off, and I'll be standing there naked."

"Why do you care? You're so young and healthy; you have a figure to die for. If you were naked, people would think I invited Venus herself. You don't need to wear underwear, but if you must, find something low and lacy. If someone catches a peek, well, lucky them. As far as a bra goes, with tits like yours, you should walk around naked. Appreciate the way God made them. Soon enough, gravity will take over, and she's a cruel mistress. We can use dressmaker's tape to make sure the dress stays put and band-aids to cover your nipples if you insist. I have a million pairs of shoes. There should be something we can squeeze your feet into. Am I right, Rita? Doesn't she look stunning?"

"Yes, ma'am, she does. Stunning."

"What are you going to wear, Rita? Do we need to put bandaids on your nipples, too?" Aimee asked.

"Oh, no. I'm not going to the party. I have to stay in the kitchen and supervise."

"Not this time. You were integral to this project. You made the three o'clock cocktails. I don't know where we'd be if we didn't have that Old Fashioned to get her talking. You should bring a date."

"Oh, no. Mr. Jimmy and I work for Miss Dodo." Mr. Jimmy was Rita's husband. He was the estate manager in charge of the grounds. He also ran errands and acted as a driver if needed.

"Well, wash and press his best overalls because the two of you have to come. The party is for everyone who worked on the book. Even the FedEx guy is coming. He's making a special trip to be my date."

"Who will do the work? Who will supervise the party?"

"You guys have been out here so long you don't realize how much society has progressed. I hired a girl in town who works as an event planner. She's coming out on Monday to get an idea of the logistics of it all. Her company has the people to do the job. She'll decorate the pool area and hire servers and a bartender. The best part of it, Rita, is they bring the food and clean up. There's nothing for you to do but enjoy the party."

"If you say so, Miss Aimee."

"You must have a black dress in your closet. If not, take Miss Aimee with you and buy one. It's on me," Dolores said.

"What are you going to wear, Dodo? Do you have a dress picked out?" Aimee asked.

"Yes, I do. I'll out-sparkle everyone. I haven't worn a girdle in ages. I hope it still fits."

Aimee laughed. "They don't call them girdles anymore. They're called foundation garments. Besides, after ninety, you're exempt. The fact that you lived that long means gravity can go screw itself."

"I still have a few more months to go." Dolores reminded her.

"The theme is 'Old Hollywood.' You'll get a kick out of this, Dodo. The company I hired is called 'An Affair to Remember.'"

"Oh, that Deborah Kerr was such a bitch. She acted like she was all sweetness and light, but she wasn't. Not by a mile."

"Well, it probably didn't help you slept with her husband."

"Probably not."

***

Chapter 6

The book people came with a mock-up for final review. Katherine went over it with a magnifying glass, checking each word and picture. She didn't like the cover photo and wanted something more up-to-date. She didn't like the inclusion of Aimee's name or photo. Dodo insisted there be a picture of the two of them together inside the backfold. It was a great photo. They had the photographer take it when he was there looking at the book inclusions. They were sitting where they always had their three o'clock cocktails, with wide smiles and wind-blown hair, looking happy as can be.

They wanted her to change the cover and the name of the book. Dodo wouldn't budge on either. She said they should call it *And the Winner is...* with her holding up the Oscar, or *Good Girls Don't, but Bad Girls Win Oscars.* The book people weren't happy, but that image of her holding up her trophy was bold and striking; they could have called it *Dodo Does Hollywood* for all it mattered. Because of Dodo's age, they kept the start time at four p.m., with Dolores making her entrance at about 4:45.

The girl decorating for their party had a few tricks up her sleeve. Dodo had a whole room full of Hollywood memorabilia, and she had free reign to use whatever she found. She placed a marquee at the top of the drive, saying in lights, "Now Playing One Night Only Dolores Reardon starring in *The Life and Times of a Hollywood Legend.*" Dodo seemed elated to be entertaining again, she gave the party planner an unlimited budget. The publishing house was paying anyway. All questions were directed to Aimee, who had never thrown a party that didn't include pizza. She trusted the planner, whose name was Jessica. The only thing

Aimee wanted was fairy lighting everywhere they could put it. She wanted the rails down to the beach lit up so anyone interested could go down to the shore.

She went inside when she saw Rita through the windows. "So, Rita, what do you think? Will Dodo be happy?"

"Oh, yes," she said, frowning.

"Is something upsetting you? You seem worried."

"I am," she confessed. "I don't go to parties, Miss Aimee, I work parties. My dress will look like a black garbage bag compared to everyone else. And Mr. Jimmy wants to park the cars. I keep telling him we are guests, but he doesn't believe me."

Aimee looked for an extra invitation. She wrote on it. "Mr. Jimmy, please come and celebrate Miss Dodo. Your job is to make sure Rita's glass is never empty. Signed Miss Aimee."

"Here. Give him this. The glam squad is coming at noon on Saturday, so be ready to knock Mr. Jimmy's socks off."

"Glam Squad?"

"Hair and makeup people."

"Hair and makeup? Oh no, Miss Aimee."

"Oh, yes, Miss Rita. You're getting the full treatment. When we get done with you, they won't be able to tell which one of us is the movie star."

Rita blushed. All her life, she had to do for someone else. Her mother had been Dolores's housekeeper, and Rita grew up on the fringe of celebrity. For the past twenty-five years, it had just been Miss Dolores. She wore the same utilitarian housekeeper's outfit and white shoes. It's been a long time since Rita had the need to dress up and feel pretty, and she was secretly looking forward to it.

It was Friday afternoon, and they watched lights get strung up everywhere. They were having their three o'clock cocktail while the workers finished up.

"Lord, I hope you know what you're doing," Dodo said.

"I don't have to. This is the Hamptons. This little cocktail party is small potatoes compared to some parties they've thrown, I'm sure. Or weddings. It will all be fine." Aimee took a sip of wine and looked around her. "I better soak it in now. I leave on Monday."

"Leave? You?" Dolores sounded horrified. "Where will you go?"

Aimee laughed at her. "Home. My carriage turns back into a pumpkin."

"Why?"

"Work. I have a long-term sub job. A teacher is going out on maternity leave at the end of the month, and I've been hired to be her substitute. It's through Christmas."

"How dreadful. Do you like teaching?"

"Honestly, no. A degree in creative writing doesn't qualify me for much, so I have to take what I can get. I suppose I'll probably go back to school and get my teaching certificate. Ugh." Aimee made a face.

"What would you do if you could do anything you wanted?"

"Write, of course. I don't mind ghostwriting. It's not an ego thing with me. I don't want fame and glory. I just like words. Putting words on paper to tell a story."

"What kind of stories would you tell?"

"Truthfully, Victorian Gothic Novels. Bodice rippers. You know, the lord of the manor needs an heir, and his wife can't give him one. So he falls for this wench and knocks her up. She has a son, his heir, but he can't legally claim him. Or one where the governess discovers a hidden passageway. It leads to a room where the seer is kept, a crazy old crone who has visions. The seer saw the bad son murder the good son to gain control over the estate. The governess tries to warn the good son but ends up trapped with the seer. You know, women who are forced into societal roles but have a whole lot more to offer and obstacles to overcome; stories like that. My mother was addicted to those books. I grew up reading them.

"I guess it's another thing I had in common with Mom. I was the youngest, and we had a lot of the same interests. We were really close, I guess, and we both read those books. At first, I didn't tell her. I was too young to be reading books like that, but we bonded over it later. She died when I was in college. It took a long time to accept that she wasn't home. She wasn't there. She wasn't anywhere. But yeah, as corny as it sounds, I'd like to write books like that."

"Then that's what you should do."

"Maybe someday. Right now, I have loans to pay back and put food on the table."

"My goodness, Aimee, I didn't even think about your life outside of this place."

"Unfortunately, I have one. I'm just one of the great unwashed. I still live with my dad. I live there, but he mostly stays with his girlfriend, but that's okay. He was so lonely after my mom died. Sally makes him laugh.

"Oh, and they're coming to the party. They got a hotel room in town. I figured they both would never have an opportunity to come to the Hamptons. My Dad said he was looking forward to 'hobnobbing with the swells.'"

"I wish you would have told me sooner. They could have stayed here. There's more than enough room. We could have opened up the lower cottage. I can't remember the last time somebody stayed down there. Tell them they're more than welcome to use it. Nobody else does." Dolores offered.

"You tell them. If I do, they'll take you up on it and never leave."

"That wouldn't be so bad."

"Have you *met* my father? You just wait. Boy, I'll be sad to leave this place. What a great summer gig. I'm going to call any time I'm free at three. We'll have a cocktail hour over the phone."

"I don't like this, Aimee. Stay here."

"I can't. I have the first half of the school year committed. Don't worry. You'll be seeing me after the holidays when we promote the book. If you find traveling tiresome, we can always do it from here. If they bring up your seclusion, like you had some horrible disease, just wave your hand around and say, 'Leave here? It's paradise. Would I leave?'"

Chapter 7

Soon, it was party day, and the traffic in and out of the house was heavy. The staff had walkie-talkies, and everyone knew their places. The ladies all met in Dodo's suite at noon, where hair and makeup were set up. Both Rita and Aimee sat and let the stylists do their thing. It was decided that because of the drama of the back of Aimee's dress, she needed to have her hair up and add her exposed neck to lengthen the drama. She wasn't sure, but Lisa, who did hair, lectured Aimee about how she was a professional and told her to wait until she was done before she had an opinion.

"I don't want it stiff. I want it soft."

"Quiet," Lisa commanded.

They switched chairs. Lisa took Rita's functional lunch lady hairdo and created a soft cap of curls, Aimee's thick hair tamed into a sleek French updo. They turned to each other and laughed after Lisa's partner Anita did their make-up.

"Look at us! Who'd believe we're so hot!" Aimee said and reached for Rita's hands.

"Come on, ladies. Time to get dressed." Anita brought out their dresses.

They dressed in their fancy clothes. Rita wore a black dress but was very self-conscious about how snug it fit across her belly.

"I don't know, Miss Dodo, I'd feel better if I could put on my apron," Rita said.

Aimee looked at her back. "Unbelievable. I better not move too quickly, or it will go sliding off."

"The tape, Aimee. The tape." Dodo reminded her. Once both women were dressed, Dodo ordered, "Follow me," and retreated deep into one of her many walk-in closets. She pulled open a drawer, and it sparkled with vintage costume jewelry.

"Oh, no. Miss Dolores. I can't wear your jewelry. It's too much money. What if I broke it or a stone fell out? I couldn't pay for it."

"Rita, stop worrying. This is just costume jewelry. The real stuff is locked away in a safety deposit box at the bank. Now, you need some fancy jewelry. Let's drip you in cubic zirconia, and nobody will look at your tummy, Rita. And Aimee, you need to do the same." She pulled a few drawers open and found two pairs of statement earrings that definitely could not be missed. "Here, put these on."

She found a necklace that matched Rita's earrings. Aimee put it on Rita and stepped back. "Dodo's right. The earrings swing, and the sparkle causes the eye to be automatically drawn up."

"I'm still self-conscious, Miss Dodo."

Aimee looked into Dodo's closet and pointed. "May I?" she asked Dodo.

"Absolutely. Aren't we having fun? It's like playing dress up."

Aimee went deeper into the closet. She finally found the scarves and chose a couple. She folded one into the size of a sash. She brought them out and looked at Rita.

"Here. Let's try this." She draped the ribbon of fabric over Rita's shoulder and brought it to the opposite hip. "Dodo, do you have a large pin or broach? If we clip it here, the diagonal line will cross over her stomach and help break up the solid black."

"That's an excellent idea." She pulled out a very large brooch made of different colored stones. "This? Or clear stones?" Dodo asked.

Aimee took the colored stone brooch. She took the edge of the scarf, and her eyes saw the label. “Dodo? This is a Hermès scarf. I don’t know if we should poke holes in it. Maybe we should use another.”

“Oh, pooh. I can’t remember who that was a gift from, but what good does it do hanging in here?” Dolores was having a ball, looking at all her fancy things again.

Aimee pinned the scarf like a sash. “Better, Rita?”

“Oh, Miss Dodo, I feel like Miss America,” she said with a huge grin.

“I take that as a yes.” Dodo turned to Aimee. “Now you. Those earrings are perfect. We need a rhinestone cuff for you. Here. This ring, too. There. Rita may be Miss America, but you might look better than I will.”

“No way, Dodo. I can’t outshine you. Besides, if people are looking at me, it’s to see if they can see my butt crack.”

“Let’s try this.” She took a pendant and put it on backwards. The jewelry consisted of six clear stones connected to each other in graduated sizes. The largest came to rest between her shoulder blades. The stones glittered in the light of Dodo’s closet. “Is this better? Because if they weren’t checking out your backside before, they will be now,” Dodo told her.

“Well, I like it,” Aimee said. “Do you mind if I look through your jewelry? It reminds me of my Mom. When I was little, she used to take me to garage and estate sales, looking for jewelry. She collected antique vintage jewelry. I have it now. I like to wear it now and again, it makes me feel close to her. I can still smell her perfume. I guess I inherited her love for it. If I go to a thrift store, it’s the first thing I look at.” Aimee smiled at the memory and almost started to tear up. “Here. I have to leave, or else I’ll cry and ruin my makeup.”

“One last thing, Aimee.” Dodo gave her a pair of shoes. A very fancy pair of heels. Thin-heeled, rhinestone-studded straps held them together.

“Dodo, I’m not sure about these.”

“It doesn’t matter. If they break, they break.”

“I’m not worried about breaking the shoe. I’m worried about breaking my ankle.” Aimee said with a concerned look on her face.

“Well, that’s what you get for your generation’s desire for comfort. You have no idea how to be beautiful. So you and Miss Rita go out there and supervise. Practice walking around in heels. It’s my turn to get ready. Out. I want to surprise everyone.”

Before they left, Aimee had Lisa promise to come find her when Dolores was ready to make her entrance. She had a special escort.

Aimee and Rita went to check the progress in the yard. An Affair to Remember was operating like a well-oiled machine. There were people in and out of the kitchen, Rita’s turf. Aimee wasn’t sure how Rita would react. She kept twisting a gold bracelet around her wrist, but it was the only outward manifestation of nervousness.

“I don’t know, Miss Aimee. All those people in my kitchen.”

“Relax, Miss Rita. Let the professionals handle it. Go find Mr. Jimmy and show him how beautiful you look. Let him appreciate it.” Aimee told her.

“He’s probably out front. He doesn’t trust the valets know what they’re doing.”

“You go out front and find him. I’ll check out back.”

Aimee looked in the kitchen, the amount of food was astounding. Either they were expecting everyone in town, or they’d be eating until midnight. She went and said hello to the bartenders. One was named Marco, and the other was Robb. Her fairy lights were everywhere. She wondered if maybe she had gone overboard. The party could be over before it got dark enough for them to be appreciated.

Framed movie posters from her five Academy Award-winning films were set up on easels. The art director found the original posters upstairs, in the memorabilia room. Aimee had them framed with archival materials so they would last forever. It was her gift to Dodo. Celebrate her, indeed.

As Aimee requested, there were a number of 'conversation pits,' four chairs around a center table. She wasn't sure of Dodo's ability to stand for any length of time; she wanted seating that would accommodate her wherever she happened to be. There were some higher bar top tables scattered about, too. There were lights floating in the pool that changed color.

Dolores didn't know that Aimee knew she swam laps early in the morning, sans swimsuit. She came down in her robe, swam her lap, dried off, put her robe on and left. Aimee asked Rita about it.

"I told her she should wear something. What if she got hurt? Anyone who came to help would see her, au natural, but she didn't care. 'Oh, pooh,' Miss Dodo said. 'It's not like there's anything anybody would be interested in.' She did put the lift in to help her get in and out, but she still uses the stairs."

"That explains her stamina. She's in great shape for being almost ninety."

Everything was coming together nicely. The people from the publishing house worked on the display of their books. They blew up certain pictures or interesting passages and had them enlarged and framed. The display was on a table with a black velvet cover. It was approaching four. Guests would soon be arriving; Aimee would act as the hostess until the publishing people were free. After all, this was their party.

One of the servers approached her and said she was wanted out front. She went through the house, and before she reached the door, she heard the booming voice of her father. Aimee went out to greet him.

"Hey, Dad! Hi, Sally. So, what do you think? None of the swells are here yet, will I do?"

Her father looked at her in awe. This was his little girl, looking like one of the swells herself. She looked exactly like her mother. So much so that he was struck mute and felt his eyes water.

"Dad? What's wrong?" Aimee asked, concerned about his silence.

"I'm sorry, Aimee. You look so beautiful. I'm speechless. You look just like your mother."

"You? Speechless. Never. Check this out, though." She turned around and showed him the back, or the lack of a back of her dress.

"Aimee! You're positively gorgeous. You could be a movie star!" Sally squealed.

"You can't walk around like that!" her father said. "Here. Put my coat on."

"Joey, don't be a prude. She's a knockout," Sally said, the only person whom Aimee has ever heard call her Dad 'Joey.' Big old Joe Dunsmore, built like a bear who bowled, called Joey. *He must really be in love if he lets her call him Joey*, Aimee thought.

"Come on, nobody's here yet. Go check out the house. The wing off the kitchen is Dolores's; don't go there. Otherwise, feel free to snoop, but keep out of the way of the workers. The bar is out by the pool when you're ready. Here, I'll show you."

They went inside, and Aimee gave them a brief tour. When they ended up out by the pool, Aimee showed them the walkway down to the water.

"Make sure you check that out. Sally, be careful. Your heels might sink in the grass or get caught between the boards. The dunes are protected, so no sneaking off behind them for a little nookie."

"Joey, she sure has your number!" Sally laughed.

Rita was waving to Aimee.

"Get yourselves a drink. Duty calls." Aimee said and walked away.

"There's someone at the door for you," Rita said. Aimee went up front. It was Connor, dressed in a tuxedo. She greeted him with a kiss on the cheek.

"Well, don't you look handsome?"

"I could say the same about you, but I'd have to put my tongue back in my mouth. Really. Aimee. You're gorgeous."

"Not so fast. Look." She showed him the back of her dress. Aimee turned back to see the look on his face.

"No fair. You look like you're getting on a jet to Cannes, and I look like I'm going to the prom. I even brought you a corsage. My mother said I should bring one for Mrs. Reardon just in case she needed one, so I grabbed one for you. I don't think it matches your outfit."

"Oh, pooh. Let me see that." Aimee put it on the wrist that didn't have the cuff and held it out to admire. "It's perfect." She kissed him on the lips this time. "We don't have anything for Dolores. She'll love it. When she walks in with you as her escort, she'll be thrilled."

"So, I wasted a whole day and looked like arm candy in this monkey suit for all of two minutes? That's what you needed me for? Can we stand somewhere else? Everyone keeps confusing me as one of the valets."

"Follow me," she said. She brought him into the front room. It was brightly lit, and they stood in front of the window. Aimee grabbed his lapels and pulled his mouth to hers. She practically growled at him, "Play your cards right, mister, and I just might show you the ceiling of the pool house. Tonight. For all your trouble, I mean." She kissed him like he'd never been kissed before.

"Oh," he said. "Yes, please. Use me."

"Thanks. You just wait here. Give the corsage to her in front of someone who will help her put it on. Don't go too fast, she has old bones. Please. I have to go check on the guests. By the way, there are plenty of industry types here, so make sure you look like a pro, all strong and dominant. Maybe you could get discovered."

"You think?"

"I don't know. Stranger things have happened." Aimee said with a shrug.

She checked out the kitchen, but she didn't even know what to pretend to check on, so she left. The pool area was filling up with people.

Many of the corner office types were present. Aimee was surprised their project got off the ground with so little fanfare, yet look who Dolores Reardon pulled in. Aimee felt no obligation to sit and make small talk with anyone. She was a free agent and didn't answer to anyone except maybe her Dad, who was over there yukking it up with what looked like a couple of proofreaders.

Someone tapped her on the shoulder. It was Lisa, the hairstylist. Dodo was ready. She left with the instructions to get Connor and put the corsage on Dodo. When they were ready, Connor should count to five and walk her out of the dining room door, the only one lit by a spotlight.

A red carpet was placed in front, the spotlight lit the doorway, and the crowd hushed. Soon, Dolores Reardon and her most current boy toy appeared in the doorway. The applause started and grew louder until she reached the edge of the carpet. The crowd grew around her. Even the caterers stopped what they were doing and honored Dolores; their applause made it louder.

It's kind of impressive, Aimee thought. The valets and employees of An Affair to Remember joined the applause with the guests and made it seem more substantial. Aimee laughed. *Just like the Olive Garden.*

Everyone rushed them, Connor, to his credit, kept Dolores tight at his side. The crowd threatened to overwhelm them, and he worried Mrs. Reardon would be trampled. He held her firmly against him and only let up when the crowd subsided.

Dodo looked up at him with sparkles in her eyes. "Thank you, young man." She signed for him to bring his ear closer. "Oh, the things I could teach you," she whispered. Dodo let go of his arm and let the crowd sweep her away.

He watched her for a second to make sure she was safe and searched for Aimee. He found her and dragged her back inside. He kissed her until she was panting and pushed him away. "How'd I do?" he said into her throat. "Did I earn a bonus?" He pressed up against her. She pressed back.

"You sure did. Let's go back outside. I'd like you to meet my dad."

She took him by the hand and located her father by the sound of his voice.

"Hey, Dad. Sorry to break in. Got a second?"

"Look, everyone! My daughter! She helped write the book!" he said as he turned away from his new friends.

"What's so important, sweetie?"

"Dad. I want you to meet Connor. My date. Connor, my dad, Joe Dunsmore. This is his date, Sally Reade."

Joe Dunsmore shook Connor's hand. His hand was lost among Joe Dunsmore's massive grip. "So, you like my daughter?"

"Yes, sir. Yes, I do."

"I don't blame you. She's a knockout, huh?"

"Yes. She sure is."

"Well, don't break her heart. I'm having too good a time to get pissed off. Nice to meet you. Bye." He turned back to his new friends.

"Connor, nice to meet you. Aimee, you look stunning. Absolutely stunning." Sally complimented her and turned back to keep an eye on Joey.

"He never gave me a chance."

"A chance for what?"

"To ask for your hand in marriage. I want to marry you."

"Down, boy. You're just hypnotized by my dimples."

"You don't have dimples."

"Sacral dimples." She put his hands down the back of her dress. "Feel those little dips? Sacral dimples."

"Yeah, I can see those distracting me."

"Feel anything else?"

"No."

"Think about it," she said and pulled him back to join the party.

"Hey! You're not wearing anything else! Are you trying to kill me?"

"Yes, I am. You'll be nothing but dust after tonight. I'll mail you back to campus in a first-class envelope."

The party went on, voices and laughter rose and fell like the tide. A number of people went down to the beach to watch the sunset. Perhaps in honor of Dodo, the sunset was spectacular. There wasn't a color that Mother Nature didn't pull out of her toolkit. Once the sun disappeared, the crowd, even those jaded New Yorkers, applauded.

Rita told Aimee where to find a wheelchair; Aimee wanted to bring Dodo down to the shore with her guests. Aimee had Connor push it over to Dodo. She frowned.

"I don't need that thing."

"Yeah, you do," Aimee said. "Half the party is down by the water, watching the sunset. When was the last time you saw the sun go down?"

"Ages."

"Then hop in. It's really easy to catch a heel or step on a rock. We covered every angle for this party except emergency medical care. We even have a man in a tuxedo to usher you. Let's go down and join the others. When you wrote the book, the advice you gave was, 'You never score any points from the bench,' so suit up and get in the game. You better hurry, or we'll miss it." Dodo sat, and Connor pushed her down to the end of the deck.

"You don't need to get to the water. You can see the sunset fine from here. Right, Connor?"

"That's right, Aimee. This is the most beautiful place in the world to see the sunset." When he said that, he looked over Dodo's head and smiled at Aimee. She smiled back.

After the sun went down, the guest turned to walk back to the house. They saw Dodo there and came over to thank her for such a magnificent display.

"You're welcome. I ordered it specifically from the man upstairs. I'm glad He didn't disappoint."

"Even God knows better than to let you down, Dodo," someone said.

"Here, Dolores, I'll bring you back. Out of the way, Junior," Joe Dunsmore said and practically hip-checked Connor into the dunes.

"Be gentle, Dad. She's not seat belted in," Aimee warned.

"You worry too much. Just like your mother. Now get out of the way." He turned Dodo around and started to push.

"Wait a minute, Joey! Wait for me!" Sally yelled. She took off her heels and hurried after him.

Aimee and Connor waited until they were alone. He grabbed her and kissed her. "I don't think I'll go back to school. I want to stay here with you and watch the sunset together every night."

"You might as well go back to school. I leave on Monday unless you want to watch the sunset with Rita."

"Rita might be mighty fine, but it's you I want." He put his forehead against hers and brushed his nose against hers.

"I think this is the prettiest part of the sunset, the clouds hanging on until the night overtakes the sky. Maybe we can come back later and see what it looks like by moonlight."

"Are you a closet romantic, Aimee Dunsmore?" Connor said.

"Guilty. Maybe we'll go for a moonlight swim."

"You stop it now. I was only half kidding about wanting to marry you. It won't take much to talk me into eloping. After all, I'm already in a tuxedo."

"Not for long."

"I mean it. Stop."

"I can't help it. This whole summer has been like a dream. I am an incurable romantic. Let's end this knee-deep in lust and used condoms."

"Shit. Condoms. I don't have any. I didn't expect to need any."

"Ask a valet. Send him into town to buy some if you have to."

"Great idea. Let's go back. I need to work on this." He grabbed her by the hand and hurried up the walk. "Be right back," he said, and he ran out front.

Aimee looked around. The servers were still circulated, and the bartenders were still serving. The fairy lights started to glow in the twilight. Some of the industry people had departed, and the crowd started to thin out. She looked around for Dodo. She found her seated at a table, deep in conversation with Sally, of all people. Aimee joined them.

"Aimee, your family is just wonderful. Sally knows more about my movies than I do, and your father is a real hoot."

"He's a real hoot, all right," Aimee agreed.

"Where did your date go so fast?"

"He had an errand to run. Are you warm enough, Dodo? Once the sun goes down, it gets a little chilly. I can run inside and grab you a sweater unless you'd rather go in the house."

"I think the party was a smashing success, but it is getting chilly. I think I want to go inside now."

"It's just about over, anyway. You should go inside. It was a wonderful party, Dodo. The book came out better than anybody expected. You hit a home run," Aimee said.

"No," Dodo said. "*We* hit a home run."

"Let me find someone to help you inside. Your escort seems to be missing." Aimee said with a laugh. Sally beat her to it.

"Joey? Joey! Come over and help Dolores, please."

Her father came running. "Yes, here I am. Let me help you inside, Dolores. You," he said to Aimee, "move aside."

Dolores stood and took 'Joey's' arm.

"Come with me, madame," he said to Dolores. He looked at Aimee and winked. Growing up, her father had this habit of complaining about his kids. He had this big, booming voice he was very proud of; he used it any chance he could.

Sally followed close behind in case 'Joey' needed supervision. Aimee was going to go inside but stopped when she saw Connor come running around the side of the house. He scooped her up and twirled her around. "I'm all set, Aimee. I hope you are."

"My father needs to go. He's having a blast, though. He's a real party kind of guy. Go grab a bottle of white, put it inside the pool house and come back. I'll push my dad towards the door. Dodo has to be exhausted."

The caterer started to break everything down. Aimee used this to prod her father along. Rita offered to stay and help Dodo get ready for bed.

"Okay, Dad. Rita needs to get home, but Miss Dolores is too polite of a host to ask you to leave. But I'm not. I hope you had a good time, and I'm glad you came, but it's time to go."

Oddly enough, her father got up and reached for Sally. "Dolores, it was a fantastic party. Love the book. Thank you for having us," he said as he walked to the door. Sally waved over her shoulder.

"Dolores! Thank you! See you tomorrow!" She followed her husband out.

"What's tomorrow?" Aimee asked.

"Sally's making us brunch before they leave tomorrow," Dodo said.

"Goodnight, Rita. You looked fantastic. Dodo. You throw a hell of a party. I am taking my date and walking him out. Goodnight." Aimee grabbed Connor's hand and pulled him out of the kitchen. Aimee brought him into the pool house and, for the first time all summer, closed the drapes.

***

Chapter 8

Aimee turned to face Connor. He was watching her, waiting for her to make the first move.

"Well, hello there, handsome. Who let you in?" Aimee said as she moved up against him.

"This really hot chick. This stone-cold fox." He moved back.

"Let's decide this right now," Aimee said. "This is a fantasy, Connor. I can make your dreams come true if you are willing to agree to one thing. We are sharing a moment. I have no reason to come back here, and you have too much in front of you to get wrapped up with some girl. Can you accept it's just a moment?"

"Can it last all night?"

"Yeah, if *you* can."

"I'm young and healthy. I see no problem. A moment lasts only a bit, but I'll have the memory forever. Show me what you got." He lifted his chin, throwing down the challenge.

Aimee took a step back, reached under the shoulders of her dress, and unstuck the tape. The dress slid down her body, a black silky pool at her feet. She looked him in the eye, the smile on her face positively wicked.

His eyes grew wide as he took in Aimee's naked body, but his smile broke, and he laughed out loud. Aimee panicked and looked at her dress in a pile on the floor but froze at his laughter. She never wanted to flee as badly as she did at that moment, but her feet wouldn't move. Aimee bent down to pick up her dress.

Before, it was a symbol of how hot and sexy she was, but in reality, it was a black rag. She stood, and Connor was right there.

"Here. Let me pass." She said as she tried to step around him. Tears pricked her eyes despite her best efforts. He reached out and grabbed her arm. "Let me go."

"What's the matter?" Connor said, holding her by her arms.

"What's the matter? *What's the matter?* I'm standing here naked, and you're laughing at me!" Aimee lashed out. "*That's* what's the matter."

He looked at her oddly and befuddled. "No. What are those?" He pointed at her chest. "These."

Aimee looked down and saw the bandaids used to secure her nipples. "Oh. Sorry about that." She laughed, wiped her eyes and used her nails to pick them off. "So there's no nipple. Poking through the fabric." She explained, embarrassed, she almost started crying.

His hand reached for her other breast. "Here. Let me help. I'm sorry I laughed. I was surprised, that's all." Her breasts were now bandaid-free. "You were a ten with the band-aids on. Now, you're off the charts. Dry your eyes, baby. You are the most beautiful thing I've ever seen," he said and kissed her. Connor removed the bobby pins from her hair, and they cascaded about her shoulders. "Perfect." He smiled.

He reached up and started unbuttoning his shirt. Aimee wanted to kiss him and pulled his head down. Connor found it hard to multitask. He decided to go with her mouth. He reached up and held her face.

"Help me with the buttons, please. My hands are busy." Connor's hands roamed all over her body while she worked down the front of his shirt. When Aimee was finished, she pulled the shirt off him and threw it next to her dress. He shed his pants. They stood there, naked, and looked at each other. Connor picked her up and threw her over his shoulder. He took her to the bedroom and dropped her on the bed. He looked down at her. "You ready?" He said.

"For what?"

"An affair to remember."

"Bring it on."

He dove right next to her. Connor wanted to absorb her. Aimee was so soft and smelled so good, like fresh lemons. He wasn't sure where to start. It didn't matter; she let his hands wander all over her. She touched him; she ground into him. Connor slid up and down her like a snake. They rolled around and slipped all over each other until she said into his ear, "Condom?"

He ran and grabbed his pants, pulled out a box and dropped them on the bed. Aimee grabbed one and held it in her teeth. She pulled him down on the bed and tore open the wrapper. Aimee pushed him on his back and unrolled the condom. Connor would have shot his wad right then, but he was too shocked.

She straddled him and hovered above him. She stared right into his eyes.

"Ready for your bonus?"

"Hell yeah."

She slowly slid down him. Aimee slid so slowly he couldn't help it, but he had to enter her immediately. His hips moved towards her until he finally made contact. Instead of the furious pumping he felt building up inside him, she slowly ground her pelvis into him. She would draw back and repeat the grind. When she had him right on the edge of that sweet blade he desired, she started to move faster.

He never had a girl like her. Usually, his job was to create the moment and do all the work, but being a man inside this woman was her responsibility, and she took command. Aimee took charge and determined the rhythm. Connor grabbed her hips and pushed into her every time he got close enough, but she kept her own pace. When Aimee got to the edge, she looked him in the eye and said, "Now," and let go.

He held her firm and drove into her. When he started to move against her, she let out a little moan, and he took over. Connor held her fast and smashed against her; the moan that escaped her was a little louder. He lost it, and as he came, he could feel her start to shake with one last grind against him. Her moan was accompanied by an orgasm, and she collapsed on top of him.

She rolled off him and grabbed some tissues. Aimee took care of the used condom and cleaned him up. He watched in fascination how she had absolutely no hang-ups. Aimee handled a used rubber the way she handled a pencil and gently cleaned him up.

Connor couldn't decide if she had enough experience or too much experience. Aimee wasn't ashamed or embarrassed, or this was simply what happened when you matured. She was a few years older than he, but those couple of years apparently made a huge difference.

"Whew," he said, flat on his back, looking at the ceiling.

"Whew," she agreed, flat on her back next to him.

Connor rolled on his side, propped his head in hand and looked at her. She was so beautiful, the best looking girl he ever had. He felt like he should say something but feared it would be stupid and immature, so he kissed her. It was her turn to look at him. Connor smiled, and Aimee kissed him back. They took some time kissing each other, just kissing. There was no beginning or end; they started and finished each other's kisses until they were a single organism connected at the mouth. She stopped and asked him if he wanted to go swimming.

"The pool's heated, and I think the fairy lights are still up."

He followed her out to the front window and peeked through the curtains. "Sure. Why not?"

She got each of them a thick cotton robe from the closet and handed him one. "The house is dark, so we have to be quiet."

Aimee went first and slid into the water, barely breaking the surface, and he slid in after her. He came up and, in a single action, flicked his head so all the water flew off in the same direction, the hair plastered against his head. She giggled at him.

"What?"

"The way you flick your hair like that. I think it's sexy."

He swam over. "Do you?"

Aimee dove under the water and came up next to him. "I do."

They swirled around together in the water so warm it was steaming, sending up plumes of vapor when they moved. They stayed close together to keep their voices low.

They ended up sitting on the stairs; he was on the last one with the water up to his neck, and she was on his lap with only her head above water. Connor had his arms around her waist, she had her arms around his neck. They sat silently, enjoying each other's experience. Finally, Aimee spoke.

"Look at all the lights. That's what I wanted. All these fairy lights and a midnight swim. I wouldn't want to be the person who has to take them down, but they look magical. They put them everywhere. Isn't it romantic?"

"Yeah, this is pretty cool. And romantic. Who did you have in mind when you planned this midnight swim?"

"Nobody. I just wanted the experience. I figured I'd let the book company pay for it. I wanted to enjoy this. You being here is gravy. I'm so bad I even send myself flowers once a month." She confessed.

"You do? Why?"

"For the experience. I haven't had a boyfriend since college. I'm not going to wait for some guy to come along to make me feel special. I do it for myself. That way, I don't need a guy to make me feel good. If I'm with someone, they don't have the pressure of me being with them because I want something from them."

"You are special. Really special. This may not come out right, but most girls I know are needy. They want a guy to prop them up. You seem like you've evolved beyond that." Connor said.

"I don't know about that. I had a pretty steady boyfriend in college. At least, I thought we were steady, but then I found out he had another steady. He was my first serious boyfriend. I guess you could say he broke my heart. He was supposed to love me. How could you cheat on someone you love? I guess I couldn't get over it. We did the 'get back together/ break-up thing' for a while, but eventually, it exhausted itself, and we both agreed it was over."

"If I had a girlfriend like you, I'd try to protect her from pain rather than be the cause of it."

Aimee laughed. "I believe you. I believe you, believe you. I've just found that life just keeps throwing curveballs you never see coming. I'm a couple of years older. It's not that big a deal, except you're still in college. In a bubble.

"The real world hasn't seeped in. No past due bills. No student loan payments. You don't have to worry about a car or health insurance. You don't have to go back and live with your parents because you just spent four years in college, but you're not prepared for anything." She leaned over and kissed him. "You're a good guy with a good plan. You'll graduate and hit the ground running. You said so yourself you wanted to get out of here, and you will. I see great things in your future."

"What about you? What's your future look like?"

"I'm living it. Ever since I learned how to write, I have wanted to be a writer, to tell stories. So I'll live in my dad's house, substitute teach for money, and write. My friends used to get so mad at me because we'd go somewhere, and I'd end up talking to some down-on-his-luck sad sack. I wanted to hear his story. If someone had an interesting tattoo, I'd want to know why. That's why I loved this assignment. It was a chance to tell Dolores's story, and it was quite a story. Like all stories, though, it comes to an end, or at least for me. On Monday, I'll take the train home and start again. When do you leave?"

"Tomorrow afternoon. I have a project due next week."

"See? Fairy lights and mind-blowing sex don't last forever."

"You did blow my mind and then some. I hope to return the favor."

"Want to go inside and try?" Aimee asked him.

"Yes, I do."

"Well, come on then." She stood, and the steam that emanated from her warm skin gave him an instant boner. He stood up as well and blushed because his dick had a mind of its own. She smiled at him and gave him a robe. "Follow me," she said, taking his hand and leading him back inside.

Aimee took two towels out of the closet and handed him one. Connor pulled her close and used his towel to dry her off. After she was dry, he continued to rub her down until Aimee said, "Hey." He looked at her and dried himself. He took her hand and led her back to bed. Connor figured since she told him all this romantic stuff, he'd romance the heck out of her.

I hope I know how he thought.

He knew he had to thrill her. Connor thought he would say all kinds of things, sweet things and tell her how lucky he was she asked him to stay. Kiss her all over until she got all giggly, and focus on that spot. Cuddle with her under the sheets. *Just be all flirty with her and quit overthinking this,* he thought.

He sat on the corner of her bed and pulled her in, wrapped his arms around her. He placed his face on her warm stomach and sighed.

"What's the matter?" Aimee asked.

"Nothing. I wanted to see if you felt as good dry as you did underwater. You do. Now you have me wondering if you felt as good laying down as you do standing up." Aimee laid back and let him worship her. Superlatives rolled off his tongue. He kissed her and tickled and teased her until she was quivering like warm jelly. Connor slid his hand down her belly; her hips rose up at the last second, and his fingers met her warmth and wetness. He really didn't do much else but leave his fingers where she could move against him and sweet talk the hell out of her.

"Hey. Why don't you grab a condom," Aimee said.

"I'm not sure you're ready yet."

"Oh, I'm ready."

"I don't believe you," Connor said, increasing the pressure against her and winding her up further.

"Oh please," she whispered. "Please."

He was going to make her wait longer, but the second please got to him, and he could hold out no longer. Connor got between her legs and slowly entered her, but she wrapped her legs around him and pulled him inside. She was rocking underneath him; suddenly, he felt her start to shudder from her very center outward, which caused the same earthquake to happen in him. He exploded just as she did, and they both saw stars.

Connor gently rolled off her and took care of the used condom. He rolled back on his side and looked at her.

"Aimee, I don't know what to say. I know we spent some time this summer walking the beach, but I never expected this to happen. Honest. I had no plans other than being your friend. But you're right, this is magic. I don't know why you picked me, but thanks."

"I had no plans for any of this, either. I like you, our walks were fun, but we were just friends. The beach, the water, and the lights set the scene, but the way you were so willing, so kind to Dolores, I guess it moved me. Don't mistake this as love, but I feel a certain tenderness towards you. It's been a long time since I felt connected to a guy. Maybe I was lonely. Or maybe I thought you looked cute in your uniform."

"You looked so handsome in your tuxedo, and I felt so pretty in that dress, I thought, why not? So what if it's not forever? Why not spend one night with you? For the record, it was the right call. You said and did all the right things. It was magic."

"Why don't we get under the sheets and take a nap? You must be exhausted." Connor yawned.

Aimee agreed, and that's what they did. She tucked herself close beside him and quickly fell asleep. It wasn't quite as easy for Connor to fall asleep. He looked at her. She looked so peaceful. She even smiled in her sleep; she looked happy and content. Connor knew this was probably it, he doubted he'd ever see her again.

It was hard for him to accept that she wasn't in it for the long haul. How could she decide not to like him, let alone not fall in love with him? Here he was, looking at her, asleep and untroubled, and all he wanted to do was stay. He didn't want to leave. Connor wanted her here beside him forever. Aimee said it was magical, and it was. Love or magic, it didn't matter to him. She took up room in his heart. It may never go any further, but last night, he fell in love with her.

Connor soon nodded off. They awoke the next morning to voices. The workers had come to take the lights down. They joined together one last time, silently but smiling at each other. When it was over, they hugged and kissed goodbye. He had to walk nonchalantly out of her door wearing a tuxedo and up the drive to his car. The only one who noticed was Mr. Jimmy, who smiled to himself. The kid got lucky with Miss Aimee. Good for him.

Her father knocked on her door and woke her, telling her brunch was in fifteen minutes. She looked around for Connor but remembered he left earlier. Aimee was glad there was brunch to distract her. To sit there alone all day, she knew she'd start to miss Connor. Aimee also knew Sally loved to cook, so it should be good. Even if it was bad, it was still better than being alone. Her father was good at post-party dissection.

Rita came out with Dodo, who was happy to talk about the party and her guests. Aimee listened to her Dad talk with Dolores. She helped Sally cut up fruit for brunch. The talk got around to the young man who was Dodo's escort.

"That was your date, right, Miss Aimee?" Rita asked, already knowing the answer.

"Connor? Yes, but he was invited because he's the FedEx guy. I asked him to dress in a tux so he could escort Dodo. He was such a good sport. I thought he looked smashing."

"He thought you looked smashing. He couldn't take his eyes off you," Sally teased.

"I know. I did look smashing." Aimee popped a ripe strawberry in her mouth. "Did you have fun at the party, Rita?"

"Yes. It was hard to relax in the beginning; I kept looking in the kitchen to make sure they didn't ruin anything, but after the second glass of wine, I said, 'Who cares.'"

"That's right. The publisher paid for it. I think the fairy lights made it special."

"Yes. They must have looked beautiful during that midnight swim," Dodo said.

"You saw us?"

"Darling Aimee, I know everything that goes on around here. You should have invited him for brunch."

"That kid hot for my little girl? I think he needs a good talking to," Joe said.

"He couldn't stay. He had to get back to school. He goes to NYU."

"I know. Mr. Jimmy said he left early this morning," Rita said.

"Geez, you people should work for the FBI."

***

Aimee put the last of her things in her suitcase. She was leaving Dodo and her part on Paradise Point. Mr. Jimmy was driving her to the station early in the morning, and Aimee did what she used to do in college—sleep in her clothes and just leave her toothbrush out. She'd wake up, brush her teeth, and go. She probably should have grown up and gotten dressed in the morning like normal people, but she preferred to grab and go. Aimee didn't like to open her suitcase once it was packed, and if it wasn't closed, she couldn't sleep.

She was having dinner tonight with just Dodo; Rita didn't work on Sundays, so they would have leftovers from the party as well as brunch. Sally cooked up enough food to feed an army, but she enjoyed doing it in an effort to repay Dodo for her hospitality. Her father was doing his best knight-in-shining armor routine, attentive to the point of obsession. If Dodo needed anything, Joe was right on it.

Sally was perfect for Dodo. Her mother used to be a huge fan, she had all the gossip tabloids like 'Hollywood Confidential' in the reception area of her hair salon. Sally grew up reading them, very familiar with many of Dodo's contemporaries and the storylines the press created with their intrusive photographs. They gabbed like a couple of hens at the county fairground. Sally said she only remembered headlines. She'd say one, and Dolores filled in the rest.

They hated to leave but promised to come back and use the lower cottage. Her father ushered Dodo to her room, made sure she was safely inside and got Sally. Joe wanted to get on the road. He kissed Aimee on the cheek and thanked her for the invite. He also thanked her for including Sally; it made her so happy.

"I'll meet you at home," he said. He looked out the window and saw his car. "Damn, he brought the car back. I wanted to drive the golf cart." It was used to transport guests to their cars.

"Maybe next time, Dad," Aimee teased.

"I'm coming back next summer. Dodo asked us to come. She said we're 'good company.'"

"You are, Dad."

He held the door for Sally. "I'm not kidding. In August."

"I'm sure you'll have a great time. Who knows where I'll be?"

"You'll be on vacation. With us. Pencil it in."

"I will. Drive safe. Find a hotel if you get tired. See you tomorrow."

***

Aimee sent Rita home; she had the day off. It was Aimee's last night with Dodo, and she wanted the two of them to spend a quiet evening alone. Dodo was still in her room; it wasn't time for her afternoon cocktail. Aimee felt like she should go down to the water and soak it all in, but she was dead tired. She fell asleep on the couch. Dodo, looking for her three p.m. refreshment, woke her.

"Poor Aimee. You must be so tired, and I just woke you up. I was looking for Rita." She held her arms open and shrugged.

Aimee blinked her eyes a couple of times to wake up. "Oh. It's Sunday. Rita's got the night off. It's you and me eating leftovers."

"That's all fine and good, but it is three o'clock now. I'm thirsty. I can make my own cocktail, but am I drinking alone?" Dodo said.

"No need. I'll get it while I get a glass of wine," Aimee said as she got up. "I slept all afternoon. I feel pretty good today."

Aimee came back with their drinks. Dodo sat in her mission oak and leather recliner, and Aimee sat next to her on the matching sofa. They sat in silence for a bit, and Aimee finally spoke.

"I'm sure I'll miss this the most, Dodo. After our drink, I'll start warming up leftovers. Half of the things in the fridge, I don't even know what they are."

"Shall we be naughty and have one more?" Dodo said, referring to their drinks.

"I guess one more can't hurt, although I have to get up pretty early tomorrow to catch the train."

"About that. There's been a change of plans. A car service is coming at noon and driving you home."

"How did that happen?"

"I thought you earned it. You put together one smash of a book, and for them to expect you to get up at four-thirty in the morning so you catch a train is ridiculous. We'll have time for coffee."

"Thanks. Thanks a lot. Now that makes me feel good. I earned myself an upgrade. That feels great." Aimee said with a smile of satisfaction.

Aimee brought out assorted food from last night and reheated it in the microwave. She refreshed their drinks, got out the dishes and silverware, placed it all on the coffee table, and sat at Dodo's feet.

"Chef's surprise. Let me know what looks good, and I'll dish it up for you." After dinner, Aimee fixed a tray of desserts.

"Oh, my," said Dodo. "I can't eat this stuff. I have a number of upcoming events, and I can't be a huge tub next to those young, slender girls."

"Life is short. Eat dessert first," Aimee advised.

The next morning, they had coffee, and Aimee hugged Dodo goodbye. She tried to be extra careful; when she hugged Dodo, she seemed to be so frail and fragile. "Oh, pooh. I won't break," said Dodo, giving her a good squeeze. "I'll miss you, Aimee. I haven't made a new friend in ages. It seems I have made a number of them since I met you."

"We start after the holiday with the press and all that for the book, so rest up. Enjoy the peace and quiet."

The driver put Aimee's bags in the trunk. She waved from the limo as she left. *Time to get back to reality,* Aimee thought and napped all the way home.

Chapter 9

Aimee came home and substitute taught for the fall semester. Part of her responsibility was study hall as well as detention. Somehow, what was supposed to be a once-a-month duty, detention, was now a once-a-week requirement. She didn't care; she worked on her manuscript while the kids ignored whatever they were supposed to be doing.

After a few weeks, Aimee noticed the students chronically in detention creeping towards the front of the room until they sat there in the front row, their objective to annoy her. When they sat in the back, they were easy to ignore, but up front, she had to pay attention to them.

She finally looked at them, three boys and a girl, and asked, "What? Why don't you go back to your other seats?"

One of them, a boy named Nick, answered her. "It's too easy for you to ignore us back there."

"Is that why you're in detention every week? Mommy doesn't pay enough attention to you at home, so you act up in school?" Aimee said. The other kids started laughing at him and teased him about his *mommy.*

"Why don't you go back there and finish up your work?"

"Why can't I finish it up here?" he said.

"Look, kid," Amiee put her pencil down. "I get paid to sit here whether you do your work or not. Do you need help with your work? Do you not understand the assignment? Should I see if the Special Ed teacher is free? Maybe she can dumb it down enough for you to understand the instructions."

The other kids laughed again. Nick turned red and looked like he started to get mad. His brow crinkled together as his mouth pulled into a frown.

"That goes for all of you, Einsteins. If you need help, I'll see if I can find someone to help you. Otherwise, piss off and let me get some work done."

"I'm pretty sure you can't tell us to 'piss off,'" one of the other boys said.

"How about I tell you to fuck off? Is that allowed?"

"You can't say that!" the girl, whose name Aimee thought was Ashley, said, shocked at a teacher swearing, especially *that* word.

"So, I guess it's not allowed. Oops. Do you think I'll get fired? Here, let me write you a pass for the principal's office so you can rat me out." Aimee picked up her pencil. "Any takers?" Nobody said anything. "I thought so. Look, kids, I'm not your mother. I don't care what you do or don't do. The only thing I do care about is where you do it, and that's as far away from me as possible. So go to your regular seats in the back of the room and screw off as much as you want. I won't tell."

"What are you doing?" Ashley asked.

"Writing a book." Aimee didn't look up.

"You?" the shorter punk said. "Writing a book? They pay people to write books?"

"Yes, but you can read one for free."

"What kind of book is it?" Ashley wanted to know.

"Some rich guy's life story, but the rich guy asked me to do it and pretend he wrote it."

"Then it's a lie!"

"No, it's not. I'm a ghostwriter. People hire me to write a book they can say they wrote. It happens all the time."

"So you get paid to pretend you're somebody else?"

"Pretty much."

"Cool. But it can't pay that much if you substitute teach," Nick said.

"True. I'm just starting out. I'll let you know in ten years."

"I like to write books," said the shorter one.

"Yeah, right. *Comic books*" said the one who wasn't Nick.

"There is actually a category of books for comics, but they are only called graphic novels. Publishers look for people who specialize in them."

"You're kidding me," the shorter one said.

"I kid you not," Aimee said. "That, however, is all the time we have today, kids. Try to behave yourselves, and maybe I won't see you next week." The bell rang, and everyone stood up. After they gathered their things, they headed out the door.

"See you next week, teach," the short one said.

"God, I hope not," Aimee answered.

***

Aimee finished up her student teaching gig. They offered her another permanent substitute position for the second half of the year, but she declined, hoping the publisher of Dolores's book would hire her, for lack of a better term, to be Dodo's handler. Or manager. Or assistant. In fact, since Aimee spent Thanksgiving with her Dad at Sally's, she was hoping they wouldn't miss her at Christmas. She called Dodo once a week as a way to ease her loneliness, both Aimee's and Dodo's. After all the excitement of the summer, there was a certain hole in each of their lives that the other seemed to fill.

The last time she spoke to Dolores, she also spoke to Rita. Rita was very excited, her daughter had her first child, a girl. She was the first girl grandchild.

Aimee offered to come down the week before Christmas and stay with Dodo so Rita could go into the city and spend the holiday with her new granddaughter.

Aimee told Rita to pack her bags; she was coming. As soon as Mr. Jimmy picked her up from the train and brought her to Dodo's, he was taking Rita to her daughter's house. Aimee gave her the week off, Mr. Jimmy, too, but he was more comfortable at Dodo's, so he would return Christmas night. When he dropped Aimee off at the train station to leave, Rita would be waiting for her ride home.

Aimee's desire to visit Dodo turned into a need. In order for the film to meet the qualifications necessary to be a contender for the Oscars, it would open in select theaters Christmas week. That meant promoting it on all fronts, so the book launch moved up as well. The first week of the New Year, all the morning talk shows would feature the book tour. The stars of the film would handle the press junket. Dolores was supposed to create a buzz that would overflow into interest in the movie. Her resurrected career would leverage the curious to put their 'asses in the seats.' Her involvement in the movie promotion would be minor.

The big focus was the book. It was necessary to have a big buzz. A huge buzz. Old fans were fine, but new fans were needed as well. The cult of celebrity was strong, so Dolores Reardon's vanishing act played right into this. Her re-emergence plugged right into the lure of 'being discovered sitting at a bus stop,' offering hope to all the unknown starlets and ingenues everywhere and igniting the vintage appeal of hipster movie buffs.

Aimee's wish came true, and the book company hired her to go on tour with Dodo. She didn't know Dodo insisted on it, and when the author, an old-school movie star, requested something, she usually got it. Aimee was so happy she didn't have to substitute teach, she didn't care who asked for what.

Joe and Sally had a houseful for the holidays. Aimee asked if they minded if she spent Christmas with Dodo; their house would be empty and could be used to accommodate any of Sally's overflowing guests. Joe said it was fine; in fact, he'd prefer to go to Dodo's, too, but he needed to stay behind and help Sally.

***

Chapter 10

Aimee sent word ahead for Mr. Jimmy to get a Christmas tree, lights, and decorations. She was planning on the visit being a surprise, and Dodo could watch her decorate the tree. Mr. Jimmy told Dodo about Aimee's visit. He knew the only person to give Rita time off was Dolores, and he wanted her permission before Rita took a whole week off.

Dodo was ecstatic that Aimee was coming and told Rita to take all the time she wanted. Dodo called a decorator to have everything done before Aimee arrived, including as many Christmas lights as there were places to put them.

Aimee got there on Thursday; Christmas was on Sunday. Mr. Jimmy took his wife into the city and would be staying for a couple of days. Aimee fixed Dodo their three p.m. cocktail. She talked about the food for Christmas Eve and Day. Dodo handed her a couple of menus from a few of the higher-end restaurants. The decorator recommended ordering in rather than cooking, and both Dodo and Aimee agreed. They needed the order placed no later than three p.m. on Friday.

"Perfect. We'll place the order for both days and celebrate with prepared meals. Should we pretend to be into the holidays at all? Order pre-made cookies and at least bother to frost them? Turn on Christmas music and bake a cheesecake? Anything?"

"Aimee, dear, I think I've lived through enough Christmases to know I'll forget this one, too. I don't feel the need to indulge in any traditions, but you might. Is there anything special your family likes to do? Anything you used to do with your mom?"

"My Mom was funny. She never missed a moment to teach me something. She used to sit me on the counter and play mad scientist when we baked cookies. She used to make me do the fractions. And chemistry. She'd talk about how the bread would rise."

"Your mother made her own bread?"

"No. She got a bread maker as a gift. We used it in the winter sometimes when it was cold out."

"It sounds like growing up was a very non-traumatic event for you,"

"I was on the fringe of being popular. I was a face in the crowd; nobody paid any attention to me, either positively or negatively, which was fine with me. I had all my drama outside the public focus. The prom queen and king's break-up is big news. I was the wedding guest nobody could figure out; neither the bride's side nor the groom claimed to have invited me, but everyone seemed to know me, so it could be figured out later if the couple felt like figuring it out at all.

"So yeah. All the kids were self-supporting and imperfect; some had a harder time growing up than others, but I had a typical childhood. My parents were good people."

"Yes, I love them. They are good people. I'm surprised you're so well-adjusted. Nobody is well-adjusted these days. Your parents provided a stable home life."

Aimee didn't bother to correct Dodo that Sally wasn't her mother.

"Yeah. They did. The middle-class American dream."

"We've evolved beyond that here at Paradise Point. Top shelf all the way. This is the best part about being rich. You get to be a guest at your own party. Somebody else takes on responsibility for providing cleaning up, and they're happy to have the work. We will need to cook a few things, but that's all. Enjoy being my guest."

"I will. My dad and Sally are entertaining her side, so I won't be missed. This will be the calm before the storm. Lots of early mornings coming up."

Promptly at three, the upper gate buzzed, and she let the van in. Aimee unlocked the second gate and went to the front door. She let the food delivery guy in, and he took the assorted pans into the kitchen. He passed by her on the way back for a second load, and he said, "Hello, Aimee."

"Connor! It's you!" she said and threw her arms over his shoulders and kissed him.

"Hey, let me finish getting this stuff." He brought in another load in the kitchen. Once his packages were on the counters, he turned to her and opened his arms. "I'm ready now," he said with a smile.

"Connor! You're delivering food now?"

"Mr. Jimmy told me you were coming. I was at the restaurant when your order was ready for delivery and offered to drop it off. I can't stay; I have to return the van. I did it so I could see you. How long are you in town?"

"I'm not sure. I might need to go home at some point and get some better clothes. After the first of the year, we do all the morning talk shows, so I'll be in the city, but I don't know where we're staying. We haven't got the final itinerary. I'm here through Christmas and a couple days after. How about you?"

"Tonight, we're having dinner at my house. Tomorrow morning, we're leaving early to go to my aunt's in Connecticut. I'm leaving for school right after. I have some work I need to do. I'm meeting with a coach who's supposed to help me find an internship for next semester. Maybe we can meet up when you're in the city."

"Sure, like I said, I don't know my schedule, but Dolores does like to turn in early. It's too bad we can't get together before you leave."

"If you're willing to stay up tonight and wait for me to finish up this family thing, I can stop over around eleven."

Aimee kissed him a couple of times. "Yeah. I think I can stay awake for you. Dodo hired security since Mr. Jimmy was away. I'll let him know to expect you and let you in. After ten, the buzzer rings his pager."

This time, he grabbed her in a huge hug. "Drink a lot of coffee. I'll see you later. I have to get the van back." He kissed her and left.

Aimee returned to the large room off the kitchen. It's where they spent the most time, and she had just served Dodo her three p.m. cocktail. Aimee joined her and picked up her glass of wine. "Food's all set. All we need to do is eat it. I'm keeping it warm in the oven."

"The delivery boy looked familiar," Dodo observed.

"He should. That's Connor. He was the guy in the tuxedo at your party."

"Wasn't he sweet on you?"

"Yes, he was. He still is. Do you mind if he stops by later tonight? He's not going to be in town the rest of the week."

Dolores gave her a sly look. "Of course not."

"You planned this all out, having Mr. Jimmy go tell him I was in town, didn't you?" Aimee accused her.

"Merry Christmas, Aimee."

"You meddler, you," Aimee said. "I think I'll find some rich old coot to entertain *you*. See how much you like other people poking around in your love life. But thanks, I am happy to see Connor."

"Once I retire for the evening, the house is yours. Do it anywhere you want. Everywhere you want."

"That's not why he's coming over. He's only coming over to say hello."

"As long as he comes, I don't care what you're doing."

Aimee caught Dodo's double entendre. "I'm definitely finding you a man."

"Sorry, hon. They're all dead."

"Maybe someone you overlooked will come to a book signing, and you'll fall in love over a black Sharpie marker," Aimee suggested.

"Maybe. I just want my picture in *People* looking fabulous."

"I'll take that. Let me put the food in." The decorator even had the table set. "After dinner, we can watch *It's a Wonderful Life*."

"Oh, that Donna Reed," Dodo started.

"Now stop that. No negative energy on Christmas Eve." Aimee warned her.

"I was going to say what a lovely woman." Dolores finished.

"Better. Should we have one more with dinner?"

"Just one. It's a holiday, after all." Dodo passed Aimee her empty glass.

They delivered a wonderful dinner of roast tenderloin of beef, mashed potatoes, and green beans. There was also a box of assorted desserts.

"Dodo, do you have a meat thermometer? We need to heat it until it's warm and not overcook it."

"Meat thermometer? Is that something you shove up a cow's ass to see if it has a fever?" Dodo laughed.

"Yes. We need to see if it has mad cow disease." It was Aimee's turn to laugh. "Maybe we shouldn't have another drink."

"Oh, pooh. I'm sure if you look in those drawers over there, you can find one. I only have red wine once a year, but it's on Christmas Eve, so open a bottle of red. Did you find that thing?"

"Yes, I did, and I found a corkscrew. I'll open the wine and let it breathe. They have us all set up in the dining room. Fancy. I'm going to pretend I'm a movie star."

"Go ahead. I am one, and it's nice work if you can get it."

"Oh, Dodo. I want to be you when I grow up."

"Just don't overstay your welcome. If you die too early, you're a washed-up has-been. You have to live long enough to become 'vintage' or 'retro.' You come back into style on a wave of nostalgia. I've got to say, I'm happy to be able to do it now. I'm not sure I could keep this pace up much longer. I might not have the stamina next year."

"We probably are lucky we can get this done now. After the book, you get a brief hiatus, and then it's all the Oscar promo; you can smile through that. Let the studio handle the rest. Your only job is to look like a million bucks on the red carpet Oscar night."

"Speaking of the Oscars, I need one of those things. A one-off."

"What's that?"

"A date. You know."

"You mean a plus one?"

"Yes. A plus one. Would you like to be my escort?"

"To the Oscars? Hell, yes," Aimee said. "Wouldn't you like to bring a guy? I can see if Connor is free."

"Connor? He only has eyes for you, Aimee."

"Maybe he has an older brother."

"This whole thing started with you; I want to finish it with you. I figure this will be your only chance to go to Hollywood and live like a star, so I want you as my guest. If you don't come, I'll get paired with some studio handler, and that won't be very much fun at all. So please be my guest."

"I'd love to, but you need to clear it with the studio. I'm not sure they'd go for it. The studio would want someone more marketable to the industry. I'm a writer, not a celebrity. They may drag in some old guy from Central Casting to play your date."

"Let me take care of it," Dodo said.

"I think the meat has rested enough. I'll carve at the table. Time for dinner."

It was just the two of them. Dodo asked about the Christmases of Aimee's childhood. Aimee had lots of stories; she had a typical middle-class childhood, and her family was content with enough. Her parents might have been able to give them more but never did. They could have gone to Disneyland but instead went to Cape Cod.

"The only person who had a problem was my sister Carrie. She wanted her life to be one big extravaganza after another and found her middle-class upbringing deficient in pretty much everything.

"Carrie always had a problem with our mother. Each school year, there were several exclusive, sought-after brand names kids wanted to go back to school. Our mom conceded one on-trend brand item. After that, Sears. Sam always got sneakers. I got a monogrammed leather backpack, and Carrie picked a necklace from Tiffany's. Something totally useless. I wondered why she didn't pick the down jacket; that necklace wouldn't keep her warm come fall.

"Carrie constantly fought about needing more clothes. My Mom said to get a job or go to the thrift store. Carrie saved her babysitting money and blew it on something expensive and totally impractical. She now sells real estate in LA, the land of the rich and famous. She's worked hard for those nice things, sacrificing her personal life on the altar of conspicuous consumption.

"That was the price. She was ready to pay and happy to do it. It would kill her if I were in Hollywood. I'll call her, and we can all have lunch; see if the studio can hook us up with the latest and greatest spot. She would die if I had A-list connections and I'm going to the Academy Awards. Carrie would try to squeeze an invite out of you but don't fall for it. Besides, I doubt they'd want to waste a ticket on me."

"Let me talk to the film people. If they want to use my newfound fame and my established reputation, they'll need to play by my rules."

"I wish she didn't fight like she did with my Mom. She died when I was nineteen, and I have a lot more memories of Carrie fighting with her than I have of her doing anything else," Aimee said. "I'll do the dishes, and we can go sit by the fire."

"Don't worry about the dishes. They'll be back in the morning to take care of everything."

"I don't think I can leave a mess. Maybe it's my middle-class upbringing, but I can't leave it like this. Just let me put the leftovers away and bring the dishes into the kitchen."

"If you must, Aimee," Dodo said. "If you must. I'll be nice and cozy by the fire."

They sat by the fire for a bit and watched the movie, Dodo could barely stay awake. Soon, Aimee walked her to her room, got her pajamas ready and turned down the bed.

"Goodnight, Dodo. Dream of dancing sugar plums, or whatever those things are. I'll see you in the morning." Aimee said as she escorted Dodo to her room.

"'Night dear. If you're expecting company, make sure you give Anton notice. He can let him in. Why don't you close those outer doors? You can be secure in your privacy."

"You mean these outer doors? How much noise are you expecting us to make?"

"You can make as much as you want now. Good night, Aimee." Dodo shut the door with a smile that made Aimee blush.

***

Aimee didn't realize the pocket doors closed off the whole suite. She buzzed Anton and told him to expect Connor and to have him come in through the kitchen. Aimee turned off all the lights except the Christmas ones. She turned the TV off and sat on the floor, glancing around in awe; she never got sick of Christmas lights. The decorator trimmed all the doorways in twinkling white lights. Aimee crawled over, put another log on and keyed the music of old English carols on low. She looked around and felt a tug on her heart, the lights, the fire, and perhaps the wine made her loose and romantic.

She heard a knock on the kitchen door and jumped up to let Connor in. "Hi, Connor." She smiled at him.

"Hi, Aimee. Why are you looking at me like that?"

"I was just wondering if it would be rude to jump on you."

"Not at all," he said and grabbed her. He started to kiss her, and she found herself floundering. He surprised her by taking the lead and kissing her stupidly. Aimee had it all planned out in her head, where she set the scene and seduced him.

He flipped the switch and had her backpedaling, trying to catch up to him. Connor knew she'd probably take the lead and wanted to catch her off guard. He wanted her off guard the entire time he was there. It took most of last semester to get Aimee out of his head; he wanted to be in *her* head for a while. Let her try not to think about him for the next couple of months. Connor picked her up and sat her on the counter while he took his coat off. He took her and deposited her on the couch in front of the fire.

"Very nice, Aimee."

"What is?"

"The decor. All those lights. The roaring fire. A very nicely executed atmosphere for romance."

"Think so?"

"Unfortunately, I'm still full from dinner, so we'll just have to make out for a while."

Connor kissed Aimee for a bit, trying to go slow and torment her for as long as possible. Aimee, however, met him kiss for a kiss until he was the one being tormented. He decided he wasn't going down first, so he matched her but turned the heat up. Every kiss went deeper, and every touch raised more goosebumps. He wouldn't let her catch her breath until she finally pulled away, panting.

"So, somebody's been practicing," she said.

"Not practice. Research. Last time, after I went home, I looked for one of those books, a Romance novel? There's always some guy on the cover who looks like Fabio. I found one that must have been my mom's, so I took it back to school with me. My roommates gave me a ton of shit about it, but I told them about how women want romance."

"I would have given anything to be a fly on the wall. What did you tell them?" Aimee asked him.

"Just that if you want to get a woman in the mood, spend more time trying to get in her head and less time trying to get in her pants."

"That's exactly right."

He stopped talking and started kissing her neck and nibbling on her earlobe. She started to giggle, and he kept at it. Soon, he found other spots on her neck that made her laugh as well. Before she knew it, they were on the floor naked in front of the fireplace.

"You look beautiful in the firelight. It makes your eyes sparkle, and your body has all these areas in shadow that just beg to be explored." Connor said and spent some time exploring her, still telling her how beautiful she was.

While he whispered in her ear, he let his hands roam all over her. He slid his fingers between her legs and could not believe how wet and slippery she was. Aimee was arching her body towards him, telling him without words how much she wanted him.

Connor wanted to hold off and show her how closely he paid attention, but her talk was pushing him to the edge. She was on her back and looking at him with an evil smile. It both excited and frightened him. He watched her face as she watched him watch her, and he almost came in his hand while putting on the condom.

He fully intended to romance the hell out of her, but between the crackle and warmth of the fire and the twinkling lights, he kind of romanced the hell out of himself. Connor felt Aimee yield and give herself over to him. He looked at her. Her eyes were closed, her lips parted, still with that smile on her face. His eyes couldn't stay on her, he would come immediately.

The other thing Connor learned from that book was it was always called "making love," not fucking. He had very little experience in making love, but he was an expert at fucking. Connor decided it was just slowing everything down and paying attention more. He tried like hell to "make love" to Aimee.

He went back to that part of her neck that caused her to giggle. Connor kissed her there and used his tongue to lick her. He could sense she enjoyed him focusing on her both inside and out. Connor started to talk in her ear, his breath warm as he whispered everything wonderful about her. She started moving beneath him, and he hoped she was close because he wasn't sure how much longer he could hold out.

"Aimee," he whispered to her, "look at me."

She opened her eyes but kept moving her hips. She held his gaze as he felt her body start to shudder, and a little moan escaped her mouth. Aimee wrapped her arms around him and pulled him down on top of her. He could feel her orgasm ripple through her like waves, like a pebble in a pond. Connor let go and couldn't help it; nature took over, and he drove as deep as he could and shuddered along with her. He laid on top of her for a minute, waiting for his racing heart to calm, and then rolled off her.

"Geez. I thought you were trying to kill me," he said, breathless.

"It was that good?" She asked.

"Incredible. Is your father here?"

"My Dad? That's a weird question. No. If he was, he'd shoot you for doing his daughter. Why?"

"Damn. If he caught us, we'd have a shotgun wedding, and I wouldn't have to ask for his permission to marry you." Connor told her.

"That again? You don't want to marry me. You're on sensory overload. The fire. The lights. My breath in your ears. Your eyes are on mine. My skin is on yours. It's magic. Love magic, maybe, but it's magic."

"Are you a witch or some kind of sorceress? 'Cause you sure put a spell on me." Connor asked her.

"No." She sighed. "Just a hopeless romantic."

"Do you ever have sex in places that aren't done up so fancy?"

"No. That's why you could never marry me. I'd be too busy with my head in the clouds. You'd come home from work and want dinner and some good loving, and I'd be like, what? Dinner? Again? Didn't we just have dinner last night? I'm not meant to operate in the real world. I spend too much time in my head.

I'm the kind of person who'd get hit by a bus because I'd be daydreaming and not notice the light changed."

"You think so?"

"Yeah. I prefer the people in my stories. The heroes act like heroes, not like egotistical, cheating, rat bastard law students."

"I don't get it. You're this great person and a whole lot of fun."

"I can be. I can also be stubborn and selfish. And a bore. I guess in order to be a ghostwriter, I have to be a blank slate. Otherwise, I'd inject too much of myself into someone else's story."

"That doesn't sound like much of a life, depriving yourself of one so you can write about someone else's," Connor observed.

"Perhaps, but I don't want that much of a life. Being a wife or a mother never interested me. I've always wanted to be a writer. That's what interested me. That's what always interested me, so that's what I am."

"But you're so much more. You're the most amazing girl I've ever met."

She kissed him. "I know you think so, and thank you for that. I know I set the mood. The inspiration it gave was all you. The rest was all you."

"But you set me up. You create these living fantasies, and I fill in the blanks. This laying in front of the fireplace has to be played out in the romance genre."

"Genre?" she said, laughing.

"Yes, genre. I told you I did some research. But how many of those books have this same scene in them? Most of them, probably."

"Yeah. So what? You seemed to enjoy it,"

"Yes, I did. You are kinda right. It doesn't matter. If I walk in on a gorgeous, sexy naked woman lying in front of a fieldstone fireplace, I'm going for it." He leaned over and kissed her. "Every time. I have to put another log on, so stay put."

Aimee sat up with her back against the sofa, facing the fire. Connor sat next to her. They sat close and talked in low voices late into the night. The sky started to brighten, signaling the imminent sunrise.

"Wow, Aimee, we've been talking all night. I have to get going."

"That's too bad. I like talking to you. You're a pretty interesting guy."

"I have my moments." Connor stood up and got dressed. "Do you have any idea if I'll ever see you again?"

"Next week, we're doing the morning shows. Turn on your TV."

"I'm not kidding, Aimee. I want to see you again."

"Talk to my dad." He made a face. "There. Over there by the phone. A pen and pad. Write your address and number. I'll let you know when I have some free time. Dodo's too old to party past eight p.m., so I imagine I won't be too busy in the evenings."

He came over and kissed her goodbye. "I'm expecting a call. Don't let me down. Aw, shit," he said. "One more." He kissed her again.

"Merry Christmas, Aimee," he said and let himself out.

"Merry Christmas, Connor," Aimee said as she kissed him goodbye.

Chapter 11

She locked up afterwards, and he left and turned off the lights. Aimee went to bed for a couple of hours. She slept for a while, but the clean-up crew woke her up with their noise, and she got up after they left. The coffee pot had been cleaned and replenished. All she had to do was press on, and the smell of fresh coffee filled the kitchen. Aimee had her head in the fridge looking for cream when Dodo entered.

"Good Morning, Aimee. Merry Christmas."

"Merry Christmas, Dodo. Coffee?"

"Yes, please. We can have it by the tree and open presents."

Aimee fixed Dodo's cup in addition to her own and carried the mugs over to the tree. She placed her cup down, handed hers to Dodo and stifled a yawn. "Sorry."

"Did you stay up late with your guest?" Dodo asked. "Did he enjoy his gift?"

"His gift? What gift?"

Dodo bent over, picked up a condom wrapper off the floor and held it out to Aimee. She blushed and took the wrapper. "Yes, he did."

"Smart guy."

"Yes, he is. Who are all these presents for?" Aimee asked, surprised at the number.

"Rita, Jimmy, their kids, and a couple of them are for you."

"Me? I hope not. I only got you one."

"Give it to me. I can't wait," Dodo said and stretched out her arms.

"Please don't get your hopes up," Aimee said as she fished it out of the pile. "It's more of a memento than a gift."

"Those are my favorite. Pass it over."

Aimee handed her what was obviously a wrapped picture. "Three guesses."

Dodo unwrapped the frame. Aimee had one of the book jackets mounted, fresh off the presses. It had the cover, back and inside fold with the picture of the two of them mounted before it had ever been folded.

"Look! It's us!" Dolores said, pleased with the gift.

"Do you like it? It's hard to figure out what to get to get the woman who has two of everything."

"Well, I don't have one of these. Soon, I'll have a bestseller and a triumphant return to film. This ties it all together. A picture with my new best friend." Dolores hugged the picture with both arms.

"You consider me a best friend? That's the best present I could ever get. Take all these presents and give them to the poor," Aimee said as she gestured to the pile under the tree.

"All your presents are in the green paper." Dolores pointed at the pile.

Aimee looked at what was left and shook her head. "That's way too many."

"You can open them and then give them away."

"Okay, if you insist." The first one Aimee opened contained a beautiful hand-tooled leather journal and a very expensive pen. "Dodo, you shouldn't have. It's beautiful. It's too much. I probably can't even afford the replacement ink for this pen."

"Aimee, I've got to say this poverty thing is a crashing bore. I'm sure you don't have the luxury not to be, do you? You only have so much; you have to make sure you don't waste it. But it is dreary."

"That's the truth. Being poor is boring," Aimee agreed. She reached out and grabbed another. "To Dodo, from Ione. Who's Ione?"

Dodo reached for it. "My stepson is, or was, her stepdad."

"Really, Dodo. She still thinks about you. You must have meant something to her for her to send you a gift."

"I do remember her. She'd get up in the morning and go for a sunrise walk with me. Every time for a couple of years, I'd pass by the lower cottage and hear a screen door slam, her feet slapping on the stairs and running to catch up with me. I asked her why she didn't do this with any of her grown-ups, and she laughed. 'We don't have anyone awake to supervise us. If I didn't go with you, it would be a waste of a trip to the ocean.' I hired a girl from the club to supervise them so they could explore when they wanted to. They would come to my house for lunch. Ione." Dodo sighed.

"What's in the box?"

Dodo read the card and smiled. "'A donation has been made in your name to the Paradise Point Dune Preservation Association.' She did love the beach."

The next box contained the same.

"Who's that from?"

"Joe Dunsmore and Sally Reade." Dolores read off the card.

"You have got to be kidding me! How did they know?"

"Your father is a very good listener as well as a very smart man. He asked Mr. Jimmy."

"I'll make sure I tell him you said so," Aimee said and reached for another box.

She opened a box from the First Street Publishing Company. Inside was a gift card to be used at Sak's Fifth Avenue. She had an appointment Tuesday at ten a.m. to meet with her personal stylist. They had been briefed regarding Aimee's role. Dress her in classics, neutrals; nothing to outshine the star.

"Wow. What does this mean?" Aimee said with a puzzled look on her face.

"The co-ed comfort look has got to go," Dolores informed her.

"Why do I have to get dressed up to go backstage?"

"Didn't I tell you? We're double billed—you have to sit next to me."

"Wait? What? On stage? With you? I can't do that! I don't have anything to wear. Even if I went home, I have nothing there, either."

"That's why you're going to Saks."

"I can't afford clothes from Saks."

"This is on the publishing house. Buy brand new things right down to your unmentionables. New shoes, and some boots. Have it all sent here."

"If you say so. What's this last box?"

"It's for you. Another gift from our publishers."

Aimee opened the box and found a check for ten thousand dollars. She picked it up with a shocked look on her face. "What's this? There has to be some mistake."

"It's partial payment for the interview. You never charged them for the actual interview."

"Didn't I have a contract? I don't remember the interview fee?"

"About that. Your lawyer was a bum. I had mine renegotiate a better deal for you."

"Thanks. I won't have to teach this semester," Aimee said and smiled.

"About that. Are you going back to school to get your teaching degree?"

"Not if I can help it," Aimee said.

"You should figure out a better way to make a living."

"Don't bum me out. I'll get up and see what the directions are for dinner. Would you like more coffee?" Aimee asked as she got up.

They spent a quiet Christmas Day watching old movies and napping. Mr. Jimmy came back early, leaving Rita behind.

A few days later, he gave her a ride to Sak's for her appointment. Her stylist, Rhoda, took Aimee's measurements and sent her to the salon for a blowout. Why she needed a blowout was beyond her, but once Aimee returned, the stylist said it was the final piece to determine what would complement Aimee's new look.

"A new look? I thought I was just getting a couple of outfits for TV. I don't need a new look."

"Trust me. You need a new look."

Aimee felt uncomfortable. She couldn't afford a new wardrobe, and she thought Rhoda completely dismissed her. To Rhoda, she was just a human mannequin. *I'm supposed to dress to the nines to run out and get coffee? I don't think so,* Aimee decided.

"Okay," said Rhoda, "we need to get you out of what you wore here. You are a beautiful young woman. There is no reason you should be walking around looking like a college kid. You need to embrace who you are now. The minute you walked in here, I said, 'No, no, no. What a waste. She needs a complete overhaul.'"

"What do you mean? I always dress like this. It's good enough for running errands, that's about all I do."

"Well, you only have one chance to make a first impression. They say that for a reason. You don't want people to think you're a bag lady, do you? Now get out of those clothes, and let's get you properly dressed for an afternoon in Manhattan."

"But I'm not spending the afternoon here."

"Maybe you should. I have something hanging up in the dressing room. It will be perfect on you."

Aimee went into the dressing room and looked at the outfit. It was the ubiquitous black big city uniform. She tried it on and looked at herself in the mirror. The slender black pants fit perfectly and paired with the black v-neck knit sweater, she looked long and lean. Even the boots were an upgrade from her trusted Doc Marten's. They had stacked heels that made her taller but were sturdy enough that she wouldn't break an ankle on her jaunt around Manhattan. She came out of the dressing room, and Rhoda exclaimed, "Here," and brought her over to the full-length mirror. She pointed at Aimee's reflection.

"See, look at you. When you put a little care into what you're wearing, you look like somebody people should know, and taking your hair out of that awful ponytail did wonders."

"I look like every other woman under sixty around here, wearing all black."

"No, you don't. You look like what every woman under sixty *wants* to look like. Trust me. I do this for a living. You exude health and confidence; most of the women who want this look can't pull it off. They look like they're wearing potato sacks. This is *your* look. You were born to wear it."

"If you say so, Rhoda. Let me change out of it and send it with the rest."

"You can't. I sent your clothes to the incinerator. You'll have to wear it home." Rhoda replied and handed her a black trench coat. "This finishes the look."

"But my boots. I need those boots," Aimee begged.

"Don't worry about those damn boots. I know how much they mean to you. My kids wear the same kind, and I know how important they are. Speaking from a purely fashionable perspective, they do nothing but weigh you down and make you look bottom-heavy, and they do nothing as far as establishing a clean line for the eye to follow. The boots you have on are functional but don't interrupt the eye. Your boots are packed with the others. Your driver is loading everything up;

you can meet him out front. You watch, Aimee. People are going to be looking at you, wondering if you're a star."

"I don't want to be looked at; I like to blend in, Rhoda."

"I hate to break it to you, Aimee, but you've won the genetic lottery. You are a very beautiful girl, but a stunning woman. Someday, they'll stop looking, and you'll miss it, believe me."

Everything was packed up for Aimee to decide what she liked once she tried it on at Dodo's. After the clothes were loaded, Mr. Jimmy's Cadillac picked her up out front. While she waited, she did what a good writer does. Aimee observed humanity; only she noticed people looking back and observing her. Rhoda was right; people looked at her differently.

Aimee wasn't sure she liked it.

Mr. Jimmy pulled up. "How was your shopping trip, Miss Aimee? You look very nice. Is there any place else you'd like to go while we're here?"

Aimee picked up her oversized bag and dug through it. She was glad she left it in the car; otherwise, Rhoda might have pitched it in the trash. Aimee pulled out a piece of paper and handed it to Mr. Jimmy.

"Is this nearby? I just want to stop and say hello."

"We are in a car, Miss Aimee. Everything is nearby. Shall we drive over?"

"Yes, please."

***

Mr. Jimmy pulled up in front of an apartment building. The streets were busy with college kids on their way to and from academic buildings.

"This is the address, Miss Aimee. Are you going inside?"

"Yes." She thought about leaving. What if Connor was up there banging some girl? Her new black outfit made her feel a little dangerous, but it gave her some courage. So what if he had some girl up there? She was only going to say hello. "I should be right back. If you have to move the car, I'll wait out front for you."

She walked to the door but didn't see his name near the buzzer. Someone came out, and she slipped into the building. Aimee still had no idea where to find him or what floor he lived on, so she turned to exit when she heard someone ask her if she needed help.

"Hello," she said to the voice. It was a younger-looking guy. "Do you know where Connor Edmond lives?"

"Yeah. He's on my floor. Follow me."

She got on the elevator with him. The walls were plastered with flyers. It looked like an elevator in any university. She glanced at the guy who was helping her and introduced herself.

"Thanks so much for helping me. My name's Aimee."

"No problem. I'm Ben. This is our floor." They exited the elevator. "His room is the last one on the left. I'm going this way. Nice to meet you, Aimee." She walked down the hall to his room. She had her hand up to knock when the door opened, and a guy stepped through, almost knocking her over.

"Oh, hey. Sorry. Whoa," he said. "Looking for me?"

"Sorry, but no. I'm looking for Connor."

"My name's Connor. Is that good enough?"

"No, Connor Edmond."

"ConEd? He never mentioned a hot girlfriend like you."

"That's because I'm not his girlfriend. I'm his parole officer."

"Oh. No, he's in class. If you want to leave a note, his room is across from the bathroom. I'd help you, but I'm late. Just shut the door behind you. It'll lock."

"Thanks, Connor."

"It's not Connor. It's Nate."

"I thought so. Thanks, Nate."

"He'll be sorry he missed you."

"No, he won't. He missed his court date. He's in a little bit of trouble. Enjoy your afternoon."

He left, and she went in to leave him a message. Aimee found a piece of paper near the printer, which was easy. She searched for a pen, but the only thing she found was a dry-erase marker. She wrote: 'Stopped by to say hi. Will be at the Ritz Sun-Thurs next week. Call me. A.' Aimee looked for tape but didn't want to waste time searching for it. She found a steak knife and stabbed the note into his door. Aimee thought his roommates would get a kick out of it.

She took the elevator down but needed to wait for Mr. Jimmy. Aimee leaned against the building and indulged in her go-to hobby, people-watching. She started to count the number of girls wearing all black. There were many, but Aimee looked different. Maybe it was the quality of her clothes, but Aimee decided it was the blowout. She had grown-up hair, whereas the college girls all had ponytails or messy buns.

"No Connor yet?" Connor's roommate asked.

"No, Nate, he never came home. Aren't you late for class?" She saw Mr. Jimmy pull up. "You better get going. You don't want to get on my list," Aimee said as Mr. Jimmy got out and opened the door for her. She got in, and he shut the door. Mr. Jimmy hustled to the driver's side, got in, and pulled out into traffic.

Aimee leaned over the seat and asked him what that was all about.

"Playing to the crowd, Miss Aimee. Show those young pups to stay in school and study hard; someday, they'll be as successful as you."

"But none of this is mine."

"They don't know that."

***

Connor got back to his apartment late; Nate and Brendan, the third roommate, were watching TV. Connor noticed them staring at him when he came home.

"What is wrong with you guys? Why are you staring at me?"

"'ConEd. You dog," Brendan said.

"I met your parole officer today. I don't know what you did over the summer, but lock me up and throw away the key if I can get a smoking-hot parole officer like her," Nate said.

"What are you talking about? I don't have a parole officer."

"I don't know who she was. She left you a note and a big black limo picked her up out front. Throw yourself on the mercy of the court, dude."

Connor went and looked at his door with a knife holding the note sticking out. He pointed at it.

"This? She left this? Aimee was here?" Connor laughed. "Figures I'd miss her."

"Dude, she's telling you to look her up next week at the Ritz Carlton. I saw her. She was wearing this black trench coat like she was a spy or something, and she kept flipping this thick brown hair—"

"You sure? I've never seen her hair not in a ponytail." *Oh, wait, I did, and it really was something,* Connor thought. "I wonder what she wanted."

"For you to call her next week. She's staying at the Ritz fucking Carlton. How dumb can you be?" Nate said. "You should stay away from her. You'd be in over your head. I'll call her."

“I saw her first, dude,” Connor said and left the message up. It made him smile every time he looked at it. His roommates never had a girl go to this length to give them a message.

Chapter 12

Aimee ran her items by Dodo and decided this all-black thing had its merits. Everything always matched. She could wear boots. They did the big morning shows, the morning talk shows, and then syndication-taped pieces. Aimee and Dodo worked very well together; they played off each other with a charming, spontaneous affection. Aimee could tell when Dodo's energy was lagging, she would tell the story and set Dodo up to execute a flawless punchline. The interaction between the two of them was seamless; their affection for each other was genuine.

Aimee had a message from Connor when she checked in at the Ritz, telling her to call him as soon as she checked in. She called, and they made plans for Wednesday night.

There were two formal dinners scheduled Monday and Tuesday; one to celebrate the best-selling memoir of Hollywood's last living legend, the other the movie people wanted in on their success. Tuesday was Dolores's ninetieth birthday.

Aimee switched the dinner to lunch on Tuesday to spare Dodo the longer day. They celebrated her birthday, the limited release at the end of the year gave the film excellent reviews, and the reception to the book was outstanding. The intent of using the positive press generated from the book as a vehicle to carry the movie into the award season was working. It was a clear all-the-bases home run. They delivered.

The only cause for concern was the schedule they expected Dodo to keep. Aimee didn't like that they had her booked from the early morning to late at night. Even if Dodo wanted to keep up, she was still ninety years old, and her body was ninety years old. It wasn't right the way the PR machine exploited Dolores, but she didn't seem to mind.

The luncheon was only for people in the film industry. Aimee and Dodo were back in their suite for their three o'clock cocktail. Dolores wouldn't admit it, but she was dog-tired and happy to retire to her room. They had a quiet night, with room service supplying the cake and candles.

Amy had two pieces of cake delivered, and they watched all these people from the infotainment industry complex. Dolores helped create all. I wish her a happy ninetieth on TV. News people during the national nightly news wished Dolores Reardon a Happy Birthday. Even Lester Holt wished "America's Last Living Legend a Happy Birthday."

They laughed and cheered each time they heard her name. There were Dolores Reardon film festivals and retrospections. Dolores Reardon was a hot commodity.

"Dolores, would you mind if I made plans for dinner tomorrow?"

"Of course not. To tell you the truth, I'm getting kind of sick of you."

"Good. I'm getting sick of you, too."

"Who's your dinner date?" Dolores asked innocently enough, but she knew the answer.

Aimee blushed. "It's Connor. I figured I'd never see him again after this trip, so why not take advantage of it? I doubt I'll have any reason to come back here in the future. He's going to Michigan after he graduates, so that's that."

"You don't need a reason to come here. Why can't he be the reason?"

"I don't want him to think there's a future with me because there isn't. He's at a point in his life where there's substantial personal growth. He needs to go out and experience life. I don't have much of one, but I like it that way. It works for me. He's too young. There is a lot more to life than the person you decide you want. She may look great on a red carpet, but she's not the 'everyday' kind of girl. She won't have your dinner ready or your laundry done, and she won't feel bad about it, either."

"I know. It takes boys much longer to mature."

"I don't know if that's it. He's right where he should be. I've already been there. Dodo, you were married five times. How did you know you wanted to marry them?"

"You'll have to read my book to find out," Dolores said with a laugh. "They each served a purpose at different stages in my life. The number of people I've been related to is amazing, and I've outlived most of them and alienated the rest of them. It was wonderful having you come for the holidays. It was nice not to be lonely."

"You have a lot to look forward to, the upcoming award shows and all the parties. It will be a busy couple of months."

"About that. Since you're not teaching, you're definitely going to be my escort to the Academy Awards, right? I know I asked you before, but I confirmed it with the studio. I put your name down so you can't back out. We've done the book tour together and had a riot. If this is my last hurrah, I don't want to go out on the arm of some senile old studio executive. Besides, when are you ever going to get an invite to the Oscars? You just can't look better than I do."

"I didn't think you were serious. I thought you were kidding. I figured the studio would turn you down flat." Aimee sounded nervous.

"I might tease Aimee, but I never kid. The studio can deny me nothing."

"But I can't—"

"The rest of that sentence better not be you can't afford it."

"But I can't, Dodo."

"The basic law of Hollywood is when you're on top, bleed the suckers dry. They'll not hesitate to dump you when you lose your shine. Right now, I have the power. They want to use and exploit me because my story will sell tickets. I know that, so I'm going to use them back. I'll demand you be my escort, and they'll have to pony up the cash until I'm happy. That means first-class accommodations. Clothing. Accessories. I'm going to insist they drape you in diamonds from Harry Winston."

"That's not going to happen. I'm a nobody."

"I know that. You know that. They don't. So we are going to soak them for all we can get. You could be the latest undiscovered ingenue, and someone's looking at you only to leverage your career to build one for themselves."

"I'll be your date, but I'm not wearing heels."

Dodo, having won the battle, sat back and smiled. As far as the shoes went, that was a subject to argue over another day. "What's on the agenda for tomorrow? Are we almost done?"

"We did all the big shows. Now you sit, and the reporters come to you. They have taped entertainment news pieces for the local affiliates. I imagine whoever you talk to will bring a cameraman with them, and then it's more blah, blah, blah. Again, we start at eight, but hopefully, we'll be done by two and make it back by three for our afternoon ritual."

"Entertainment news? There is such a thing? How ridiculous."

"Well, there's only about four hundred TV channels. They have to broadcast something. You can handle this by yourself, right?"

"I could, but I'm not going to. You're going to be part of this media circus until it's over."

"I'm supposed to be a ghostwriter. How can I be a ghostwriter if everyone knows who I am?"

"I don't know, but you'll figure it out. What time is your date? Where are you going?"

"Probably nowhere. We'll get room service and hang out."

***

There were three entrances to the suite. The main one and two unmarked doors further down the hall, one on each side, allowed direct access to the smaller bedroom suites. This allowed for the guests' privacy. They heard a knock on the main door, and Aimee answered it.

"Look, Dodo, somebody sent you roses." She gave Dodo the card and placed the flowers in the center of the table. Aimee stood back and looked at them, then proceeded to rearrange the bouquet to her satisfaction.

"Who sent you the roses, Dodo?"

"Nobody. Your name is on the envelope. They're for you."

"That can't be right." She opened up the card. "Oh, no."

"Who, Aimee, who?"

"Connor. It says to be in the lobby at five p.m. I can't believe he did this. I told him not to get attached."

"Looks like he disregarded your instructions. Goody."

"Goody? What goody?"

"The boy isn't a pushover. Everything has been on your terms if I'm not mistaken. It seems like he's trying to woo you." Dolores said, rubbing her hands together, pleased that Connor was going to knock her for a loop.

"What woo? Woo who?"

"Woo you. He wants to show you he can give as good as he gets."

"Well, I'm not sure I like it."

"I'm not sure you have a choice. I can't wait for tomorrow night. Let's see what else he has in store for you."

"It better not be a carriage ride in Central Park."

***

Aimee wasn't sure what Connor had planned, but she wore another version of her new all-black uniform. She was so nervous she went downstairs fifteen minutes early. Dodo kept teasing her, which only made Aimee more nervous. She sat in the lobby, waiting for Connor to arrive. He walked in right after she sat down. She saw him look for her, and once he saw her, he smiled so big she could see it from the other side of the lobby. He hurried over and sat down.

"Aimee! I'm so glad to see you! I'm sorry I wasn't home when you stopped by. You look beautiful. I saw you on TV a bunch of times. I made Nate get up and see you on GMA. He was like, yeah, that's your parole officer. Now he thinks you're a movie star."

Aimee could feel her face getting red. "Thank you, Connor. The flowers are gorgeous, by the way."

"I'm glad you liked them."

"Do you mind if I ask you what we're doing? I thought you'd hang out, and we could order room service, but it seems like you have other plans."

"Does it make you nervous, Aimee?" he said with a smile.

"Kind of. I'm not used to flying blind."

"Let me explain. The time we spent together was always some elaborate fantasy you created. Being with you feels like I woke up in the middle of somebody else's dream. You've got some strong magic there, girlie."

"Thank you, but—"

"But nothing. I'm taking you out on a date. We're going to bum around the city and window shop, and when you get tired, we can grab dinner. After dinner, we'll come back here and see what happens."

"Okay, but I'm not much of a shopper."

"Enough. We are going to leave here and see what happens. No midnight swims, no twinkling lights, no roaring fires. It's just you, me and whatever chemistry we have together." He stood up and held his hand out. She took it and got up. They stopped once they got out in front of the hotel.

"Right or left?" Connor asked her.

"You pick. You're the one who's taking me out."

"Fair enough. This way." He took her hand and went left. Aimee noticed him smiling and looking at her out of the side of his eye.

"Okay, what gives? Why are you looking at me like that?"

"Are those the clothes you wore when you came over?"

"No, but I was wearing all black. Why?"

"My roommate Nate thought you were with the CIA. Or a spy. He said a big black limo picked you up, and the driver got out and held the door for you."

"Oh, that was Mr. Jimmy goofing around."

"Well, you sure impressed him. I have to say I'm a little scared of the new you." Connor admitted.

"These clothes? When I had to get a new wardrobe for the TV shows, Dodo had this stylist do a complete overhaul. She said my shirts and sweats looked like I slept in my clothes, and if I wanted to be taken seriously, I needed to dress my age. She also said no more ponytails and sent me to get a blowout. I guess I look a lot older if I look like a government operative."

"That's it; your hair. You always wear it up. The stylist was right. I think it's part of your M.O. to dress as ambiguously as possible. Now I kind of see what you mean. You don't look like the kind of girl you bring to a frat party. You look way older and out of my league."

Aimee stopped and pushed Connor against a brick wall, grabbed his head and kissed him like the Aimee who kissed him in the pool. She stopped and smiled at him.

"See. Same old me. I do like the new clothes. All black means everything matches, and deciding what to wear becomes a no-brainer."

"You look great. Really great. Not that you looked like a lazy slob before, but now you look like what all these other women are trying to look like. A native New Yorker."

"I know, but I'm just a hick from upstate."

"Don't worry. I won't tell anybody."

They turned down a side street. It was lined with funky little shops and a few galleries. Aimee wanted to go in one, so they picked the closest and entered. They looked at the current show, trying not to say too much.

"Usually, you'd have to have a heart attack in front of the most expensive piece to get attention from the staff," Aimee said under her breath, "and some might leave you there because it could be interpreted as performance art. I'm not fond of abstract art."

The gallery consultant must have been eavesdropping because she approached Aimee.

"You need to look at it from the artist's point of view."

"Are you the artist?" Aimee asked, thinking, *I'll probably say something insulting like it looked like someone gave a monkey a paintbrush.*

"Oh, no."

"See, that's the problem. I have no idea what the artist's point of view is, do you?"

The woman looked like she was sorry she approached them. She shook her head no.

"What this piece says to me is noise, like sirens and fire alarms, even car horns," Aimee said. "Maybe the artist is trying to communicate to the world at large noise is everywhere; you can't escape it. Even in the serenity of your own home, you can't get away from it. It's right here on the wall. Noise."

"That's the beauty of it. Each person can interpret it however they want. It isn't anything; it's everything," the gallery associate said.

"If that's the purpose of abstract art, I suppose this meets the requirement," Aimee said.

"Yes, it does. If you'll excuse me, " she said and walked away.

"What does it say to you, Connor?"

"It's dumb. There's no design or flow to it, no thought process as to why it was created in the first place. Maybe the point is that the garbage men are on strike, that's what it's saying."

"I like that answer. Let's go. I guess when it comes to art, I'm more of a traditionalist," Aimee said and headed for the door.

They walked down the street a little further. They entered a handmade goods store. There was a large bald man at the register who looked like Mr. Clean. He smiled and welcomed them into the store. He had a gold front tooth.

Aimee looked in the jewelry case while Connor wandered to the back. Somebody made items out of meteorite, at least, that's what the sign said. It looked like black glass or obsidian to her. She glanced at a cuff bracelet made out of sterling silver with a chunk of meteorite in the center. She liked it a lot but decided to pass. She caught up with Connor, who was looking at the vintage rock concert posters on display.

"Find anything interesting up front?" he asked her.

"Yes. There's this cool bracelet made out of meteorite, but I'm too cheap to buy it. See any posters?"

"Yeah, I saw a few. Check them out, I'll wander around up front."

She didn't find any posters and meandered to the front, stopping to look at the handmade pottery and hand-poured candles. Connor was talking to the bald man when she walked over.

"What's up?" Aimee asked.

"I was asking about someplace to eat, and he said there was a nice place down the next block."

A few stores down, there was a fortune teller who read tarot cards.

"Let's do this," Aimee suggested. "You wait out here, so it looks like I'm alone. I don't want you to influence her either way. Then you go in, and we'll compare results over dinner."

Aimee went in and came out a few minutes later. "Your turn."

"Okay, but just to let you know, I don't believe in this shit. Besides, how does it seem random if I come in after you? But I'll have an open mind and see what happens." He entered the shop. Aimee looked at the displays in the neighboring shops. Connor came out, took her hand, and walked down the block.

"Well, what did you think?" she asked him.

"Let's find that place he recommended and sit down first."

They walked, holding hands, and found the restaurant, a little hole in the wall. He looked at her to see if she found it acceptable. She nodded her head, and they went in. The hostess seated them in the back, where it was dim and lit by candles. She took their drink orders and left.

"What do you think?" Connor asked.

"I like it. It's romantic." She smiled. "What about you?"

"I told the guy I was looking for someplace romantic, and he suggested here."

"Good call." The server came with menus and went over the specials. She left them to look over it all.

"So, what did she say?"

"The special is grilled salmon with baby carrots."

"Not her. The card reader," Aimee pushed.

"Order first. Then we'll talk."

Aimee ordered a cheeseburger with extra pickles and a side of fries. Connor ordered the same, minus the pickles.

"Just a burger? You're a cheap date."

"I don't eat this much. That's all we do. Eat in the green room. Go out to lunch. Order dinner. I just feel like something normal, not covered in some rich sauce. What about you? Why not something more substantial?"

"You made the cheeseburger sound good. So, what did your cards say?"

"She said something about water, how I love it and spent time there. She said I was going to a party soon, but don't be fooled by false people. As far as love goes, she didn't see marriage and children, and I wouldn't find love until I was older. She said I have love now, but it wasn't meant to last. I would be happy with my life. The cards didn't read negatively. I would be satisfied with my choices. How about you?"

"She saw water around me, too, but it wasn't in my future. I was going away from the water. She saw tall things around me, trees, maybe. I would get married to a woman I would meet away from the water and have a few kids. She saw a break in my future, but that necessarily isn't a bad thing. It could be that I quit my job and start my own company or move anything. What do you think? Is she full of shit?"

"The water thing was kind of spot on. We met, walked the shore and swam under the stars. Plus, you're leaving the water. You're going to Michigan."

"What about Lake Michigan? That's water, too," Connor said.

"True, but I'm a Pisces, that's a water sign, there is that. Tall things? Buildings. Trees? Wood is used to build things. You marry someone you haven't met yet. Reasonable. And a break? You could break your leg skiing. Too far ahead to tell."

"What about yours? What did you think about that?"

"The water thing. Again, there's our connection, but she didn't say I was leaving it, so maybe I'll be back to visit Dolores. She said "I have love now, but it won't last." Aimee looked at Connor and smiled. "I'll be an old lady when it comes around again, but that's okay. She said I'll be happy with my choices. Oh, and a party with fake people, Dodo invited me to the Oscars. The land is full of phonies. I think she did pretty good."

"She said you were in love now," Connor said, watching her face for a reaction.

"No, she said I had love now. Connor, you have no idea how much I wish I could fall in love with you and live happily ever after, but it's not in the cards. So I have love now. You."

"You love me?" he asked incredulously.

The server saved her from answering by bringing the food over. "You were the extra pickles, correct? Can I get you anything else? Another round?"

Connor ordered more drinks.

"Another round? You may have to carry me home."

"Gladly. But back to my question. You love me?"

Aimee took a bite from her burger and chewed rather than answer. She took another bite and again to prevent her from talking.

"I'll order another round and another until your burger's gone and you're too drunk to lie."

"Okay. Yeah, I guess you could say I have love for you. You're like the best book I'll ever read, but I'll eventually reach the end, and the world spins round, and you just go on. But I'll miss you for a while, Connor."

"So you love me a little."

"I think I do."

"I got you a little gift." He handed her a box.

"A gift? Why?"

"Just open it."

She took the lid off the square shaped box. In it was the silver cuff with the piece of meteorite set in the middle, the one she admired in the store. The salesperson told him that was the one she liked, so Connor bought it for her while she was in the back looking at posters. He slipped it in his pocket, and off they went.

"How did you know?"

"The fortune teller told me."

"We went to her after the store."

"What do you think?"

"I...I..."Aimee started to cry.

"Why are you crying? I thought you'd love it." Connor sounded nervous, like he made a huge mistake.

"I do love it. It's the most romantic thing anybody has ever done for me. You were paying attention." He moved his chair next to hers and put his arms around her.

"Aw, Aimee. I thought you'd think it was a nice gesture, and it would end up in the back of your sock drawer. You are so good at this romance thing, I wanted to romance you. I must not be very good at it if I made you cry."

"It's not the gift, I love the cuff. It's perfect. I guess you proved my point."

"What's that?"

"The easiest way to get into a girl's pants is to get into her head, and boy, are you in for some good lovin' tonight. This whole day. The flowers, exploring this little street of all these cool shops. Those wonderful burgers, this thoughtful gift. It wasn't any old gift, you were paying attention. That's the romantic part. You bought it for *me.*"

"So, I did all the right things. Huh. Yay me. Let me get the check, and we'll get out of here."

Aimee put the bracelet on and admired it in the dim light, the stone seemed to capture the light and release it tenfold. Connor came over, got her hand, and they walked out into the night. It was a little colder, and they walked close together. Connor was surprised. *You put a little effort into romance and girls go nuts,* he thought. *Even Aimee, the queen of romance, got done in. Good to know.*

They got to her hotel. When the elevator doors closed, and they were all alone, he pushed her against the wall and kissed her hard. She kissed back harder. The bell dinged, and they separated as another couple got on. Then, it opened on her floor. She stopped in front of the unmarked door.

"Isn't the room that way?"

"I've got my own entrance. Follow me."

They entered her room. Aimee pushed him up against the door and started kissing him. He wrapped his arms around her and tried to walk them over to the bed. Connor wanted to slow things down, but Aimee was on fire. When they got close enough, he picked her up and tossed her on the bed. She came at him again and tried to pin him on the bed with her mouth.

"Jesus, Aimee, what's gotten into you?"

"You did. You romanced me and seduced me. Now, love me. You've got me just where you want me: in the palm of your hand. So come over here. I want *you.*"

Connor just closed his eyes and went for it. He just held on for dear life and gave as good as he got. Aimee was all over him. Connor was all over her. He got her to the edge and slowed down. It didn't matter. She was there, and instead of her body quieting down, it seemed to have a life of its own. It moved and writhed beneath him and on top of him. He was half out of his mind with lust and decided she better come because he crossed the line, and there was no coming back.

"Now, Aimee, now!" he ordered her. Her body trembled and bucked against him, and she could feel him practically vibrate under him. Then he started to vibrate, something he never encountered before in his young life. His only option was to try to impale her to the bed with his dick, but she was like nailing Jell-O to the wall. He stopped thinking entirely and let go. His orgasm seemed to start in his toes, and he drove into her so hard that ejaculate should be coming out of her tear ducts. He collapsed on top of her, completely depleted of both energy and bodily fluids. He laid there until he could breathe normally again and rolled off her.

He looked at the ceiling and said, "Holy fuck, Aimee. Give me back that bracelet. I think I saw God."

"I saw Him a couple of times. He says 'Hello.'"

"A couple of times?"

Connor rolled on his side and held his head up with his hand. He looked at her. "Really? More than once?"

"Scout's honor. You're pretty good."

"Aimee, that was unlike anything I ever experienced. It *was* magic."

"No staging. No fairy lights. Just you, me and a little chemistry."

"It felt like we split the atom," Connor said. "We did have a pretty romantic evening. I had no idea such minor details yielded such maximum results."

"You're a good student, grasshopper."

"Well, I'm keeping this a secret. I'm only going to use it on very special occasions. I want to ask you, Aimee, if it happens like that all the time. I don't mean to be rude, but does it happen like that? You're like a ten in the sack. I've never been with anyone like you."

"We've been together a couple of times before, and it was pretty good. I hate to keep saying it, but being older just means I've had more time to figure it out. I know what I like and what needs to be done to get me there. I'm a little more comfortable with myself, and a lot of college girls are new to this.

"They don't know what they want. They know enough to know what they don't want, but not many guys want to make the investment in figuring it out. Face it—you guys just want to get laid. I just figured out the romance part on my own; that's what I needed. So I create the atmosphere and pretty much seduce myself."

"Is that what happened tonight? You seduced yourself?"

"No. You did. It only happens like that when feelings are involved."

"Feelings? You have feelings for me?" he asked.

"I told you I had feelings. You just want me to say it again."

"Yeah, I do."

"Connor, I have love for you in my heart. A piece of you will always be with me. The reality of the conclusion is close. Do you have to go? I'm not ready to say goodbye."

"Tell me you love me a little, and I'll stay."

"I love you a little," Aimee said.

"I love you a little, too. I have to leave at six, but I'll stay."

He got up quietly at 5:50 and dressed. He went over to her side of the bed and sat down. "Aimee. Aimee, I've got to go."

"I know. Kiss me. I'll see you soon."

"Yeah. We'll see each other soon," he said. Connor kissed her and let himself out. "Bye, Aimee."

It was the last time he ever saw her.

***

Connor was with Nathan at the student store when he saw the Academy Awards issue of *People*. He picked it up and immediately recognized Dolores. A few steps behind her was an incredibly stunning woman. "That's her, Nate. Aimee."

Nate looked at the cover. "Yeah. I saw her. She's hot. Very hot."

Connor bought the magazine and ripped the cover off. He used another steak knife and stuck the cover next to the note she left. They had love, maybe not forever, but in the moment. Fresh, optimistic, rich, love. Before, the conflict of life intruded on the lover's delusions and turned them to ashes.

***

Chapter 13

Connor left Aimee and walked out into the night. It was the best night of his whole life. Having a girl—no, a woman—like Aimee respond to him like that made him think he should turn around and run right back to her, but he had an important paper due, and she was going home. Their paths diverged right here, and with every step, he got further away from her.

Dodo had arranged for a car service to deliver Aimee home. She had two more tasks left, the award shows. Rhoda had her measurements and sent four formal gowns. She was to evaluate them for style and basic fit, any altering could be done the day of, barring any major reconstruction. If that was required, another option needed to be chosen because it was too close and not enough time.

Aimee called Sally to come over and help her. Sally was there before Aimee hung up the phone. Her Dad came with her; after Dodo's party, he was high on all things Dodo. He was also pleased Aimee asked Sally for help. They were both his girls, and he wanted them to get along, but he didn't have much to worry about.

Aimee was lucky Sally came. She had no idea how to even put one of these monstrosities on. Over her head, or step into it? Sally helped get her in, and her father gave two of them the thumbs up, so she chose those, packed all four gowns up and sent them back. The next time she would see it would be when she would be getting dressed for the Academy Awards.

It was nice the way they wasted money on her. She flew first class to LA. A driver waited with her name on the sign, and somebody else got her bags. As she exited the terminal, she was blinded by camera flashes. Celebrities put their heads down and blocked their faces as they raced into the terminal or waiting cars. Aimee stopped and put her hand up to block the lights.

"Sorry, guys, nobody special. Just a joke writer. Don't waste your film," she said and followed the driver to the limo. He took her to the same hotel as Dodo. They had adjoining rooms and shared hair and makeup. Someone came from deBeers and adorned them in jewels.

Aimee didn't realize Dodo wanted her to be her escort from the red carpet into the theater. Unfortunately, Dodo's appearance sent the paparazzi into a frenzy. Dodo smiled and posed while Aimee looked like a deer in the headlights.

"Don't stand so stiff. Smile, Aimee. Enjoy this. Imagine Connor seeing us on the cover of *People* and him saying that's her! That's my summer lover! And nobody will believe him."

Aimee started laughing and relaxed. She went as Dodo was stopped by everyone requesting an interview. Aimee tried to hang back as Dodo was interviewed, but Dodo wouldn't let go of her arm, so Aimee felt compelled to engage. Soon, it was time to enter the theater, and Aimee couldn't stop smiling at the smile she kept plastered on her face. Being next to Dodo on the red carpet meant tons of photographers; Aimee needed to be ready in case she got caught in the crossfire.

They sat at the table with the director and her wife, the supporting female lead, Dolores Reardon, with Aimee next to her. The supporting male nominee was a young established actor, movie magazine cover boy, and all-around horn dog Tony Maracuso, and his date, a past Miss Universe winner, rounded out the table.

Tony's seat was next to Aimee. He completely ignored his date, the former Miss Universe, and worked his incredible charm on Aimee with no success. Not even a yawn.

Aimee couldn't be so dense she didn't know he was curious about her. She had absolutely no use for his attention. He'd say something funny, and she'd laugh and turn away.

"Do you know who's the hottest girl in the room?" he asked Aimee.

"Yeah. Me," Aimee answered, shook her head and turned back towards Dodo.

In another attempt, he tried to be cordial, genuine even.

"So, Aimee, right? Aimee, how do you know Dolores?" An article he read about picking up chicks advised saying a girl's name often makes a positive impression and increases the odds of scoring.

"We're lovers," she said in his ear, her breath warm and pleasant, and turned back to Dodo and the conversation going on at the table. He inhaled sharply behind her. He loved girls like her. It was too much fun, breaking them.

Nobody was more surprised than Dodo when she won the award for outstanding supporting actress. *Good lord,* Dodo thought. *How am I ever going to get up there?*

Aimee stood to help her; Dolores reached for her arm and held it in a tight grasp. The gentlemen at the table forgot what a gentleman does, assist a lady in need, and just sat there. Aimee, with Dodo on her arm, moved toward the stage. Suddenly, tuxedoed men everywhere jumped up to help. One such man stood with his arm out at the bottom of the stairs. Aimee smiled at him and mouthed, "Thank you," and placed Dodo in his care. She had no idea who he was until she got back to her seat and stood with everyone else applauding.

"Are his eyes really that blue?" Miss Universe asked her once the applause died down.

"Who?"

"William Burke. The man who took Dodo up on stage."

“I don’t know. I was so grateful I didn’t have to walk her up those stairs in these shoes. I didn’t look at him. I’m not very graceful in heels.”

The crowd quieted so Dolores Reardon could be heard.

“I would like to thank the Academy and apologize to my fellow nominees. They only gave me the award because I’m as old as dirt. You all gave such strong and powerful performances I should probably give it back. You lived this long, survived this long in this business, and I’m sure you’ll get one, too.

“You know, I have so many people to thank, but they’re all dead, so I won’t bother. If I’ve learned anything in the last ninety years, it’s that life moves you forward. I’ve had to say goodbye to so many people, but I am blessed with new people to move forward with me. The cast and crew were like family. I’d like to thank them individually, but due to time, I can’t. This is for you, Aimee Dunsmore, Connor Edmond, Rita and Jim, Joe Dunsmore and Sally Reade. I thank you all for this honor.” She stepped away from the podium and stopped. She turned towards the audience and held Oscar over her head, mimicking the photograph from the book. She laughed and walked away.

Everyone sat back down while Dolores stayed backstage. That left Aimee alone at the table. Tony was all set to try again, but Aimee stood at the sight of a waiter. He gave her directions to the side entrance where she could slip in and find Dodo. She left before Tony could stand and come to her rescue. He sat back down, frowning. *Women love me. Maybe she is gay, and Dolores Reardon is her sugar momma, that has to be it. Women love me,* he decided.

Aimee finally found Dodo. They wouldn’t let her in, though. She waited and slipped in when someone exited the room. Aimee searched the room and noticed her sitting while being interviewed. Dodo looked like she was running on nervous energy and about to crash. It was late, much later than Dodo was used to. Aimee interrupted and told them to talk to her press agent; Dolores was running late. Aimee said to skip the after-parties. Someone called an elevator that brought them into a below-level parking garage to an awaiting town car to take them to the hotel without encountering a soul. Aimee asked if they could go to a drive-thru, all the food was at the after-parties, and she was starving. They ate In-And-Out burgers in the back of the limo.

***

Award season is finally finished. Everyone got home safely, and Dodo put her award on a shelf in the bathroom. Aimee got paid more money in a month than she did in a year of teaching; plus, with the book royalties, she didn't have to worry about money for a while.

She did end up on the cover of *People*, just another face in the crowd, but dressed like that, people wondered if she was the next big thing. She bought one for Connor and sent it to him in his family's care. She highlighted Dolores's speech and where she thanked him.

Aimee hated the whole thing and was glad her chosen career was a solo occupation. She told Dodo if she ever needed an escort to any formal function, Joe Dunsmore was available. The noise, the crush of people, the insanity of it all was just too overwhelming. She much preferred the sounds of Paradise Point, and Dolores concurred.

Aimee and Dodo remained close. She spent two more Christmases with her so Rita could have some time off. Both times, Mr. Jimmy told her that Connor wasn't coming home. He came for Thanksgiving instead. She knew before he told her; she kept in touch with Connor. Aimee knew their connection was fading. Their communication was getting further apart, but that was the way it was supposed to be.

***

Chapter 14

Aimee was grateful Dodo invited her to spend the summers and use the pool house as a writer's retreat. She was getting frailer and frailer each time Aimee saw her. Joe and Sally came for a visit and stayed twice during the month of July. It was the third summer she was there, and Dodo's condition experienced a steep decline. She spent a lot of time in her room, and most nights, they ate dinner there. Dolores Reardon died in her sleep on August 30th.

In her will, Dodo wanted to be cremated and her remains scattered at Paradise Point. Rita, Jimmy, and Aimee went down to the shore. Aimee walked out up to her knees and scattered Dodo's ashes as best she could when suddenly, a rogue wave appeared out of nowhere and knocked her flat on her ass, soaking her. Aimee looked up at the sky and yelled, "Very funny, Dodo!"

***

They went to the lawyer's office for the reading of the will. Aimee was surprised she was included. She could understand Rita and Jimmy. Aimee thought she probably wanted to return Aimee's gift of the book cover. Dodo told her she was leaving her estate to charity.

Dodo left Rita and Mr. Jimmy's lifetime use of the caretaker's cottage. He got the car, and she left Rita a sizable chunk of money with the instructions to "hire somebody to wait on her for the rest of her life."

Also present was Ione Graham, Dodo's step-grandchild. Dodo had the upper and lower cottages, with the land split off from the main estate and established as part of the Forever Wild Paradise Point Dune Preservation Trust, with

Ione as trustee and use of both cottages. Anyone with the name Dunsmore had lifetime use of the unoccupied cottage should Ione choose to reside there.

She named Ione the trustee because she loved the shore almost as much as Dodo. She left Aimee her costume jewelry as well as the contents of her safe deposit box, the real stuff. Dodo left her any and all movie memorabilia she wanted and created a trust to provide an income for Aimee so "she could write all she wanted and never have to teach again."

Aimee was touched by Dodo's generosity, and Ione as well. Amy started crying, Ione joined her, and soon Rita started. Losing her mom so young, Aimee had, without realizing it, transferred her need for a strong female role model over to Dodo. She loved her, and she poured all the love she had for her mom into Dodo. Aimee didn't want to think about how it felt to lose her Mom twice. Instead, she focused on how much Dodo must have loved her to give her such a gift. She was free to follow her dreams, much like Dodo did when she set out over seventy years ago. Aimee thought she deserved none of it and felt terribly guilty.

The lawyer pushed over a box of tissues. Aimee took some and passed the box to Ione, who was even more upset than Aimee.

"You don't understand. I haven't seen Dodo in years. We aren't even related. My dad was her third husband's kid. Why would she do this?"

"You remembered her every Christmas," Aimee said. "You donated to the Dune Preservation Society. That was her pet project, and she'd smile when she read the card. She told me about how you would walk the beach with her every morning. Dodo said you sat there and waited for her."

"Yes, I did. My parents and their friends partied like rock stars. I was stuck watching four kids, two in diapers until they woke up, and I was only ten. The adults were always hungover and didn't want us in the house, but we were forbidden to leave the yard. We had peanut butter sandwiches for breakfast and lunch every day until Dodo got involved. I remember she reamed out my Dad for child neglect. She hired someone to watch us so we could leave the yard and play, and Dodo fed us lunch.

"I loved the beach, and the only time I could enjoy it was with Dodo. She loved the dunes and was involved in the early preservation of them. You don't know how grateful I was that Dodo got involved. I was so nervous someone would wander off and drown, and I would get blamed. I never forgot what she did for me. That's why I made the donation every year. It wasn't very much, but what do you get someone who could buy anything she wanted? I had no idea it meant that much to her."

"It did. I spent the last couple of Christmases with her, and it did mean that much to her. She would smile and tell me a story about you."

"Ione," said the lawyer, "I've handled the Preservation Trust for Dolores for years. If you don't mind, I can continue, and your name will be kept out of the press. This place is going to be crawling with developers and people with way too much money wanting to get a piece of this property. I can handle them. I believe the house and the contents will be sold at auction, and the money will be added to the trust.

"I know Dolores wanted to put a codicil in the will that the house can't be torn down, and anything built new must be on one level, but I don't think once it's sold, we can enforce that. She loved the way the house was all on one floor and preserved the view. Dolores knew that some rich asshole, her words, would tear it down and build some monstrosity. Everything in the house will go to auction, so if there's something you want, grab it now. Any proceeds go back into the Trust. Ione, you're free to be as involved as you want. You could even move into one of the cottages."

"I wish I could. My job and everything is in Cincinnati."

"Ione quit. Relocate," Aimee said. "I don't know if it's sunk in yet, but the biggest thing Dodo left us is security. You don't have to work a nine-to-five anymore or worry about rent. You can retire to the beach and paint seascapes if you want. Sucky, shitty, God awful works of art. Who cares if it gives you pleasure?"

Ione sat back and considered what Aimee said. Aimee wanted to go to the bank with the lawyer and see the contents of the safe deposit box. Mr. Jimmy would take Ione back to the main house while Aimee went with the lawyer. He would return her to Paradise Point afterwards.

They went to the bank and unlocked the box. Aimee almost choked. It was full of seventy years' worth of jewelry Dodo had collected from her lovers and husbands. She recognized a few from the scrapbook others from pictures. She gasped.

"I don't know, Jim," she said to the lawyer. "I can't even guess what these are worth. They're worth a lot."

"They're worth more than that. Dolores was famous for her jewelry. She had fake ones made of her favorites. Anything of value went here."

"What am I supposed to do with this? I'm afraid to touch it. I can't hang on to it. I think people will be interested in these pieces, and if I have them, somebody will want them. I'm afraid I can't even afford to insure these, and I'll get robbed, or worse, when they find out they're not in my possession."

"Aimee, much like you told Ione, money isn't a factor. If I may suggest something, why don't we have Sotheby's come, photograph each piece, and determine the value of each one separately. You can decide if there's anything you want to keep and auction off the rest. Nobody will know if a few pieces are missing, and you have them. Your name will be kept out of it. I'll certify the provenance as from the original owner of this estate. If you ever need to sell them, they have the papers to get top dollar." He joked Dolores was meddling from the grave.

"Dolores was famous for her jewelry; everybody knew that. There will be a lot of interest in those particular items. Many were gifts from men long dead. After the auction, you can decide what to do with the money. Invest it, donate it, or some combination of both. Even some of the better costume jewelry; there's a market for those, too. She created some knock offs of her favorites. There is always interest when a movie star's possessions are up for auction. These can be listed as part of the estate but not you specifically as the seller."

"One thing I forgot to mention is she left you the last Oscar she won." The lawyer said.

Aimee sat down, completely overwhelmed. She thought how unimportant this place, and this stuff, was now Dodo was gone. She might come back if her family used one of the cottages for a gathering, but as this was a destination for her, no more. Aimee told the lawyer to behave as if he were working for Dodo to make decisions the way she would.

It was suggested she hire an accountant to keep track of the finances, make sure the money was square, and have the lawyer watch the accountant. Aimee did and ignored the thing entirely and lived her life. The money was there if she needed it.

The following summer, the Dunsmore clan rotated and overlapped when they stayed for the month of August. Aimee walked down to Paradise Point on the 30th and watched the sunset. She wasn't surprised Ione was waiting on the stairs and came with her to remember the woman that changed both their lives.

***

Mr. Jimmy died about five years later. Aimee went to the service. It was held in the part of the city where they originally came from, Washington Heights.

Miss Rita retired to a nice senior living facility in Florida and could go back and forth to be with her family as she pleased.

Now that the caretaker's cottage was vacant, it went to the owner of the house. From what Ione said, an environmentally conscious Silicon Valley multi-millionaire bought Dodo's house. He respected her desire to keep any building to one level. He kept the original house, gutted it and changed the inside. He also expanded the floor plan but kept it all on one level.

After the family reunion they had at the lower cottage, Aimee knew she would never return. She had lost touch with Connor over the years. The last time she heard, he was married and living in Phoenix.

Everything had changed so drastically since Dodo died. There was no Dodo, no Connor, Mr. Jimmy, or Rita left. The only good thing was Ione planned on spending summers in the upper cottage. She extended an open invitation to Aimee; she was welcome to stay with her. The lower cottage was to be used by a prominent university as a base of operations for their marine biology program. Aimee thanked her for the invite but never went. It made her too sad.

***

Aimee continued to live in her dad's house. She placed Dodo's Oscar in her bathroom like Dodo did. He survived a bout with colon cancer, Sally, breast cancer. They moved back in because Sally's house had too many stairs. The downstairs master bedroom with its bathroom was perfect for them, and Aimee had the upstairs. The publishing house kept her as busy as she wanted to be ghost-writing, and she published a number of bestselling romance novels under the pen name Dolores O'Rourke.

Aimee was so grateful to Dolores for providing her the means to do what she loved without worry. She would have been fine with the money the trust provided for her, but the money from the jewelry sale was mind-boggling. Aimee kept half and donated the rest to the Forever Wild Paradise Point Dune Preservation Society.

The money allowed her to hire the best caregivers when her Dad's cancer came roaring back a few years later and later the best hospice care when he ran out of options. Sally's children wanted their mom to move in with them, but Aimee said she could stay right where she was, and that's what Sally did. *If she couldn't physically have Joey Dunsmore,* Aimee thought, *Sally seemed content with his ghost.*

When Sally's health started to decline, Aimee provided her with the same level of care her father received. It was only when she entered home hospice she moved in with her daughter; her family wanted to be with their mother at the end. Aimee still paid for Sally to have the best care possible, and when she died, Aimee paid for her funeral costs.

Sally was like Dodo in that Aimee looked at her as a mother figure. Aimee thought about Dodo and Ione. If she was going to write Romance novels, it seemed like she should live alone, out in some desolate spot like the upper cottage with only the wind and surf as a company. Aimee decided against it. She could feel just as lonely and desolate at her dad's house, looking out over the Vasily family's backyard.

Aimee bought the house from her father's estate and paid off her siblings. Everyone kept telling her to move; she could afford to live anywhere she wanted, but Aimee stayed. *Why move?* She thought. *I can write from anywhere. I'm not sure if it's the ghosts of my parents that makes me want to stay. All my brothers and sisters are spread out across the U.S.; they have families and lives that don't need their spinster sister along for the ride.*

It was a train ride into the city if she needed to talk to her publisher. Aimee stayed and considered herself happy. Life went on, days and then years passed. Whenever she could, she had a drink at three p.m. and toasted Dodo.

***

Part Two

Chapter 15

Aimee finished for the day. She was trying to decide what to have for dinner. Nothing looked appetizing in the freezer, but it was so hot outside she stuck her head in there and enjoyed the cold air. It was too hot to cook and almost too hot to eat. She wanted some ice cream for dinner, but the freezer contained none, and it was too hot to go to the grocery store. Aimee heard her phone ringing and reluctantly took her head out of the freezer to answer it.

"Hello?" she answered.

"Hello. Is this Aimee Dunsmore?" an unfamiliar voice said.

Shoot, I should've checked the caller ID, Aimee thought. She looked. It said UNKNOWN. "No. Why don't you call back and leave her a message."

"I'd rather leave it with you. Tell Aimee Dunsmore Mitchell Raleigh called."

"Mitchell Raleigh? What does he want?" *Mitchell Raleigh? Why do I know that name?* She searched her memory but came up with nothing.

"He wants to talk to Aimee Dunsmore."

"About what?"

"You're awfully nosy for someone taking a message. Tell her Mitchell Raleigh, the aging hipster called."

Aimee couldn't help it; she burst out laughing. *Oh, him.* "Wait a minute. I'll see if she's free."

"Enough fun and games, Aimee. I know it's you."

"No, it's not."

"I recognize your voice. It has a distinct nasal quality about it."

"Hey! It does not!"

"So you are Aimee Dunsmore."

"Busted. It's me. I usually never answer the phone, especially an unknown number. I had my head in the freezer and wasn't thinking. I guess it's your lucky day."

"Maybe it's *your* lucky day. Anyway, why did you have your head in the freezer?"

"Oh, I was looking for something to eat. It's so hot out that I kinda just left it in there. Don't worry. It's still attached to my body. What can I do for you, Mitchell Raleigh?"

"For starters, you don't have to call me Mitchell Raleigh all the time. Mitch is just fine, and I'm passing your exit in about ten minutes. I was hoping you were free for dinner. I'll get off and meet you somewhere."

Aimee didn't say anything. She wasn't sure she wanted to learn more about Mitchell Raleigh than she already knew, but she was bored and hungry.

"Aimee? You still there?"

"Yeah, I was debating about whether I wanted to meet up with you, but I'm hungry, and the only thing in my freezer was my head, so sure, I'll take a risk and say yes. Remember where we had coffee? I could meet you there, in the parking lot. I'll think about where we could eat, and we'll take it from there."

"Sounds good. See you there." He hung up.

Aimee looked at the sundress she was wearing and wondered if she should change it, but she decided against it. She wasn't going to get all dressed up to try to impress some stranger. Maybe if Aimee looked like her plain, ordinary self, he wouldn't call the next time he passed through. She grabbed her bag and left.

She got to the plaza ahead of him; she didn't see the Tesla. She left the car running and the air on high while she waited. She noticed a red sports car turn into the parking lot and head right to her. He pulled up opposite her so their driver's side windows lined up. They lowered their windows to talk.

"What the hell is that? A Lamborghini?"

"Close. A Maserati, with AC like you wouldn't believe. If you got in, you might think you put your whole body in the freezer. Care to test it out?"

Aimee took her phone out and took his picture. She typed something.

"Sure," she said and got out and took a photo of his license plates. Aimee got in the passenger side. "One sec." She hit send, put it back in her bag and turned to him.

"What was that all about?" he asked, gesturing to her bag.

"I sent your photo to my best friend, and if I go missing, they'll know your face and plates."

"Think about it. If I was going to kidnap you, it would not be in a car like this. Isn't it usually a white van?"

"Usually." Aimee conceded. "Take a right out of here and go about five miles. Get on the 311 North. It's about four exits ahead."

Once he hit the open road, he put the pedal to the metal and let that car fly. He glanced at her. She was looking straight ahead with her eyes open wide. He decided to back off and only do ten above the limit.

"Sorry about that. The adolescent teenage gearhead comes out sometimes, and I want to show off. You never really outgrow it. It's only fun now if you're introducing it to someone new. I'm sorry I scared you."

"I wasn't scared, mostly awed. Who would buy a high-performance car like this? If I owned it, I'd want to drive it fast; that's what it's made for. What's the point if you're only going to the grocery store?"

"Is that a dig?"

"Huh?"

"A dig. For driving a Tesla to the grocery store."

"No, more like an obvious conclusion. Plus, it's red. A red car is the color most pulled over by the police. A car like this is saying, 'Look at me! I'm rich!'"

"It's more like 'look at me pretending to be rich.' If you were rich, you'd make the payments, and the car wouldn't be repossessed. More than likely, you'd pay cash if you were rich."

"I guess so. It would be an addition to a collection of cars. Someone rich who took automotive science in high school, somebody who likes motors. Although if I were rich, I'd buy a muscle car, you know, like a '68 Camaro. Maybe a '73 Firebird."

"This is an interesting discussion. Let's continue it over dinner. Where are we going?"

"Two more exits we'll be getting off; the place is on a lake."

He hit the gas, and they were there in five minutes. It wasn't peak hours, so they were able to get a nice table with a view.

"I should apologize to you. I didn't ask if there were dietary restrictions, like if you were a vegetarian or lactose intolerant, or something like that. Or in the mood for Italian. This is real casual, like burgers and stuff. I just thought you'd like the view," Aimee said.

He looked her directly in the eye and said, "I do enjoy the view. Very much."

Is he talking about me? Aimee thought alarmingly and blushed bright red. She looked to the exit. He followed her gaze to the door like she was going to make a run for it, so he changed the subject.

"I should have checked with you if *you* had any dietary considerations, like if you were allergic to fish or seafood," Mitch said.

"I wouldn't suggest a place where I couldn't eat," Aimee replied.

"True. So, you should have been the one to be considering my needs."

"And yet, I managed not to. Anything on that menu jump out at you?

"A burger. Do you see anything special?"

"I'm good. I'm a creature of habit. I always get the same thing. A BLT or a salad. I get sick of food. You always have to make it or get it or eat it."

"That is true about food," he said. "It's required for survival."

"You know what I really hate?"

"What?"

"Foodies. Those people who invite you to dinner, and when you get there, they start cooking, and you have to stand there and watch them 'prepare' the meal. Like it's a master class or something. They narrate every little thing about the meal like they're on the Food Network, and it bores the hell out of me. I'm like, give me a peanut butter sandwich and let me get the fuck out of there." She clapped her hand up over her mouth. "Excuse me. I didn't mean to swear."

"That's fine, I'm not offended. I know what you mean about foodies. People take it way too far. What else do you hate?"

"Not too much else. I have things I'm not fond of, but it's no big deal. What do you hate?"

"Slow drivers and fake people."

"Then you should probably take me back to my car. I'm the biggest phony you'll ever meet."

"I don't think so, and I'm a pretty good judge of character."

"You'll see." Aimee laughed.

The server brought their drinks. She had lemonade, and he had ice tea.

“Okay, I know what you hate,” Mitch said. “Now I want to know what you know about muscle cars.”

“Muscle cars? I have an older brother, and he and his friends were into them, like a Buick 444 or a ‘67 Mustang. Eddie had a ‘68 Camaro. GTOs. Road Runners and the like are rebuilt with big motors and fat tires. Headers. But yeah. Now, those cars sounded like badass cars. These new cars are all about the packaging.

“The old ones, it was about the *motor.* You should have been on my street on a hot summer night. They’d start those V-8s, and it sounded like an earthquake. They’d sit there, these cars rumbling, and one by one, they’d leave, and the last guy peeled out, leaving rubber on the road.” Aimee said.

“That’s true. If you love cars, you have to respect them. Sounds like a young boy’s dream childhood. Or girl. It sounds a lot like mine. However, instead of my friends, it was my father. He loved motors.”

“Nowadays, it’s all electronics and computers. Back then, all you needed to do was shove a screwdriver into the choke,” Aimee said and took a sip of her lemonade.

“I’m impressed.”

“Don’t be. That’s all I got, and what I learned was mostly from eavesdropping. I was a lot younger than my brother Eddie, so I may not have the details correct.”

“Sharp hearing. Good memory. Impressive.”

“Were you one of those guys? Rumor had it, or maybe it was a little kid’s misinterpretation, but those guys drove those cars to get all the hot girls.”

“I plead the fifth. Although a girl saying things like horsepower and choke might be misconstrued by such a guy as talking dirty.”

“Roadrunner. Corvette. MoPar. Two strokes. Four strokes. Hemi. Clutch. I’d have to think about it to see if I remember anything else.” Aimee recalled.

"Can you drive a stick?"

"You mean a standard transmission? Yes. I took my road test in that '68 Camaro."

"Let's talk about something else. Your fragmented knowledge is more than enough to get a guy turned on."

"We don't want that. Let's talk about knitting. Do you know how to crochet?" Aimee asked.

"No. Do you?"

"Yes. What kind of boat do you have?" Aimee asked him.

"How do you know I have a boat?"

"I already told you. You have sunglass tan lines. Inboard or outboard motor? Let me guess. Inboard/Outboard twin Mercury's."

The server came with their meals. Mitch had a cheeseburger and fries, and Aimee had a BLT. She took a bite so she'd stop talking. He didn't eat. He just sat back and stared at her. She swallowed and asked him why he wasn't eating.

"I'm not sure what to make of you, Aimee Dunsmore."

"Don't make anything. Eat your food before it gets cold," she said and took another bite. He started to eat his cheeseburger but continued to stare at her. She swallowed and then spoke. "Quit staring at me. You're making me self-conscious, watching me chew."

"Sorry. You're just so pretty I can't look away," he said as she took a drink. She started to laugh, and lemonade almost shot out of her nose. Aimee started to cough and choke. He jumped up and pounded on her back. After a minute, she held her hand up so he would stop.

"Are you okay?" She nodded. "Are you sure?"

"Yes," she said hoarsely. "I'm good. You just surprised me. I haven't been called pretty in years."

"What's wrong with the men in this town? Are they all blind?" He said as he sat back down.

She laughed again. "No. Just used to me, I guess. Or dead. I'm a local. I live in the house I grew up in. There are four kids in my family. One is in DC, one is in LA, one is in Boston, and here, it is me. My parents are dead. So there you go. What's your story?"

"Three boys, one girl. Allie lives in Buffalo, and my brother David lives in Buffalo, too. I live in Rochester, and my brother Andrew is in Albany. My dad had a bunch of car dealerships all over the East Coast. He started Raleigh Automotive in Albany, and it grew bigger than he had ever imagined. When he retired, he sold off all but his initial core dealerships, which were located in upstate NY. We each run one, even my sister because there are two in Buffalo. I started West Lake Luxury Auto on my own. My mom died a few years ago, and my dad retired to Florida. I'm divorced, and I have two step-kids I legally adopted and I'm still close to. You never said anything specific about you. Tell me some details."

It was her turn to sit back and stare at him, evaluating how much about herself she wanted to reveal. She laughed inwardly. There really wasn't that much to disclose.

"Specifics? My middle name is Marie. Never married, no kids. I just turned fifty. I'm self-employed as a ghostwriter. Being ambiguous is my superpower. That's about it."

"That's about it? You don't look fifty."

"No husband and no kids equals no wrinkles. Relationships age you, that and smoking." Aimee laughed.

"How old do you think I am?"

"I don't know, and I don't care enough to find out."

"That wasn't very nice," Mitch said back to her, a frown on his face.

"Just being honest. I know you're older than me. The number doesn't really matter much at this age."

"I'll never tell you. It's not important anyway."

"How long have you been divorced?" She asked.

"'The number doesn't really matter,'" he said back to her, but by the bland look on her face, he could tell he'd have her attention for about five more seconds if he didn't come up with something quick.

"Five years. I hung in there as long as I could, for the kids' sake. You can say what you want about staying together because of the kids, but they already had one dad disappear on them. I didn't think it was fair to them to have to live with watching another one walk away. It wasn't their fault. It wasn't their fault their mother suffered from a mental illness that could be managed with medication, but she refused to take it."

"Oh."

"Yeah. I think that's why the kids' dad left. She was hard to live with, but the kids were just little. It was no excuse to leave *them* alone with a mother that couldn't be a mother. I think after he left, her parents got involved, she saw the right doctors and her moods stabilized. She was fine. That's when I met her. The kids were six and four. We got married, and everything was great. I adopted the kids. The oldest is Bella, and the youngest is Ryan. I think Bella was twelve, and Ryan was ten the first time she went off her meds without telling anyone.

"She was all manic about redecorating, and I came home to a huge hole in the wall. She took a sledgehammer to the kitchen; she said she wanted an 'open floor plan.' She lost interest in it and just left it like that. She started to paint the living room and walked away, leaving that half done, too. Then, for a week, she'd argue and pick fights. Now, Bella was starting to get all hormonal, and the fights were pretty bad. Afterwards, she'd stay in bed for a week, sobbing we didn't love her. Then she'd come out all contrite and sorry. Get back on her meds, and life would settle down for a few years. The last few times were bad because she wouldn't stay on her meds. She'd scream at me to mind my own business, they were her kids, not mine."

"Wow. Those kids were lucky you were such an anchor for them."

"Anchor?"

"Yeah. When the sea was whipped into a frenzy, and life was smashing them against the rocks, you were there to shield them, protect them from the storm raging around them."

"Yes, but as far as I'm concerned, they're my kids, and it was my responsibility to keep them safe. Ryan works with me now, and Bella is a lawyer in Pittsburgh. And my ex-wife Sandy lives locally. I don't have much to do with her, but every once in a while, she'll make a scene."

"The typical 'I love you, you're perfect, now change? Or: I don't want you, so you can't be wanted by anybody else scenarios?'" Aimee asked.

"More like if I'm miserable, you should be too. Sandy focuses all her hate on me, and she leaves the kids alone. I don't care. Everyone knows she's nuts. Her parents feel horrible. They can't help her. They have to sit there waiting until she exhausts herself and sleeps for days. When she wakes up, she'll cooperate with taking her pills. Keep her on a schedule, and she's fine."

"She's not nuts, she's sick. I feel for your ex-in-laws. They've got to be getting too old for that," Aimee said.

"They are. I feel bad for Ryan. He loves his mom, and he'll ultimately be responsible for her. He'll try his best, and we'll see how far he gets."

"I guess you found marriage quite taxing."

"Taxing and then some. But, like I said, I got two great kids out of it. Let's talk about something more current. When was the last time you went out on a date?"

"Date? Is that what this is?"

"Close enough. Answer the question."

"Last date? Fifteen years. I don't consider that current. That's what happens when you live in the same town you grew up in. Anyone worth dating you've run through by the time you graduate high school. Nobody ever lives there on purpose. If you leave and come back, it usually means something bad happened, and you have nowhere else to go."

"Is that what happened to you? Something bad happened, and you returned home, hanging your head in disgrace?"

"I wish. I came here after I graduated college. My mom died when I was in college, and my brother Sam stayed here to keep my Dad from being alone. I came back so my brother could get on with his life. I could ghostwrite from anywhere, so I stayed. It was okay. My Dad found a girlfriend and was usually with her, so I mostly lived alone. I never felt the need to leave. I can get downstate by train if I need to get to my agent or the publishers."

"So you're not a retarded adolescent stuck in your head at eighteen living in your parent's basement?" Mitch asked.

"A loser? Yeah, pretty much," Aimee answered.

"That's not what I said. Or what I meant."

"It doesn't matter. Put it all down on paper, and that's what it looks like."

She took another bite of her sandwich. While she was chewing, his phone rang.

"Hey, Ryan, what's up? No, I'm having dinner with a friend. A few hours, why? No, I can't help her, she knows that. Call your grandfather. Yeah. I'll talk to you later. Love you. Bye."

Mitchell looked up at Aimee. She glanced back, her gaze clear and nonjudgmental. She didn't ask for an explanation, but he felt obligated to give her one.

"Sorry about that. My ex-wife is in one of her moods, and she's been hounding Ryan about where I am. She gets like that, and sometimes, she gets fixated on something and won't let it go. Right now, it's me. Sandy has some problem that's my fault and wants me to fix it, but I'm not going to do it."

The whole tone of their dinner shifted. Before the call, it was two people getting to know each other. Now, it was two acquaintances having a sandwich. Aimee sat quietly while he ate his fries. He offered her some, but she declined. He sensed her moving away from him, and he didn't like it.

"Look, Aimee, I'm sorry about that. I told you my ex was crazy. It doesn't happen too often that she wants me. Mostly, she goes on about how much she hates me, that I ruined her life, and that I'm a horrible human being. Do you think I'm a horrible human being?" Mitch asked her.

"No. If she suffers from being mentally ill, it's probably easier to hate you than to think about being divorced and alone. She creates her own reality, I suppose. It probably changes day to day; what's bothering her." Aimee answered him.

"Thanks for understanding. You don't need to worry about her. She lives over an hour away. Enough about her. Let's talk about you."

"I'm a cipher. You're not supposed to know any more than that."

"What's your favorite color?"

"Yellow. Yours?"

"Blue. Pizza or tacos?

"Tacos. You?"

"Italian. Land or sea?"

"Sea."

"Me, too. We have a lot in common," he said. "Last time you were kissed?"

"About fifteen years ago, and I don't want to know your answer. Are you almost finished?" Aimee asked.

"Yup. I've been done for a while. Let me get the check." He waved for the server.

Aimee put her hand in her bag and pulled out a bunch of bills. "I'll get the tip," she said, dropping a twenty on the table.

"Don't you want any change back?" He said, pointing to the bill.

"No, that's another thing about me—I'm a big tipper."

"Suit yourself. Okay, let's go."

They went through the door, and immediately, any relief from the restaurant's AC vanished, and the sweat started to drip again.

"Whew. It's hot. Maybe even hotter," Aimee said.

He walked to her side and held open the door for her. She sat while he got in, turned the air on high and angled the vents towards her. "That should feel better."

"It does, but I don't want to hog all the air." She angled a vent back.

"That's okay. The heat is making your hair all poofy. By the way, that's a pretty dress." Mitch said and smiled.

"Thank you." She said in response to his compliment. Aimee put the visor down and looked at her hair. She put it back up.

"It's the humidity making my hair all poofy."

"I think you'd look good in an afro."

"We'll find out," she said, and they drove home in silence.

He pulled up next to her car and put his hand on her thigh. She looked at him and looked at his hand. He took his hand back.

“Aimee. Don’t leave it like this.” Mitch said, looking in her eyes for an unsaid answer.

“Like what?”

“We went out for a bite to eat, and we had a great time until that phone call ruined the mood. I’m sorry, but don’t let it ruin our evening. I like you, and I’d like to see you again. My ex-wife does not want me back, and if she did, she’s S.O.L. I have no interest in her, but I do in you.”

“You do, do you?”

“What about me? Do you have any interest in seeing me again?”

Aimee sat back and chewed her lip. “Do you promise no crazy ex-wives popping out of the woodwork?” He nodded. “Okay, I’m interested in seeing you again.”

He got out and walked to her side, opened the door and helped her out. He held her hand and walked her to her car. He put both arms out and leaned against her car, with her in the middle.

“So we agree to see each other again?” She nodded.

“Can we agree that fifteen years is too long between kisses?” She nodded again. He leaned in and kissed her, a nice, simple kiss that left her wondering where the rest of it was.

“Thanks for a nice time. I’ll call you the next time I’m passing through, and maybe we can do this again,” he said as he shut her door. Her car was an oven, and it had to run a few minutes for the air conditioning to kick in. She looked up and saw him sitting there. Aimee wondered if he was going to follow her home, but he was simply making sure she left without a problem. Aimee turned left out of the parking lot, and he turned right.

***

Mitch got back on the highway and put the radio on, but he wasn't interested in music. He thought about Aimee. She was too sweet a girl to drag into the mess that was his life, but after meeting her, he couldn't stop thinking about her. Since his ex-wife Sandy was a loose cannon, he gave up dating. He had to deny himself a lot of things because of Sandy; one of them was a social life. Mitch stayed on the water and fished. In truth, he had been so burnt by Sandy that he felt there was nothing left to offer to someone else. Mitch felt this incredible draw to Aimee. He didn't know if it was fair to her considering his situation, but Aimee made him want to try.

She was the first woman since his divorce that struck him that way; he felt everything he denied himself rise to the surface and dissipate into thin air. Mitch liked Aimee a lot, and as much as he felt he should let her go, he didn't want to. Fuck Sandy. He was not going to give her the power over his love life anymore. He liked Aimee, he wanted to be around her. She was so easy to be with, and if Hurricane Sandy showed up, he'd call the cops. He'd do just about anything to be with Aimee and would work out the details later. She woke up some long-dead area of his brain, and he felt the pull of her on his emotions. He looked her in the eye, and she responded with a smile. Mitch was a goner.

Mitch felt guilty he knew more about her than he admitted. She was telling a half-truth when she said she was a cipher. She had no social media presence, that was true. He did find her high school yearbook online. He thought about her when she was eighteen. *If she's pretty now, she was beautiful back then. A girl who looked like that usually had one divorce, a marriage early in life based on optimism to a guy who couldn't deliver.* He couldn't figure out her lack of a social life or a history.

It took a bit of digging, but he found a book she wrote; it was a memoir of an aging movie star. It was written over twenty years ago. He ordered a copy and had it shipped to his office at the dealership. He found her picture with the movie star on the back fold.

Man, how could a girl who looked like her manage to avoid men who decided they wanted to give her a go? Mitch wondered. It seemed like the only person Aimee had a relationship with was Dolores Reardon, who was now long dead.

He googled Dolores Reardon; now, she had quite a media presence. He sifted through the most recent posts, mostly pertaining to Dolores Reardon film festivals or revivals. He googled her with the year the book came out, which led him to her last Oscar win with Dolores on the cover of *People* with her Oscar. He studied the picture and almost missed Aimee. She was right there on the cover of *People* magazine, standing near Dolores. *That's her!* No wonder he didn't recognize her. She looked like a movie star herself.

Mitch didn't get where he was in life without developing the ability to sift through the fluff while finding the nut and then the swiftest way of getting said nut. In this case, since her trial stopped with the publisher, perhaps her ghostwriting was done for them.

He called the publisher and dropped a few names. He said he had a client who wished to have a memoir written but not do it himself. Someone suggested Aimee Dunsmore; was she available as a ghostwriter? Would she be interested in the project?

Mitch was sent to her agent's voicemail. He hung up without leaving a message. He gathered enough info to learn she was with an agent, so she must still be actively writing. He looked again at her with Dolores Reardon on the cover of *People* magazine. *She sure was beautiful*, he thought and left the image as his screensaver.

He was a half-hour out from home when the phone rang. It was his son Ryan.

"Hey, Ry, what's up? I'll be home in half an hour."

"Dad, who is Aimee Dunsmore? Mom was here, and she tore your office apart."

***

Chapter 16

Mitch hit the gas and sped back to his office. He pulled in, and Ryan came out to meet him.

"I'm sorry, Dad. I didn't realize she'd come here and cause a scene. She was screaming on the showroom floor. She was positive you were hiding in your office. In order to calm her down, I unlocked the door to show her you weren't there, but she pushed by me and went over to your desk.

"She tried to get into your computer, but all she saw was some picture of some old movie star. She found a napkin with the name Aimee Dunsmore and a phone number, and then she saw a book about the movie star on your desk and saw it was written by Aimee Dunsmore."

Ryan looked at him anxiously. He made a mistake, letting her in his father's office, but he had no idea she would flip out like that. "Mom lost it and trashed your desk. She threw that book at me. Grandpa finally came and got her to leave, but the damage was already done."

Mitch could see the worry in Ryan's eyes; Mitch would be mad if Ryan let his mother in his father's office. Mitch went over to Ryan, put his arm across his shoulders, and gave him a squeeze.

"Don't feel so bad about it. We can't control her, all we can do is try to minimize the damage she caused. It's your poor grandfather that gets the brunt of it. I don't know what's going to happen if something happens to him."

"Who is Aimee Dunsmore, Dad? Why did she make Mom flip out?"

"Aimee is a woman I know, and I like her. She's very interesting, and very pretty. She's also who I had dinner with tonight. Aimee doesn't live around here, so I don't think your mother will bother her. I don't know what your mom wanted from me in the first place. She gets stuck on something and can't let go. She'll forget about her and find something closer to home to be mad about. Everything will be fine, Ryan, trust me. I'll clean this up later. Come check out the ride I picked up."

Mitch locked the door after they left, leaving the mess for another day. He wanted Ryan to know his mother's behavior rested solely on her shoulders, and the hour she wreaked havoc was bad but only one hour out of his otherwise good day.

If she would only take her medication, she could have good days, too. She said it made her feel dull and numb and wasn't like the real her, Ryan thought.

If that complete histrionic display was the real her, it made Ryan incredibly sad. When she was taking her prescriptions, she never struck Ryan as dull and numb. There were stretches of time, years, of calm and peace. Happiness, even. *Why didn't she choose that? Why didn't she want to choose that?* Ryan thought.

***

Mitch acted as if his ex-wife's antics were no big deal, but he couldn't believe Aimee drove her to it. The idea of Aimee, but not Aimee herself. The problem with Sandy was she was as whip-smart as she was unstable. Thirty seconds. One look at his screensaver, the book on his desk, and a crumpled napkin, and Sandy decides Aimee is a threat.

This was a new one for Sandy, jealousy. Before she went into his office, she wanted to go off on him. That Mitch was used to, and he let her. Her anger and vitriol focused on him as the cause of her misery; Mitch allowed her to direct it at him to protect his kids, but he tried like hell not to take it personally. It was hard, though. Mitch's self-esteem had suffered over the years.

Sandy was sick; she couldn't help it. Actually, she could not help it and chose not to. She would rather punish the people who loved her, like her parents or kids, and then accuse them of not loving her. Even Mitch loved her at one point, but her deliberate behavior drove him away. She did it on purpose so she could accuse him of abandoning her. Sandy cast herself in the role of the perpetually persecuted victim, and there was no way on earth to convince her otherwise.

***

If this woman would just stay away from Mitch, we could work things out, Sandy thought. *Mitch is mine, even if we are divorced. Why did we divorce? When?* She hated it when things got all jumbled up in her head. It will settle into place soon, and in the meantime, this Aimee Dunsmore has to go; the sooner, the better.

Sandy memorized Aimee's number from Mitch's office. It was a good thing, too, since she forgot to grab the napkin. She called Aimee's number twice, but it was a generic *you have reached number such and such, please leave a message*. She could tell by the area code it was about an hour away.

Sandy used her computer to find out about Aimee Dunsmore. She searched a bit but found nothing. Sandy googled another tack—Dunsmore obituaries. She found one for Joseph Dunsmore. Survived by four children, one of them an Aimee M. Dunsmore. *Well, there you go. He has Aimee Dunsmore stashed about an hour east of here.*

Sandy needed to know where. She googled Aimee, and other than what Mitch already found, there was nothing. She figured Aimee must live near where she grew up if the information from the obituary was correct, and from the area code, it looked like she still did. She did a property search. If Aimee lived there and owned a house, she had to pay taxes. The two certainties in life were death and taxes, Sandy always heard, and the assessor's office did not disappoint. *Aimee M. Dunsmore, 1430 Washington Avenue. Gotcha!* Sandy thought.

Sandra rubbed her temples. Whenever she had these episodes of explosive anger or excitement, a killer headache followed. She needed to lie down and shut out the noise. She would figure out what to do about Aimee Dunsmore later.

***

Mitch was experiencing a conundrum. Contact Aimee so she'd be on alert, or stay quiet and see how Sandra wants to play this out. He decided to do nothing. Often, after Sandy was finished with her outburst, she was embarrassed and apologetic, not even aware of what caused her meltdown. Mitch hoped that would be the case this time.

He found it hard to believe he was the object of her obsession; she told him many times how much she hated him. A lot of the time, Sandy didn't even know what she was upset about, he was her default. She heaped her rage onto his shoulders, but he found her episodes quite over the top and so exaggerated they were hard to take seriously. That was the root of her problem. The less emotion she provoked, the more enraged she became.

Early in their marriage, her episodes were minor, and she needed Mitch to hug her and tell her everything would be alright. He didn't mind; that was his job as her husband. He loved Sandy and was more than willing to be her rock. He prevented the fallout from reaching the kids.

They were a family, and he wanted to preserve that at all costs. After Sandy got worse, no reassurance from him could satisfy her; in fact, it provoked her further. He was the reason she was unhappy, or so she said. One day, the inevitable happened. She slapped him across the face, and Mitch finally decided he had enough. He moved out.

He rented a house for them and got Bella a car with the expectation she'd help with Ryan's sports schedule. Mitch signed a lease, and since he was legally their father, Ryan could move in, but Ryan couldn't leave his mom alone. Bella would be leaving for college soon, and Ryan felt terrible for his mom.

All the shit Mitch absorbed was now placed on Ryan. Mitch talked to his in-laws about the harm that was being done to their grandson. Ryan needed their support, and he needed their permission to leave. Sandra leaned entirely on him, and Mitch knew if Ryan wanted to have healthy relationships in the future, he had to leave. It was too much weight for Ryan to carry and not cause damage. He was a teenage boy, not a psychiatrist.

Mitch had to get him out before he started to internalize Sandy's hate and venom. Since Mitch was not welcome at Sandy's, there was no buffer between his son and his mother. With the full endorsement of his grandparents, Ryan moved in with Mitch. If Sandy saw Ryan, it was never alone. His grandfather always went with him.

When they divorced, he gave her the house, the car, and anything else she wanted, but they didn't sell revenge at Bed Bath & Beyond. A lot of his assets were tied up by the dealership, and he would have more than enough to be comfortable. Now that he was out, he was out. Mitch was nice and polite to Sandy but kept her at arm's length. She could rage at him all she wanted, and when he grew tired of it, he walked out the door. Many times, Sandy followed him out, still spewing filth and disparaging remarks. He served her notice they were only to contact each other through either their attorneys or a mediator.

He needed to set an example for Ryan on how to set boundaries with people and what to do when people don't respect them. People such as his mother would call at three in the morning on a school night, screaming about random nonsense. It was okay to turn his phone off. It was okay not to take her calls. His mom had serious issues, Mitch told him, and none of them were his or his sister's fault. It's a chemical problem in her brain. There is medication she could take but wouldn't. It was not Ryan's job to monitor or enforce his mother's behavior.

"It's tough, Ryan, to watch someone you love suffer. It's even tougher to watch them do nothing about it, but you have to step back and tell her you love her, but you can't help her. If she gets out of control, you may have to call the police. I know we always call Grandpa for help, but he's getting old. And he's very sad. He loves your mom more than anything, and he can't help her either."

"It's easy to say, Dad, but hard to do. I want to help her, and I don't know how." Ryan said.

"That's because you're a good kid. There is nothing anybody can say or do to help her. It's her choice. Until she decides to do what the doctors tell her, things aren't going to change."

"I know you're divorced and all, but I'm glad you didn't walk away from her. I don't know what I'd do if I was all alone."

"If I walked away from her, it would mean I was walking away from you and your sister, and I could never do that. You two are the most valuable things in my life. I've never met your biological father. Maybe he was willing to leave you behind, but I'm not. I never will. I will always be there for you and your sister."

***

Aimee thought it odd she had a number of calls from an unknown number. At first, she thought it was Mitchell, but nobody left a message. She thought it strange but unimportant. Aimee was putting her things together for her meeting with her agent.

Aimee went into the city twice a year. She met with the key players, like marketing. Social media coordinator. Genre review. Category Leaders. Up and comers. Sales. They discussed last year's sales compared to this year's. Year to date. Aimee delivered two books a year as Dolores O'Rourke.

She had quite a number of books published as Dolores O'Rourke at this point in her career, many bestsellers in the Women's fiction/romance genre, and her books consistently sold. Aimee was going to cut back to one book a year in the upcoming year.

She loved writing, but she felt the need to be a little more social lately. Maybe travel a bit. Go visit her sister in L.A. Aimee could write from anywhere. She was a bestselling author. A success in her field. The Tom Hanks of romance writers. Maybe become a script doctor. Or maybe sit by the pool and watch the lemons ripen. She was independently wealthy. She'd rent her own place in the canyons. Or the hills.

Aimee's phone rang again. UNKNOWN CALLER. Curiosity got the best of her, and she answered. "Hello?"

"Aimee. I'm so glad you picked it up. What do you have going on tomorrow?"

"Hello, Mitchell. Early train. Afternoon meetings. Room Service. Sleep. Train. Home."

"I have to go into the city tomorrow. Do you want a ride? You won't have to get up so early, I can drop you off and see a guy about a car. We can meet up for dinner, and I'll give you a ride home."

"Where are you going to stay?"

"I'll find a place. I'll pick you up at eight. Don't worry. It'll be fun."

"I wasn't going to worry, but since you said that, I might start."

"Don't. I'll see you in the morning."

***

Mitch picked her up exactly at eight. He had a coffee and bagel waiting for her. He picked her up in a late model Mercedes, loaded with all the bells and whistles. They got on the highway and started out. The car rode as smooth as melted butter on glass.

"Is this your car? I don't think I should eat in it. I spill things. The fancier the car, the bigger the mess."

"Maybe you shouldn't. You look very nice today. It would be a shame to show up for your meeting with a big coffee splotch down the front of you," Mitch said.

"Eh. I'm a writer. I'm allowed to be eccentric. I'm just worried somebody will test drive this car and not buy it because it smells like Starbucks."

"Don't worry about it. If it gets messy, I'll have it detailed. If you get messy, I'll have you detailed. It's all good."

Her phone rang. She fished it out from the bottom of her bag and looked at the number. It said UNKNOWN. These calls were starting to annoy her. She answered it, and the caller hung up.

"You know, for the past week or so, somebody keeps calling me. It would go to voicemail and not leave a message. If I answer it, they hang up. Sometimes, they call five times in a row. It even happens in the middle of the night," Aimee told him.

"Aw, you have a secret admirer. Aren't you flattered?"

"No. The only people who know this number are my brothers and sister, my agent. And you, on accident. I originally thought it was you, but it can't be. You're right here." Her phone rang again. She showed him the caller ID as UNKNOWN. She answered it, and the person on the other end hung up. "See?"

"You just eat your bagel and try not to spill your coffee. I'll get the phone if they call back."

She took a bite, and the phone rang. She handed it to him, and he answered. "Hello?" He heard an audible gasp, and he thought his name; the caller hung up.

"You're right. Nobody's there. It's probably some kids dialing a random number as a prank. Just let it go to voicemail. They'll get tired of it and prank somebody else," Mitch said with a confidence he hoped sounded real. He knew who it was. Sandy. He prayed it would go no further than this. When Sandy got stuck on something, there was no telling where the end point would be.

They stopped once on the way down; Aimee needed to use the restroom. He asked for her phone, to add his name so he came up instead of UNKNOWN when he called her. He was afraid Sandy would keep calling, but at least Aimee could tell if he was calling. The phone rang again. *Speak of the devil.* He answered.

"Hello? Sandy?"

The caller said nothing but didn't hang up.

"Look, Sandy, I know it's you. Please stop calling Aimee. You have no problem with her, so please leave her alone. You don't need to do this." He hung up the phone. Aimee came back out and got in.

"All set."

Her phone rang again.

"Don't answer it. Whoever it is called while you are inside. If it goes on much longer, we'll get you a new phone."

"Can't I block the number?" Aimee asked.

"You could, but we don't know the number. The best thing would be to get a new phone."

"But I don't want a new phone. They'll get bored and move on to someone else. I'll turn it off if I have to." She stopped talking so he could negotiate his way around the city without distraction, but he must have spent some time here before. He knew exactly how to get to her publisher's building.

"What time should I pick you up?"

"Five."

"Enjoy your meeting. See you at five," he said as she exited the car.

Before she headed to the elevator, she called the hotel and changed her room to the Honeymoon Suite. *There's something about this city that makes me horny,* she thought. *I wonder what Mitch is going to think. Who gives a shit? He died and went to heaven, that's what he'll think.*

She proceeded to the elevators and went up to meet with her agent, Helen Drod. Aimee could detect a slight accent, maybe Eastern European. Perhaps her last name had been changed from Drodowneiski or something equally as long or unpronounceable. New world, new name, her ancestors might have thought. Or maybe just a lazy clerk at Ellis Island who didn't feel like typing that much shortened it for them.

Helen was a short, roly-poly-ish woman between forty and seventy with a clipped shag hairdo and her signature vampire-red lipstick.

"Aimee, darling, so good to see you. You look well, like life is agreeing with you." Two air kisses on each side of Aimee's head were Helen's standard greeting. "Let's meet in the conference room now. We have time to discuss things before the others are scheduled."

They had their meeting interspersed with reports from the different departments. Aimee told Helen she wanted to be done by four-thirty. She walked out the front door at five and glanced up and down the street but didn't see Mitchell's car. She leaned against the side of the building, and people watched while she waited.

She heard this low rumbling sound and looked around for the source. Right in front of her was what looked like a cherry-red '70 GTO. She narrowed her eyes. It wasn't something she saw every day, let alone in Manhattan. She put her hand up to block the glare. Son-of-a-gun. It was Mitch.

Aimee walked over and knocked on the window. He waved to her to get in. She opened the door and got in, the leather shiny and slippery. It had a bench seat, the kind of seat that a guy used to take the corners so sharply the girl would slide over, practically landing in his lap. Standard bucket seats eliminated this from happening. The things sacrificed on the altar of technological advancements.

"Wow. Nice car."

"Yes, it is, but don't get too attached. It's already been sold. I'm relocating it for the buyer."

"You're the repo relo man."

"That's me. Where to?"

"The Plaza."

"The Plaza?"

"You're not the only one with a few surprises up their sleeves."

"I can't wait," he said as he pulled out into traffic.

The valet parked the car, mostly young kids who had no appreciation for the history of the automobile, the combustion engine, the standard transmissions and the sheer adrenaline rush you got when you went heavy on the gas; when the speed kicked in, it was like you were seconds from lift-off.

The older gentleman's eyes lit up when he got in the car. He was the only one who could drive a stick, and he remembered these cars. He put it in gear and patched it out.

"I guess he had no idea how powerful that car is," Aimee said.

"Are you kidding me? That guy was going to do that the minute I handed him the keys. Those young kids wouldn't know the first thing to do."

"I guess the first thing is to burn rubber," Aimee said.

"Exactly."

They went inside to the beautiful lobby. A bellman took the bags away. She told him to wait and went to the desk. She came back, and they got on the elevator. The elevator went up, up, up.

"Where are we going?" he asked.

Aimee took him and spun him until he was backed up against the wall. She pulled his head down and kissed him full on the mouth. He was in shock at her advance and froze. She kissed him firmly and let go of his head.

"Wait, what. What was," he stuttered. The elevator dinged their floor. She dragged him by the handout, and their steps were lost in the thick pile of the carpet. Aimee took the key to the door marked *Honeymoon Suite*, inserted the card, and the door clicked open. She pulled Mitch through the door and closed it. Aimee walked over to the floor-to-ceiling windows and looked over as the city transitioned from day to night. He came over behind her and put his arms around her.

"Aimee, what are we doing?"

"Anything you want. You're not the only one full of surprises."

"We're getting married?"

"No. We are pretending to have a moment. No, we'll definitely have the moment; just don't make it a bigger moment than it is. That'll ruin it. We are going to take it minute by minute and see what happens."

"Oh? And then what?"

"Don't know. You can't think about now if you're thinking about later."

There was a knock at the door. She gave him a twenty and told him to let the room service guy in. He took the twenty and went to the door. There was a six-pack of beer on ice, a chilled bottle of white wine, and a bottle of champagne, as well as some chocolate-covered strawberries. Mitch opened the wine, gave her a glass, poured one for himself and sat on the loveseat.

"Come here, over to the loveseat, where I'd love you to sit and talk." He invited her.

Aimee went and sat next to him. She took a sip from her glass of wine and looked at him. "What?" she asked him.

"What? What? What are we doing? The Honeymoon Suite? Rose petals on the bed? Champagne? What's this all about?"

"Isn't it obvious? I'm trying to seduce you. Too much?"

"But why?"

"'But why?' Boy, did I call this all wrong? Here. Let me get the remote. Maybe NASCAR's on." Aimee went to stand, but Mitch pulled her back down.

"Wait a minute. I didn't say I was unwilling. I'm confused."

"What do you want? A checkered flag waving you in?"

"Stop it," he said. "I kissed you once. Once. One time, I ended up in the Honeymoon Suite at the Plaza. I can't help it if I'm a bit confused."

Aimee looked at him and sighed. She shook her head. "Jesus. You're not making this very easy, and you're sort of ruining the mood. I guess I gotta explain. Maybe it will clear things up."

"Explain what?"

"I do this for a living."

"You're a high-end call girl?"

"If you don't shut up, I'm going to toss you off the balcony. Let me get my bag." She got up and got the large tote back she'd been carrying around with her. She sat back down and pulled out a folder and an armful of books.

Aimee took a book and showed it to him. "See this? Wrote it. Bestseller." She threw it over to the bed. She held up another one. "Same." And tossed it towards the bed. Another book. "Same." Another book. "Same." She reached into the bag for a few more. He grabbed her arm to stop her.

"You wrote all these books? I don't get it."

"Yes. Notice anything?"

"No."

"Geez, you really are a guy. I write bestselling Women's Fiction/Romance novels. ROMANCE is the operative word."

"These are written by Dolores O'Rourke."

"Ever hear of a pen name? A nom de plume? There's more. Look in that folder. There's a lot of numbers. Units sold. Weeks on the Bestselling List. God, there's nothing like numbers and facts to be a major buzzkill.

"See, I was trying to set the mood for romance. You know how I told you I haven't been kissed in fifteen years? I haven't been laid in even longer. I kind of like you, I thought you kind of liked me. I got inspired and figured, why not? I think booking the Honeymoon Suite was too much; I scared you. I figured go big or go home. I should have just gone home."

"Stop that. I'm incredibly flattered that you did all this for me. I'm also blown away by the fact you haven't been with a guy in ages, and you picked me to end your dry spell."

"Don't get carried away. It's probably full of cobwebs or rusted shut."

"Hold up there. What did you have planned?"

"Planned? Nothing. I set the stage and created the ambiance. Whatever happens or doesn't happen is because of chemistry. Is there any? If there was, we could have just gone to a Super 8 motel. Or we could order room service and drink 'til we pass out. We could get naked, and you could worship me for a while. Or we could leave and pretend this didn't happen.

"See, in a book, this is where the guy takes over. This is where he starts to thrill her and make her feel like she's the only woman on Earth. Like he's been dying the whole book to get to this point, and now that it's here, he's gonna tame her, he's gonna love the shit out of her so she'll never look at another guy again." Aimee leaned over and handed him a book. "Maybe you should read one, and we'll revisit things some other time."

She stood up and walked over to the window, the city in lights below her. *If I have to explain it all, it's a bad idea,* Aimee thought. *Maybe I should switch genres. I'm losing my touch.*

Mitch walked behind her and put his arms around her but remained silent. Aimee did, too.

"Talk to me, Aimee."

"I think I said enough."

"I wish you'd tell me how you feel."

She pushed his arms away and stepped aside. "You want to know how I feel? I'll tell you how I feel. I feel stupid. Embarrassed. I feel too old for this shit. I thought we could fool around and have some fun. Now, I think I'm calling an Uber and going to the train station."

"Aimee, don't."

"Don't what?"

"Don't stop talking. I'm kind of digging this."

"You know what? Fuck you. I'm standing here like an idiot, and you're getting off on it? Boy, did I get you wrong?" She moved to her bag and started putting her books away. "I'm leaving. Order whatever you want." Aimee was about to cry, and she had to get out of there before her tears fell. She moved quickly to the door, but Mitch was faster. He blocked her from leaving.

"Get out of my way, Mitch." Instead of sounding like she had steel in her voice, she heard it tremble and crack. "Please," she whispered. "Please."

He took the bags out of her hands and put them on the floor. He took her in his arms and crushed her to his chest. He could feel her shake and start to cry.

"Please don't go, Aimee. I'm sorry. I don't want to be the reason you're crying. I want to be the reason you get goosebumps. I want to roll around on the bed with you. I want you to laugh and feel special because you are. You are the most special girl in the world. I'm sorry I didn't recognize it. Nobody ever tried so hard to make me feel special, and I feel like a huge jerk. You did all this for me, and the only thing I did for you was make you cry. I feel terrible."

He could feel the tension start to ease from her body. "Let's sit a minute, I have an idea."

Aimee pulled away and sat on the loveseat. Mitch sat next to her. She wiped her face with the back of her hands.

"Here's what we'll do," he said, leaning forward on his knees so he could look at her when he spoke. "We'll get room service and eat it in front of the window and just watch the lights turn on in the different buildings. It will be a regular dinner, and we'll see if we can't regain our momentum. After we're done, let me know if you want to go home, and I'll drive you. Let's just see what happens. Is that acceptable?"

"Yes...I think so."

“Let me get the menu and see if anything looks good.” He got up, got the menu, and held it open. “Anything?”

“Yeah. The grilled chicken salad.”

“Okay, anything else?” She shook her head. “Let me go order.”

Mitch came back with the wine and filled their glasses. “Feeling better?”

“Yes.”

“Good. It feels nice sitting next to you. You’re so soft.” They sat there. He had his arm across the back of the sofa, and it gradually slid down until it encircled her. He used it to hug her closer. She yielded to him and snuggled up. They stayed like that until room service came with their dinner. The waiter brought their dinner in and replaced all the ice before he left.

Mitch arranged the furniture so the table and chairs were in front of the window. She sat while he served her. He placed his own dinner down and removed the dome. It was a cheeseburger and fries. She laughed. He took that as a good sign. She asked him if he wanted a beer with his burger.

“No. I may be driving later and need to be sober.”

Aimee looked at him. He was trying so hard. “Have the beer. I don’t think you’ll be driving. I don’t know what you’ll be doing, but it won’t be driving.”

“Okay, if you’re sure I won’t be driving.”

“I’m sure.”

“Are you sure you had enough to eat? You only had the salad.”

“I had bread, too. I want some of those strawberries.”

“They do look good,” he agreed.

“You can stop now. It’s okay.”

“Stop what?”

“Being so nice.”

"I will not. I'm leaving no room for doubt. My intentions are sincere, Aimee. I like you. I like you a lot. If my behavior earlier made it seem otherwise, I apologize. The Honeymoon Suite scared me. I didn't think you liked me that much, and here you go, reserving the Honeymoon Suite at the Plaza. I panicked. What are the rules? Am I supposed to pay for this? Offer to chip in?"

"No, this is a gift for you, but the publisher is paying for it. You want to know another secret about me?"

"There's more? I don't know, Aimee, if I can take any more. You already outclass me. If you tell me you're a member of MENSA, I'm afraid it's over. You can be better looking at me, but not smarter."

"What if I'm richer than you?"

"You probably are. You're a bestselling author."

"No, independent of that."

"You won the lottery?"

"Kind of. When I started out, my first big job was writing this tell-all memoir of this old movie star. We became really good friends, and when she died, I was in the will. I'm an heiress. I even have one of her Oscars in my bathroom."

"Aimee, you just keep getting better and better. An heiress. With an Oscar."

"Before you decide you like Ben Franklin more than you like me, it's all tied up in a trust, and there's no point in plotting some scam to separate me from my money. There's a lot of lawyers whose sole purpose is to make sure I don't fall in love with some scoundrel with dubious intentions on a cash grab."

"I don't get it. You live in the house you grew up in. You drive a Honda that's at least five years old. You don't even have air conditioning. There's no way, looking at your simple lifestyle, a person would guess you've got money."

"I never needed much to begin with, so it's in a vault somewhere, and I hardly think about it."

"Let me recap: a beautiful heiress is holding me hostage in one of the fanciest hotels in the city, and the only way I can escape is to love my way out of it?"

"Pretty much."

"It sounds like the plot of one of your books."

"It does, doesn't it? If I use it, I'll dedicate the book to you."

***

"Is this the part where we roll around in bed?" Mitch asked.

"What kind of guy are you? Riddled with Catholic school guilt and afraid of a headstrong woman, or the strong, silent type who is going to engage in a war of wills with said heroine?"

"You tell me."

"You certainly aren't the strong, silent type. This heiress will mop the floor with you."

"That's all part of my master plan. You're going to dismiss me as some weak-willed fop, and when you least expect it, I'll strike like a cobra. I'll turn the table on you so fast you won't know what hit you."

"Not bad, not bad. Do you have a brother?"

"Yes, in Albany. Why?"

"It never hurts to throw in a rival for the heroine's affection."

"Can't. He had his manhood damaged in a farm accident."

"Fop? Manhood? Are you sure you've never written one before?"

"No, but I want to star in one."

"Then write the script. If I write it, you'll end up trapping me in a barn, and I'll stab you with a pitchfork."

"I have a secret, too, but you probably don't want to hear it. I'll make you mad, and you'll stab me with a fork anyway."

"What is it?" she said uneasily.

"I googled you. Sorry."

"What did you find?"

"Not much. Only the book about the movie star. When I googled her, I found a whole lot about her. I even found the *People* cover from her last Oscar win. I thought she was standing next to one of the movie stars, and I realized it was no movie star; it was you. You were kind of turned away, but I recognized you. You went to the *Oscars.*"

"Yes, I did. I was a glorified seat filler with better jewelry."

"I just find you delicious."

"Delicious? What does that mean?"

"I don't know. It sounds like something the lord of the manor would say to the lowly scullery maid."

"The naive, young, fresh-faced scullery maid who figures out she's being played and smashes the lord of the manor's skull in with a fireplace poker?"

"That took a sudden dark turn."

"Sells books."

"Kiss me."

"No. You ask a woman for a kiss, and she'll say no. Automatically. In this off-set power balance where the guy thinks he can just order the girl around, the girl isn't going to give up what limited power she has, which is the power to say no."

Mitch walked over to Aimee and reached out his hand to her; she took it and stood up.

"What are you doing?"

"I'm not asking," he said as she looked up at him, and he brought his lips down to hers. He kissed her, slow and romantic. She couldn't tell if he was in the moment or laying the groundwork to storm the castle, but it didn't matter. She was in the moment and started kissing him back. Mitch was caught off guard for somebody that hadn't kissed anyone in years, she was pretty damn good at it.

They stayed in the moment, trading back and forth who was in charge when soon, he felt any fight left in her vanish only to be replaced by desire. She relaxed and gave herself over to him. She turned up the heat, kissing him so determinedly he felt her suck the air right out of him like she was a vampire who fed on air rather than blood. Mitch responded by backing off, figuring she would kiss him harder and make her demands known, but she didn't. Instead, she sighed and stopped, resting her mouth against his lips.

"You are so beautiful, Aimee. The most beautiful girl I ever met," he whispered into her mouth. "Come with me. Let me show you how beautiful you are." He led me over to the bed.

Aimee sat down on the bed, he sat next to her. He moved her hair aside and started to nibble on her neck, kissing her and sucking on her earlobe. "You taste as good as you look. Delicious."

Aimee giggled. She sounded sweet and girlish, more like a fifteen-year-old girl than a fifty-year-old woman. He kept kissing and nipping at her; it wasn't too long until he had her half-undressed.

"Um, Mitch?"

"Yeah, baby?"

"Probably should have brought this up earlier, but would you use a condom? There's some in the bathroom, in that basket. They think of everything here."

"Yeah, sure. Anything for you. Anything else?"

"Yes. Dim the lights."

"Can we negotiate the last one? I'm interested in every square inch of you."

"How about a bit? I'm a little self-conscious. I just ate dinner, and now there's a definite pooch."

"I will because you asked me to, but it's not necessary. You're beautiful, so incredibly beautiful," Mitch said as he got up. "Don't move."

"Because you were so willing to indulge my neurosis, neuroses, whatever, if you want to appreciate me as is, leave the lights on," Aimee said when he returned. "If you'll find pleasure in that, who am I to deny you?"

"Compromise," he said and fine-tuned the lighting. "Good?"

"Good. I know men are visual creatures, so I'll indulge you."

"Thank you, but it's not solely visual. You smell wonderful. Your skin is so soft and silky. You feel amazing. Your lips are full and lush," he said, kissing her until she was flat on her back.

"This is the part," Aimee said.

"What part?"

"The part where we get naked and roll around on the bed."

That's what they did. Aimee was still a little self-conscious, but once the sensations started to build, she forgot about her nerves. Mitch had a lot to offer to take her mind off things. They both had little pads of flesh where they didn't twenty years ago, but they both had enough muscle that things hadn't gone totally to flab.

She enjoyed the feel of him, of his skin and the soft hairs that covered his body. Aimee closed her eyes and let Mitch discover every square inch of her however he wanted, with his hands, his mouth, and maybe even his feet. She let go and stopped thinking about her tummy rolls or if her thighs jiggled. She existed at the moment with him and enjoyed the male energy that emanated from him. It felt so good to connect with him.

As he reveled in the soft femininity of her, she let herself be engulfed in his maleness.

"Aimee. Open your eyes. Look at me."

She did, and he stared at her as he filled her with his body. She gasped at the sensations she thought she lost years ago, and in her joy of knowing she could feel them, she let loose like a cat in heat. Her explosion of sexual energy both surprised and spurred him on. When he heard her moan start deep in her chest, he focused on her finish, and he wouldn't be finished with her until he had to peel her off the ceiling. He was glad she squealed and bucked and shook because he hoped it meant she was there because there was no holding him back, and he came like he was coming from downtown.

Mitch rolled off her and wondered if he was having a heart attack or maybe it was Cupid's arrow, but he was done. He knew she was it. Mitchell had his share of women over the years, and none made him feel like he was struck by lightning, not even his wife. He loved his wife, he did. He was sure of it. He was also sure it was in the past.

"A penny for your thoughts," Aimee said, unsure how to interpret his silence. *Was it bad? Do I smell? Did he decide this was a mistake?*

"Oh. Sorry. I think I had an out-of-body experience, and I haven't fully recovered." He rolled over to look at her and smiled. "You, Aimee, are a very rare breed."

"What does that mean? Like 'Best in Show'?"

"It means I like you, I really like you. I really liked you before, but now I really, really like you."

"That's a lot of reallys."

"You deserve every one of them. Would you like a strawberry?"

"I forgot about those. Pass them over."

He brought the whole tray over. "Thanks," she said. When she bit into one, the juice dripped down her chin. He leaned over and licked it off.

"See? Delicious."

Aimee ate a few more and decided she had had enough. "I'm going to brush my teeth and go to sleep. I'm pretty tired. There's toothbrushes in that basket if you want one."

She was under the covers when he got back. "Would you please hand me my bag? My phone was ringing." She fished it out from the bottom.

"That's odd. It says I have three missed calls from UNKNOWN again."

He slid in next to her. "You were squealing so loud you couldn't hear it ring."

"Uh-huh. That was you."

He checked his phone; he had it on silent. Four missed calls from Sandy.

Aimee's phone rang again. He took it out of her hands, turned it off and tossed it in the direction of her bags. "No distractions. I'll put the timer on, and we'll watch *Seinfeld* for a bit. Goodnight," he said with a kiss.

"G'night, Mitch," she said and drifted off.

He watched TV for a bit, and once he was sure Aimee was asleep, he checked his phone. He listened to one of the messages Sandy left; it was loud and rambling, so he deleted it. He deleted the others without listening to them. He looked over at Aimee, sound asleep with a slight smile on her lips.

"Dreaming of me, Aimee?" he whispered.

“Umm,” she mumbled and turned towards him.

“Here you go, get up close,” Mitch said and tucked her tight against him. He turned the TV off and tried to go to sleep, but instead of luxuriating in the afterglow of one of the best nights of his life, he was worried Sandy would spook Aimee, and she'd decided he wasn't worth the headache. Maybe he wasn't, but Aimee sure was. She spent the last twenty-five years living a drama-free life, exactly the way she wanted. Why would she, at this time of her life, want to go down that road?

He looked over at Aimee sleeping next to him. *Too bad there isn't super glue in that basket in the bathroom,* he thought. *I'd like to glue you right to my side so you can't run away when Hurricane Sandy hits.* He curled himself around Aimee and finally drifted off to sleep.

***

Mitch got up the next morning before Aimee did. He took his phone in the bathroom so as not to disturb her and turned it on. He returned two more messages from Sandy, which he disregarded, and the one from Ryan.

“Morning, Ryan. What's got you up so early?”

“I hate to keep doing this to you, but it's Mom. I guess you had your phone turned off because she called me about five times in the middle of the night looking for you.”

“Yes. You know I went to pick up the car for Ainsley. I finished up late and stayed in the city because I didn't feel like driving home in the dark. I'm going to get on the road soon, and I'll go straight to the store, and we'll figure it out. Don't worry about it. I'll see you soon. Love you, Ryan.”

When Mitch came out of the bathroom, Aimee was up, gathering her things. “What are you doing?” he asked her.

"I didn't mean to eavesdrop, but it sounds like you have some fires to put out and need to get home."

"The only thing I need is for you to brush your teeth and get back in bed."

She looked at him, puzzled. "Are you sure? That sounded important."

"Nothing is more important than you right now. I'll meet you in bed."

Aimee went into the bathroom, did her thing, and returned to bed. He grabbed her in a tangle of sheets and started to kiss her neck. His beard was tickling her, and whatever unease she felt was replaced by laughter.

"We aren't going anywhere, Aimee. If you think I'm going to leave this bed with you in it to hurry back to give some guy a car, you're crazy. Now stop worrying. You enjoyed yourself so much yesterday. I insist you enjoy yourself a couple more times before we go."

"And you got nothing out of it, Mitch?"

"I got a lot out of it, actually, but the best thing was the look on your face when we finished. You were practically drooling."

"That was probably you."

"It doesn't matter. I want us both drooling all the way home," he said and disappeared under the sheets.

***

Mitch said they needed to conserve water and take a shower together, so that's what they did. He wanted to wash her hair for her. Aimee didn't want to deal with a wet head of hair, but she felt having someone wash her hair for her was right up there with chocolate-covered strawberries, so she let him. It felt so nice, and she was glad she did.

Being with Mitch put her senses on overload. Every time he touched her, she began to tingle and get little flutters inside. Aimee wondered if it was a bad idea.

Now that he opened the box, she wasn't sure she could stuff all the feelings back inside and have the lock hold. Aimee wasn't even sure she wanted to.

Aimee wondered if her writing career as Dolores O'Rourke was over. She laughed that her success as a romance novelist was her ability to write the sexual tension, the build-up, and the mental foreplay that drove the novel and its characters to the climax. All those unfulfilled urges and desires she buried deep down spilled out onto the page, driven in part by her lack of ability to express them physically. *If I no longer feel the need to put them on paper because I am no longer a dried-up husk of a woman hungry for love, how ironic will that be?* Aimee thought. *If Mitch finds me desirable, other men will, too.*

***

They picked up the car from the valet. Unfortunately, there was no valet that could drive a standard transmission, so one had to drive Mitch to his car. The concierge gave them a bag containing bagels and two coffees for the ride. The problem with vintage cars was they lacked amenities like consoles and cup holders; Aimee had to balance the bag on her lap and coffee in both hands until they got on the Thruway. By then, the coffee was cool enough to drink, and he was done shifting gears and could hold his cup. He offered to put the top down and dry her hair that way, but she shook her head no.

Another thing about old cars was they weren't really meant for conversation. They were loud. Aimee was glad, she was tired and just wanted to close her eyes and let the engine's bass line rumble lull her to sleep.

Aimee woke up alone and parked in a nice shady spot at a Thruway rest stop. Mitch was outside on his phone, leaning against the front bumper. She yawned and caught the name Ryan. Aimee searched her bag for her phone and pulled it out. She hadn't looked at it since Mitch turned it off. She had five missed calls. All from UNKNOWN. *Why were they calling in the middle of the night?*

Mitch got back in the car. "Morning, sunshine. Poor Ryan. He hasn't developed the confidence to say, 'No. Those terms won't work,' and walk away from the deal. It takes time. He'll be alright."

"Maybe he's not comfortable. He's got the numbers part down. Tell him there are only four numbers to consider: what it costs, cost plus what you put into it, what you'll ask, and what you'll take for it. That's all."

"You need a job? You've got it right down."

"I was actually thinking about a job change. It's funny you ask. I told my publisher I'm only turning in one book next year. Maybe I'll travel; go see my sister."

"She's the one in DC?"

"LA."

"LA? That's too far away."

"It doesn't matter. I can write from anywhere."

"No, I mean, it's too far away from me."

She looked at him. "You've got to be kidding me. Am I that good? It's that good? How long a dry spell was yours?"

"I'm sorry, Aimee, but you can't leave. We're not done."

"Done with what?"

"You tell me. What happens in the book when the scullery maid is revealed to be an heiress, and the hero has mended his ways from a scoundrel to an all-around good guy?"

"There's this creepy but harmless cousin always around, and we find out he knew about the scullery maid's privileged status, and if it's revealed, she'll inherit ahead of him, and he loses it all. He tries to kill her, but the hero has to save her."

"This is good. How does he save her?"

“Depends on how he tries to kill her. You know, we could sit around and write storylines, and you could be Dolores O’Rourke. Just type it up and pretend to be me. Let me ponder the cousin’s options.”

***

Chapter 17

Mitch pulled into her driveway. The ride was over. Lots of things were over. Aimee felt like she had outgrown something; she needed to decide what to put in that space. She knew it had to involve people. Aimee spent almost all her adult life in isolation. She had maybe two friends here that she saw on a regular basis. The one thing that Aimee knew for sure was it was Mitch's fault. He plugged back in the cord that kept her in the dark and allowed her to be an introvert. Now, the empty corners of her life became obvious, and with that knowledge came the desire to fill them.

Mitch followed her in with her bags.

"Just put them over there," she said and pointed at the kitchen table. "I'd give you the full tour, but you have to get going."

"I don't need a tour. Just show me your bedroom."

"Ha ha," she said sarcastically. "Maybe someday."

"At least you could invite me for dinner."

"Probably not. I think I'm going to gut the kitchen and redo it. This place is old. I never really thought about it, but lots of things need updating. I just lived with things the way they always were. Everything was functional, so I never cared, but since I'm not living so much in my head anymore, I'm seeing things with fresh eyes. I see how run down everything is," Aimee said. "This was my childhood home. It was easy to live with things the way they were, but I'm not a child anymore. Perhaps I left it like this because this was my parent's home, and I was afraid if I changed anything, I'd lose the memories that went with it."

"Maybe it's time to make some new memories," Mitch said. "Sell the house as is, so your memories stay of this place. When you drive by, you'll think of the ugly Formica counter where your mom taught you how to cook. If you start demoing the place, it won't be the same. That's okay, too. It's your house, make it your home. Instead of being your family's home, it will be yours if this is where you want to stay. Personally, I think you should sell it and move to Rochester."

"Move to Rochester?"

"Yes. That way, you'll be closer to me, and I can see you whenever I want."

"What happens when you get sick of me and move on? I'll be all alone. I'd rather be rejected from afar."

"Aimee, Aimee, Aimee," Mitch said and came over and hugged her. "Why would your mind go there? Didn't we have a moment yesterday? Didn't we have a couple? What if I asked you to be my girlfriend? Would you say yes?"

"I'd say, 'What is wrong with you'?"

"What's wrong with me? You. You're what's wrong with me. I think about you way too much. I wonder what you're doing when you're not around. I wonder if you're thinking of me, and if you're not, why aren't you? At least if you're my girlfriend, I know I'll cross your mind when I'm not around."

"That's why? So you know I'm thinking about you?"

"Yes. That way, I can call you anytime I want so I can make sure you're safe."

"Safe from what?"

"Tornadoes, a plague of locusts, stuff like that."

"Things like the end of days?"

"Yes. If the world's ending, I want to go out with you." Mitch told her.

"Huh. That's plenty to think about. You go home and help Ryan. Call me later tonight. I promise to think about you all day."

"All day?"

"All throughout the day."

"Okay, but you have to kiss me goodbye," Mitch said as he grabbed her.

Her phone started to ring, but Aimee didn't stop kissing him to check who was calling. She grabbed it out of her bag as she walked him to the door. She missed another call from UNKNOWN.

"Damn. This is starting to bother me," Aimee said and showed him the screen.

"That's what I'm talking about. If it goes on much longer, we're getting you a new phone," Mitch said. "I'd say let's do it right now, but I have to go."

"No hurry. I'll just keep it off."

"See? If your phone's off, I can't get a hold of you, and that's when I start to worry."

"Don't waste your time worrying. I have no plans on going anywhere other than to bed. I need to recover from last night."

"That's another thing. I don't want you to go to bed without me."

"Goodbye, Mitch. Drive safely."

She waved as he pulled out. He burned rubber, the teenage gearhead in him unable to resist the opportunity to impress a pretty girl.

***

The phone calls happened less and less, to the point she didn't mention them when she talked to Mitch. Once, Aimee answered it and buried it in the sofa cushions without disconnecting, so they couldn't call back.

She saw him a couple of times a week; they each drove half an hour and met in the middle for dinner or ice cream and talked on the phone other days. Every so often, he'd ask her if she was ready to move to Rochester, and she'd answer, "Not yet."

"I told everybody I have a girlfriend, and it's you. I hope you don't mind, but I got tired of waiting for you to make up your mind." He laughed when he said that. He spent weekends on his boat; she had an open invitation to join him, but Aimee always said next week.

Sometimes, he'd be going east to his network of luxury auto contacts. Mitch would leave the night before and stay with Aimee. He got a feel for her place and could see why she stayed. She was relaxed there. In her native habitat, she would cook wonderful dishes every so often, but not as a daily chore. It wasn't something she felt compelled to do.

When he was going to her house, he sometimes bought food and cooked for her; he had a few dishes up his sleeve he used when entertaining. Mitch liked just sitting across from Aimee, when she was happy, she beamed. Aimee beamed when he brought her ice cream for dinner. He felt happy around her. No negative energy hung like a mist about her.

Maybe things seemed so happy at Aimee's because of Sandy's absence. When he arrived home from his trip, he went straight to the dealership to talk to Ryan. He settled down, so when Mitch walked in, he was calm and in charge. Mitch greeted Ryan and asked to meet him in his office after he dropped the keys off to detail the GTO.

Mitch closed the door and sat down. Ryan was waiting for him.

"Let me guess, Ryan, it wasn't the dealership. It was your mother, wasn't it?"

"Yeah. She usually has this thing where she hates you, but lately, she's consumed with you. She's convinced you have a new girlfriend. I keep telling her you don't, but it only makes her angrier."

"Well, she's not wrong. I do have a girlfriend. It was bound to happen sooner or later."

"Aimee Dunsmore, Dad?"

"Yes. Your mother calls her phone constantly and hangs up. I told her to leave Aimee alone, but she still calls. We had to turn our phones off.

"You know how hard it is once your mom gets her mind stuck on something for her to let go, but I'll talk to her and get her to refocus on me and leave you and Aimee alone. Is she at your grandparents? I'll stop over there and talk to her. Need me to do anything here? I'll probably go home after, we can talk business over dinner."

Mitch grabbed some keys and took one of the cars off the lot. He called his ex-father-in-law, George, to tell him he was on his way over to talk to Sandy.

"I hate to tell you, Mitch, but you're the only person she wants to see." George knew that Sandy could be relentless and irrational, moods too unpredictable for his young grandson to manage, even with his father's help. George feared when Mitch decided he had had enough of his ex-wife. He would walk away, and Ryan would have no help at all.

George knew how lucky he was that Mitch came into their lives. His sense of normalcy was a counterweight to Sandy's moods. He remained a buffer between the kids and their mother. He saved those kids. When their biological father left them, Mitch stepped up and raised them. He never mentioned they weren't his kids. To him, they were.

Mitch knew of Sandy's mood swings. Back when they were married, her behavior wasn't as extreme, and it was under control as long as she stayed on her medications. For the most part, she did. It was only when Bella entered puberty that Sandy's condition worsened.

Unmedicated, Sandy looked at Bella as a threat to Sandy being the only woman in the house. She looked at Bella as a competition for female superiority. Sandy wanted to maintain her alpha female role, but Mother Nature would not rewrite biology on Sandy's behalf.

Mitch and the kids went to family counseling. He felt Bella was at grave risk of interpreting her mother's behavior as a lack of love, and young girls were predictably vulnerable to not recognizing those who loved them from those who used them until it was too late. Mitch insisted Bella see a therapist during high school to answer questions about why her mother hated her. Sandy didn't hate her, but her brain wasn't wired right. Her brain chemistry was messed up, and Bella needed to know it wasn't about Bella at all. Bella's biggest question was, if there was a medicine that could help her mother, why wouldn't she take it?

Between the therapist and Mitch, Bella maintained a healthy level of self-esteem and didn't turn to others for validation. She had friends and loved to play the piano. She loved Mitch, too. She could always count on him to be there when she needed a parent's guidance. When Sandy found out Mitch took the kids to counseling, she flipped out.

"How dare you take my kids to a shrink? There's nothing wrong with them. You're trying to convince them there's something wrong with me, and there's not. The only thing wrong in this house is you. You're not their father, and you never will be. I hate you, Mitch. You're trying to take my kids away from me, and I won't let you!"

This was one of the only times they heard Mitch fight back. Usually, fighting back was an exercise in futility. Mitch didn't want to add more to their already stress-filled lives, so he would take them for ice cream or pizza and remove them physically from their tumultuous home life. This time, Sandy cornered him in the kitchen, unaware that the kids were watching TV in the next room.

"You think I'm trying to steal your kids? Sandy, you are really out of your mind if that's what you think's going on here. I'm trying to save them and give them some stability. This whole place is toxic. They're going to grow up and think everybody lives like this. You're either screaming your head off or in bed crying nobody loves you. These kids need to be kids, not walking around tiptoeing looking for landmines. That's no way for kids to live, and these are my kids, too."

Mitch usually was sympathetic to her, patient even, but even he had his limits, and that afternoon, he reached his.

"Those *are* my kids," he said, rage etched in his features, "and I'll do everything I can to ensure they don't grow up thinking your problems are theirs, and they're allowed to feel sad or mad, or however your actions make them feel. I'm trying to make sure your shit doesn't roll downhill and bury them. I wish you'd get help. They're great kids, and they miss their mom. They don't understand why you don't miss them. You're sick, Sandy. Get some help before you destroy us all."

"Fuck you, Mitch. I know what you're doing. You want to take my kids away from me, and I won't let you. I hate you, Mitch! I hate you!"

He tried to get past her and exit the door. She hauled off and slapped him across the face. He stopped and looked at her. For all her noise, she had never crossed over into violence before. Rage boiled up inside him, and he knew if he didn't leave now, he'd slug her back, and he wasn't going to let her seduce him like that. If she was to the point she felt she could physically and emotionally abuse them, that was over the line. He would not allow his kids to witness it. He had to get away from her and fast. She let him pass, and he exited the house.

Mitch sat on the steps, put his face in his hands and cried. He did not know how he got to this point. He failed her. He was failing the kids. Mitch cried tears that originated from his soul, and he couldn't stop. All the things he let pass to not to make things worse backfired on him. There was a mushroom cloud of pain, anger and helplessness over his head. He had no idea how to get out from under it. He sat on the steps and wept.

Bella and Ryan heard the fight and saw their mother slap their father; their mother howled with rage in the kitchen, and their dad was gone. Ryan started to cry. Mitch was *gone*. Who would help them now?

Bella put her index finger against her lips and mimed quiet. She brought him to the window and pointed at Mitch's car. "He didn't leave us. He's just outside," Bella whispered. She opened the window screen and helped Ryan out. She climbed out after him and went to the stairs where their Dad sat with his face in his hands, his shoulders shaking with grief.

They went over and stood in front of their father. He was always so strong, seeing him weak like this scared them more than anything their mother ever did. Bella put her hand on one shoulder, Ryan on the other. Mitch looked up at his kids and grabbed them both by the waist, hugging them so tight Ryan went, "Oof."

"It's okay, Dad. We know what happened. We saw Mom hit you," Bella said, panicked at the sight of their father crying real tears, his eyes red. "We're sorry you're sad."

Mitch used his t-shirt and wiped his face. "There's no reason for you to be sorry, you didn't do anything. I'm sad because I don't know how to help your Mom. I've tried everything I can think of, and I only make things worse. How'd you kids get out here?"

"Bella took us out through the window."

"I need to ask you how often you sneak out, Bells, but another time. I need to get my keys and go to Grandpa's, but they're inside. Bella, if I help you back through the window, can you grab them off the table?"

Bella looked at him. "We all know Mom's sick. Sick in the head, but it doesn't give her permission to hold us hostage. It doesn't give her permission to treat us like this. It's one thing if she's trying to get better, but let's be honest. She's not even trying. I'm going in this door and get the keys, and if she doesn't like it, she can go *fuck off.*"

She opened the door and marched in there. Mitch and Ryan listened to her talk to her mother. Sandy yelled at her about what they couldn't discern, but Bella yelled right back.

"Will you SHUT UP!" Bella screamed. "I'm getting the keys, and we are leaving. It's none of your business where we're going. Why don't you sit here and try to figure out what you've lost because it's your family that's leaving? You don't DESERVE US!" She came back out after slamming the door the way only a pissed-off teenage girl could.

"Get in the car. I'm driving," Bella told them.

She drove to her grandparents. Before they got out of the car, Mitch asked them to wait.

"Bella, I'm proud of you. I know how much you love your Mom, and for you to go in there and tell her how you feel must have taken a lot of guts. I don't know what else we can do, nothing we do seems to work. I want you to know you need to love yourself first. It's okay to put what you need ahead of somebody else's problems. It's okay to say I love you, but I can't fix you.

"That's where I am now. When she goes into those rages, I can't listen to the hurtful things she says anymore. I feel really sad for her and you guys. She slapped me. She crossed my personal line of no violence, and I will not allow my kids to have that kind of stress in their homes. I have to be able to provide a stable home life for you. That's my number one priority.

"I know she's mentally ill. We all do. Our family is in crisis, but it's like you said, Bella. She's destroying us. It has to stop now. I am moving out and taking you with me. We aren't abandoning her, but we need to put some distance between us for our own mental health. That's why I want to talk to Grandpa. You guys need a place to go if I'm away on business.

"It's time to put us first. Never let anyone treat you like you aren't as important as they are. Your mother, your boyfriend, your best friend, nobody. The same goes for you, Ryan. Nobody is worth more than you. Not even me," Mitch joked to lighten the mood.

"I refuse to live in a house where it's okay to hit someone, and if I stay, I'm sending you the message that yes, it is. Just know that whatever I do, I'm bringing you with me. I will not leave you behind. I love you guys. I don't care what you heard. You are my kids. Forever.

"Look, here comes Grandpa. I feel the worst for him. Maybe if we leave, it might help him, too. He won't have to come over and calm her down when something we do gets her all riled up. He's getting old and deserves to enjoy his life. They need to get a place in Florida where they can put their feet up and drink Pina Coladas."

Mitch, the kids, and Sandy's parents sat around the kitchen table and outlined a plan. He was going to legally separate from Sandy and get a place for the three of them. The kids could go back and forth and see their mom as much as they wanted. He was giving Bella a car so if they felt that Sandy was having a bad day, they could leave and go to either their dad's or their grandparents.

It will soon be summer vacation. Bella was going to sleepaway camp for July, and Ryan was going to work at the dealership detailing cars for the summer. Bella, too, when she returned from camp. Mitch left the kids with their grandma to order pizza for dinner, and he and George were going back to the house to inform Sandy of the changes.

It was as ugly a scene as they imagined; Sandy accusing Mitch of turning her kids against her. George and Mitch stood firm with changes.

"I hate you, Mitch, I fucking hate you!" Sandy screamed at him.

"Good," he said as he walked out the door. "You won't miss me when I move out."

***

Mitch found a three-bedroom flat not too far from the center of town. The kids could walk to get ice cream or meet friends in the park; they each had their own room and, more importantly, a place of refuge for peace and quiet. Bella felt more comfortable around her friends now they could come over and have no anxiety around the hand grenade with the loose pin that was Sandy.

Ryan had a harder time. He missed his mother terribly; he felt guilty about giving up on her. Both his dad and grandpa were fully supportive of him maintaining a relationship with his mom but reinforced the fact her issues had nothing to do with him. If she went off because he left his sneakers in the middle of the living room, leave. Call someone to pick him up.

Unfortunately, Mitch had some legal battles with her. She would show up and start screaming at him in the middle of the showroom while the dealership was open and customers were present. He got a restraining order requiring her to stay away from the dealership during business hours. He avoided her, and she started to hound Ryan about his father and what he was doing.

The only thing Mitch did was go fishing. Sometimes, he brought Ryan and his friends water skiing. He found his peace on the water. Sandy had wrung him emotionally dry. The idea of another woman never crossed his mind. Mitch felt Sandy damaged him; he had nothing left to give another woman, and it would be a complete waste of time even to try.

Bella finished up and graduated high school. Sandy threw her a huge party and didn't invite Mitch. She went off to college in Pittsburgh, intent on becoming a divorce lawyer, a dream she later achieved. Ryan graduated and went to school in Buffalo for a business degree to set him up to take over the dealership when his dad wanted to retire.

When Bella was a senior in college, Mitch and Sandy got divorced. He had been divorced for five years when Aimee Dunsmore stuck around to explain what happened with her cart, and it was over that cup of coffee he decided he liked her in a way he never liked any woman before. *Fuck Sandy,* he thought. *She may have covered 90% of my heart with scars, but she missed 10%. I'm taking that and risking it all on Aimee Dunsmore.*

***

Chapter 18

Aimee enjoyed having someone introduce her as Mitch's girlfriend. As much as she said she wasn't his girlfriend, she was, which meant she had a boyfriend. When she told him that, he got all happy.

"I'm a boyfriend. Your boyfriend. You have to introduce me as 'my boyfriend.'"

They met for dinner at this Italian restaurant, an out-of-the-way place they discovered midway between them. He held her hand on top of the table, stroking the back of it with his fingers, a big smile plastered on his face. The server came over.

"Hi, I'm Krista, and I'll be your server tonight. Would you like something from the bar?"

"Hi, Krista. This is my boyfriend, Mitch. Do you know what you'd like? Perhaps a beer for my boyfriend. I'll have a glass of white wine."

She took their order and left.

"Well," Aimee said, "how did it sound? My boyfriend. I said it twice."

"You made me very happy. Twice."

"I never thought I'd have a boyfriend at fifty."

"I never thought I'd have another girlfriend. Ever. I know you know my ex-wife's problems. I spent a lot of time minimizing her behavior with the kids, playing monkey in the middle. I absorbed a lot of anger, figuring I would take on the burden and take it off the kids. It was good for them, but it was a total mind fuck for me. I couldn't imagine speaking to a woman and it not end with her saying, 'I hate you, Mitch.'"

"Well, I don't hate you, Mitch. I think you're a great dad and a wonderful guy. It's sad the way it ended; you got kicked right in the nuts, but you got the kids successfully into adulthood. I'm not sure at what cost, but you came out the other side. Sick or not, she didn't know what a gift you gave her, what a gift she had in her hands. She lost the best thing she'd ever have. You focused so much on the kids' well-being I think you lost sight of yourself. I hope you realize now how much you're worth."

He wanted to grab her and kiss her; she was so soft and lovely. Aimee was a soothing balm for his soul, and he could feel himself little by little plugging back into the goodness life offered.

"One of these days, Aimee, I'm not going to ask. I'll get some zip ties and throw you in the trunk and take you back to Rochester."

"One of these days, I might just surprise you and say yes."

"Goodbye, Aimee," he said and kissed her again. "Have a safe drive home."

"Goodbye, Mitch," she said as he opened her door for her. "You do the same."

They drove out of the parking lot. She turned right, and he turned left. Neither of them noticed the nondescript silver sedan parked there. If they did, they might have seen Sandy watching them, her face tight with anger. As she exited the lot, she turned left and followed him home. *One of these days,* she thought, *I'm going to follow her home, and little miss Aimee Dunsmore will regret she ever met you, Mitch.*

The hang-ups returned with a vengeance. Whoever it was liked to call at three a.m. Aimee ended up turning her phone off at ten p.m. Mitch had an issue with that, what if he needed to talk to her? She went to the store and got a new phone. She only had about ten contacts to switch over, so it was no big deal.

She thought no more about it until she got a postcard that read, "Your number is no longer working. Good thing I know where to find you," mailed from a local zip code. She didn't know whether to be scared or not, but the calls stopped, and she forgot about it.

Aimee was at the drugstore when a strange woman approached her.

"Margaret! It's been ages! How have you been?"

"I'm sorry, but you have confused me with someone else. My name's not Margaret."

"You're not Margaret Brown from St. Agnes?"

"No, I'm not. Sorry," Aimee said.

"Sorry to bother you. You have one of those, what do you call it? Someone who looks just like you?"

"A doppelgänger?"

"That's it! I'm surprised nobody's told you that before."

"I'm sure I'll run across her soon," Aimee said, smiled, and headed down the aisle.

Sandy watched her walk away. *Not impressed, Mitch. You could do so much better.*

***

Aimee's love affair with words wasn't just typing them, it was reading them, another trait of her Mom's Aimee inherited. Her Mom pretty much read everything, from cereal boxes to the *New York Times*. It made her Dad mad when they went places, her Mom always found to read, even if it was Popular Mechanics.

"Look, Joe, I didn't marry you for your money or your good looks, I married you for your personality," her mom once said to her dad. "I don't really like other people, they bore me. I'd stay home if I had a choice, but because you like parties, we go. You go with your larger-than-life personality, dazzle people with your wit and charm, and I let your wonderfulness spill over onto me."

It was how her parents met. Marie was sitting on a park bench reading, and Joe went over and asked her for the time. She told him to sit down, she might want to date him. After she said that, he was hooked like a trout on opening day. They were two totally different people; each admired the other's strengths.

Joe fell in love with her brains and beauty, she fell in love with his physical presence and solidness. They were in love until the day he found her on the kitchen floor. Joe Dunsmore cried like a baby at her passing and for days afterwards. When he met Sally, the Joe Dunsmore they knew and loved came back piece by piece until he became their Dad again, and none of them judged his choice in Sally. She made him happy, and that's all they wanted.

***

Aimee returned some books to the library and looked at the shelf that held her titles. She always got a thrill out of it; she wrote them all, and nobody knew. Aimee knew her mom would be proud of her. She wished she was here to see it.

She needed to go to the grocery store and left the coolness of the library. The heat waved off the hot pavement as Aimee approached her car. There was something on her windshield. She looked at it; it seemed somebody had egged her car. *Shit,* she thought. *Now I have to go to the car wash, too. If I don't get it off soon, it's going to fry. Hot enough to fry an egg, indeed.*

Aimee took a detour through to the car wash before she stopped at the grocery store. As soon as the pneumatic doors opened, cool air greeted her. Aimee shopped, checked out and went to her car. Under the windshield wiper was a flyer advertising the car wash she had just come from. She looked around to see if other cars had them, but none did. *That's odd. You'd think I'd notice that when I left, but I guess not,* she thought.

Aimee went home, parked her car in the garage, and put the door down before she unloaded her purchases. She put everything away and went to her computer. She started typing. Once she started writing, her mind thought of nothing else.

The silver sedan sat parked across the street for a while. It left once Sandy decided Aimee wasn't leaving any time soon.

***

Aimee got up early to go for a run. It was predicted to be another scorcher today. She liked to run in the park before it got too hot; she liked ice cream for dinner, so the needed run completed the circle.

Aimee felt good after her run. The heat made her loose and limber. She saw an unfamiliar car as she turned down her street. It was a silver sedan parked in front of her house. As Aimee approached, the car pulled out and went further down the street, took a right, and disappeared. *Probably Jehovah's Witnesses,* Aimee thought and pulled into her garage. She put the door down just in case they came back.

***

Mitch was going out of town for the weekend to attend an annual muscle car convention. He said he was only going because of the auction, but he was meeting his car fan friends and looked excited whenever he talked about it. When he got all excited in front of Aimee, he tried to temper his mood since he was leaving her behind.

"Will you cut it out?" Aimee said. "You'll be gone for five days. Go. Play some golf, have a few beers, tip a couple of strippers."

"Can't. I'm a boyfriend now. I need to behave myself."

"You're a *boyfriend,* not a *Boy Scout.*"

"Still, I have an obligation to you. I'm your boyfriend."

"You better not talk like that around your friends. They'll think you're whipped."

"Let them. I'm calling to invite myself over and spend the night tonight. I'm leaving tomorrow afternoon and want to see my girlfriend before I go. And as my girlfriend, you have to say yes." Mitch said.

"Them's the rules. I don't have anything for dinner."

"I'll pick something up. I'll see you around seven."

"Later."

A few weeks ago, Aimee gave him a promise present.

"What's a promise present?"

"Usually, it's a ring a guy gives a girl before he proposes. He promises to give her a true engagement ring in the future."

"You're giving me one of those? A promise ring?"

"No. It's something more symbolic."

He pulled something out of the wrapping. "What's this?"

"It's a garage door opener. To my garage. I promise your car will always have a spot next to mine."

"This *is* symbolic. It's significant. It's from you. It took a lot for you to make such a concrete gesture. I promise to always be worthy of it. This is way better than jewelry."

"Some girls might disagree."

He crushed her to him and kissed her. "There. We sealed the deal."

***

Mitch hit the garage opener and watched her door go up. He felt inordinately pleased she gave it to him. It was actually the perfect gift for a car guy. A more sentimental gift he could not remember. He felt like she asked him to go steady. *Good Lord. I'm making myself sick,* he thought.

He brought the groceries in first, followed by his gym bag. She ran into the kitchen and slid into him, he grabbed her to catch her from knocking them both down. "Hey!"

She looked up at him, smiled, and said, "Well, hello there."

"Hello to you too. I bought groceries for dinner. You can have a steak and blue cheese salad, I'll have a baked potato and some salad, and cook the steak on the grill. There's also a bottle of red. Got all the bases covered."

"I always thought the bases were more fun uncovered."

"True. Want to work up an appetite for dinner?"

"Race you!" Aimee turned and ran down the hall. When Mitch came over, they slept in the bedroom on the first floor. Aimee purchased a new queen size bed, a bigger TV, and some new lamps. She jumped on the bed, and Mitch joined her. They started making out on the bed; one thing led to another, and soon they were naked.

"I'm going to thrill you, Aimee. I'm going to make you see stars." He learned the things that got her going and how important verbal cues were to her. Maybe it was because she was a writer or a woman, but the phrase sweet nothings, whatever they were, applied here. He put his mouth by her ear and told her how wonderful she was, how lucky he was to have her. He nibbled and kissed her neck between the words that made her feel cherished.

He went to his doctor and got a clean bill of sexual health and a prescription for Viagra. She went to her doctor and got a clean bill of sexual health and the news she was now post-menopausal. They could now enjoy being together without fear of disease or pregnancy.

"Oh, Mitch," she sighed. "You make me feel so desirable."

"That's because you are. Every inch of you, inside and outside."

"Piston, O-ring, valves, hubcaps, carburetor..."

"Talking dirty, are you?"

"I'm trying."

"Well, it worked. Are you ready for some good loving?"

"No, I'm ready for some great loving."

The thing about adult love is that everything slows down. It could be a bad thing if the point was to get your rocks off if the purpose was to get laid. It could be a good thing because, finally, the guy took the time to give the woman what she needed, the extended foreplay young love lacked. Men who were lucky enough to figure it out were loved in return, in a depth of emotional satisfaction they never experienced as young men. Having a woman wrap herself around a man like this, enveloping him with her essence as well as her body, was like making love to an angel. Mitch truly felt he died and went to heaven.

Afterwards, they cuddled under the sheets. Sometimes they talked, other times not.

"Aimee, you are the absolute best," Mitch began. "I hate to talk about my ex, but I need to explain something. In order to manage her needs, I had to shut down my own. When it was over, I suppose I could have made up for lost time by fucking anything on two legs, but I couldn't. Instead of feeling elated and free, I was gun-shy and depressed. I never saw myself with a partner unless it was a lake trout. I figured that was my destiny, to be alone. I was so burned out I didn't care. When I retired, I'd get a dog and go fishing, and that would be that."

Aimee was lying across his chest; he kissed the top of her head.

"But you made the world open up for me. Colors are brighter, and the air fresher. You made me feel again. Before, I didn't want to feel anything; numbness was better than pain. You took the playbook I was living by and tossed it out the window. You didn't even look at the cover. I'm getting the chance to rewrite whatever chapters I have left, and it's all because of you."

"Yeah. It is, isn't it?" Aimee laughed. "No, I only showed you the possibilities. You took the actions. You made yourself happy. You could have just looked at the mark I made on your car and said, 'Fuck it. It's not my car, why should I care,' and drove away."

"I almost did, but there was something about you. You could have driven away yourself, but you didn't. You waited to make it right. It made me think. You were a person of integrity. It made me wonder if there were other things I might be overlooking, and I was right."

"You're getting a dog when you retire? Can I pick it out?"

"Only if you move to Rochester."

"That's emotional extortion. Are you almost ready? I'm hungry."

"Five more minutes."

"Okay."

As they ate dinner, he asked her if she would come to Rochester the following weekend. His daughter was coming in from Pittsburgh, and he'd like Aimee to meet her. Dinner. Nothing special.

"Is there something specific going on?"

"A wedding. Her high school girlfriend. She's coming in on Friday to hang out with her family; the wedding is going to take up the rest of the weekend."

"Okay, if you want me to meet her, I will."

"I do want you to meet her. She deserves to see her father happy."

"You want me to drive in on Friday?"

"Yes. Come early and spend the day with us on the boat."

"No, I want them to have you all to themselves. I'll meet you guys for dinner."

"Don't you know how to swim?"

"I have a Varsity letter that says I do. I used to be a lifeguard."

"Why won't you go on the boat whenever I ask?"

"I will. There's lots of weekends left in the summer."

"Don't wait too long. Summers go quick around here."

***

Chapter 19

Aimee met them at the restaurant. She didn't know what to wear to meet his kids. Was she supposed to dress nice, and they'd be in bathing suits from their day on the water? She decided to wear a simple, black v-neck linen dress. Aimee grabbed one of Dodo's scarves and folded it into a triangle to throw over her shoulders if she got cold, and Birkenstock's. She had a pair of rhinestone dropped ball earrings that swung around her face, sparkly but not too obnoxious.

She pulled out the silver meteor cuff that was a gift from Connor all those years ago and smiled. He was one of her favorite memories. She supposed she could google him, but she didn't want to find a recent picture of him and find he got fat and bald. She let him exist in her memories as the boy who was so sweet, so willing, with so much of life ahead of him. She hoped he found the best of everything; he deserved no less.

Aimee parked her car in the gravel lot. The restaurant was located on the water but not near the marina. There was a dock for patrons who arrived by water.

She went inside and checked with the hostess, who led her to an umbrella table outside.

"Aimee. We just got here. Perfect timing," Mitch said and stood up. He introduced her to his kids, Bella and Ryan.

Bella had ash blonde hair long enough to brush her shoulders. She was a beautiful girl, actually a beautiful woman, but her eyes were dark. She could see Bella evaluating her. Aimee figured she thought her dad was unaware of the new dating rules; he'd been out of the game for so long. Bella wanted to make sure her father wasn't thinking with his dick, caught up in a love affair with a woman waiting to fleece him dry. Aimee looked at her and smiled.

"You're in town for a wedding?"

"Yes, an old high school friend."

"What color is your dress?"

"Dark blue."

"Navy or sapphire?"

Bella looked at Aimee, curious why she continued asking questions when anybody else would say, "How nice" in dark blue and changed the subject.

"Sapphire. Why?"

"You were in the sun today and got a bit of color; a beautiful jewel tone like sapphire will make you look like a walking ten. Navy, not so much. I mean, it's a nice color, perfectly acceptable, but more suited to board rooms or courtrooms. I know it's unacceptable to look better than the bride, but unless the bride is Heidi Klum, she doesn't have a chance. Just make sure you don't stand too close to the bride in the pictures. She'll be bummed out for sure."

Aimee looked at Ryan. He was much fairer than his sister, and where she was tan, he looked sunburned. "Hello, Ryan. I hope you aren't going. I think you'll be soaking in an ice bath tomorrow. It seems like you'll be too sunburned to wear much more than shorts. And you, Mitch. Handsome as always." She felt a slight chill. "If you'll excuse me, I'll be right back." She got up to get Dodo's scarf out of her car. She came back with it over her arm.

"Where'd you go?" Mitch asked her when she returned.

"I went to the car and got this." Aimee held up her scarf. "In case I get chilly."

"I would have gotten it for you. I wish you asked," Mitch said.

"Why? There was no reason I couldn't get it."

Bella looked across the table at her brother. Aimee seemed very nice, and the only thing she wanted from their Dad was, well, nothing.

The server came over, and Mitch ordered another round. Aimee passed. She needed to sober up to drive home.

"No, you're not. Stay at my place." He signaled the server to bring another for Aimee.

"You have company; you don't need me. I'll only be in the way."

"Good. When I trip and fall, I'll land right on you."

"Please, Mitch, stop. You're embarrassing me," Aimee said, her face red.

He laughed. It was hard to rattle Aimee, and he succeeded. Bella saw the exchange. Her dad—having fun and teasing Aimee—looked happy. She's seen him happy before, but it was because he was usually satisfied with something, like Ryan having success at work or her getting into her first choice law school. Happiness, from a general point of view for him, was different. *He looks happy,* she thought, *because of this woman. Is she using him for something?* The lawyer in her wanted answers.

"So, Aimee, how did you meet my dad?" Bella asked. Her father answered and told the story.

"Karma? How interesting. How many children do you have?"

"None. I don't particularly like kids. No husband, either. I'm an old maid," Aimee said.

"I imagine you must work a lot. What is it you do?" Bella asked.

"I'm a ghostwriter."

"Do you find it fulfilling? Doing all the work and not getting the credit for it?"

"Yes. I'm at the point in my career where I can pick and choose which jobs I feel like taking on."

"See, Aimee undersells herself. She purposely presents herself as some sort of drone, and she's not. Not at all," Mitch said.

"Why did you tell them that?" Aimee looked at the kids. "He's wrong. I haven't achieved drone status. I aspire to be a drone. I'm still a grunt."

"Grunts don't get to be on the cover of *People* magazine."

"You were on the cover of *People*?" Ryan said, his mouth agape.

"That was ages ago. I happened to be standing next to the person they wanted on the cover."

Mitch showed them the cover, and he called upon his phone.

"This is the Oscars," Bella said, looking at the phone.

"See the old lady with the Oscar? Look at the pretty girl standing next to her. That's Aimee," Mitch said.

Bella looked at the picture and back at Aimee. "That *is* you."

"Hard to believe, huh? One of my first projects was ghostwriting for Dolores Reardon, the actress. We got to be good friends, and she asked me to be her date for the Oscars. As I said, that was a long time ago. I can't believe you have that."

Mitch scrolled through his phone. "Look at this. She didn't ghostwrite it. Her name is on the front, and this is her with Dolores on the back." He passed it back to Bella. It was the picture of them having their three p.m. cocktails. Bella looked again at Aimee and handed the phone to Ryan. He passed it back to Mitch.

"That's enough, Mitch. I can't believe you have all those on your phone. What else is in there? Wait, I don't want to know."

"Just one more." He must have gone to the bookstore and found her section. He took a picture of the shelf with all her titles. "This is the last one. Aimee's also a bestselling author. She wrote all these." He passed the phone to Bella, and she handed it to Ryan, who passed it back to Mitch.

"Really? You wrote all these? That's not your name," Bella said.

Aimee looked at Bella. "You're like a pit bull. I'd hate to go up against you in court, and I mean that as a compliment. No, that's my pen name, Dolores O'Rourke. I figured if I had a name established in a specific genre, ghostwriting jobs might dry up. People would have a preconceived idea of who I was; I wouldn't be a ghost anymore. I like being a ghost. Your father had to dig deep to find those photos."

"Wow. When everyone is out there trying to capture their fifteen minutes of fame, you had it. You could still have it if you revealed who you are," Bella observed.

"Please don't tell anyone. I truly enjoy being a ghost."

"Sure. Success means different things to different people. If you choose to remain anonymous, so be it."

"Thank you. Now, Mitch, have any baby pictures of your kids you'd like to share..."

"No!" they both said at once.

The server came with their drinks and promised to be back with their food.

While they waited, Bella commented on Aimee's bracelet.

"This? It's a meteorite, or so the guy said. After I wrote with Dolores, we had to promote the book. She lived in the Hamptons, so we did a lot of it in New York City. I had a friend at NYU, and I met him for dinner. We just walked around all afternoon and went down some side street. It had all kinds of cool shops; one of them had only handmade goods. That's where this came from; the guy said it was a meteorite on sterling silver. Oh, I almost forgot. We went to a fortune teller and had our cards read," Aimee said.

"Really?" asked Bella. "I always wanted to have my cards read. How accurate was it?"

"It's kind of funny when you think about it. Everything they talk about is supposed to take place in the future, and there's no way to know how accurate it is at the time, but I've already lived my lot, so now I can tell. She said I had love, but it wouldn't last. I would find love, but later in life, I'll be happy with the choices I made.

"She told Connor he would be moving away from water, and there would be a big break in his future. I know he grew up in the Hamptons and couldn't wait to move away, so that part was true. Last I knew, he lived in Arizona. As far as a big break, it could mean divorce, starting his own company, or even a skiing accident. We don't keep in touch, so I don't know."

"Connor? You never mentioned him," Mitch said.

"Why would I? We hung out for a summer years ago."

"Tell me about him now."

"Objection. Relevance?" Aimee said and looked at Bella.

"She's got you there, Dad." Bella laughed.

"I also never mentioned I was on *Good Morning America*. Why don't you make a big deal about that," Aimee said to Mitch.

"Wow," said Ryan. "You did a whole lot of things before you were as old as me now."

"Yeah, but I peaked early. I haven't been to the Oscars or on TV since."

They had a lovely dinner, and the conversation flowed freely. Mitch told them about her being an heiress, but she laughed.

"If I'm an heiress, I wouldn't be driving that piece of shit Honda."

Aimee felt the kids relax. She thought it sweet the way they worried about their father. Bella seemed happy her Dad found contentment. Aimee was the exact opposite of their mother, not needy at all. She had complete control of over her life as an adult. Bella secretly envied her.

Aimee was able to pick and choose her projects, whereas Bella grew up in chaos and worked in the same. There are either nice, amicable partings or parents intent on destroying each other in a scorched earth policy, leaving the kids in the middle of something so harmful the ramifications wouldn't be seen until they marry and repeat the patterns of their parents.

That's why Bella wanted to be a divorce lawyer. She wanted people who didn't belong together to part ways with some civility and the least amount of damage to their children. Much like Bella and Ryan, who happened to be the victims of unstable home life caused by a mentally ill parent, there were many kids stuck in homes where their needs were considered last while the parents waged war.

Sometimes creative solutions were found, parents split up, sold the family home, and bought two smaller houses across the street from each other to limit the back and forth the little ones suffered. Those were two people who absolutely hated each other but loved the kids. Bella picked this area of law because she thought she could make a difference to the innocent bystanders of love gone wrong. Maybe Bella was burning out, but her clients seemed to get more bitter and vengeful as time went on.

She wondered about changing careers and maybe going back and practicing environmental law. What good would healthy kids do if they had a sick planet?

Ryan liked Aimee very much. She made his Dad happy. He was a guy and didn't overthink things. His mom lived in her parents' house, and his grandparents went to Florida for half a year. His mom saw a new doctor, and she said she was trying some new medication. It seemed to be working; she hadn't had an episode in a while. He still lived with Mitch, but when his grandparents were away, he stayed there so his mother wasn't alone. Even as an adult, he had to navigate between two households.

They finished dinner and had coffee. Aimee and Mitch split a piece of cheesecake. Bella was staying with her friends downtown at the hotel. Ryan was going to drop her off, go to Mitch's, get ready, and go out. They said their goodbyes, and nice to meet yous. After they left, it was just Mitch and Aimee in the parking lot.

"Why don't you follow me home? Ryan won't be there most of the night. In the morning, he'll still be sleeping, and you can do the walk of shame on the QT."

"I can't. It'll be the creep of shame. I don't even know where you live."

"I know. For being a person who doesn't like to live out loud and broadcast their every move, you've done a lot of things lately, things you don't usually do. You drove here to meet my kids and had dinner with them. You had more than one glass of wine and shared more personal information than I've ever heard before. Now you're going alone to some guy's apartment, and you're nervous about what would happen if the guy's son walked in on them. Have I covered most of it?"

"Pretty much. Except the guy could be a serial killer."

"Follow me home. We don't have to do anything, just hang out and watch TV. Aren't you at least curious about where I live?"

Aimee felt terrible saying no, she wasn't. "Maybe a little. What if I come across your stash of *Playboys* or your porn collection?"

"The porn is Ryan's, and the *Playboys* are vintage and a collector's item."

"Oh, all right. I'll stay. I need to stop and get a toothbrush."

"Thank you. I've never had an overnight guest before. I'll be the perfect host, you'll see. I promise."

"Never?"

"Never. I've never come across any girl who was worth the effort to ask out on a date, let alone look at her first thing in the morning. I've seen you first thing in the morning. I've already decided you're acceptable."

She entered Mitch's apartment and looked around. It was pleasant enough, perfect for two bachelors. It lacked a woman's touch, decorated in a way that could only be considered as Early Motel. Once Ryan was in college and Bella established herself in Pittsburgh, they no longer needed the house in town. Mitch moved here to a traditional apartment in a complex. He did have a few framed pictures of the kids at different times of their lives, but as decor, that was as far as it went.

Ryan came in after he dropped his sister off. He said hi, showered, told Aimee it was nice to meet her and left.

"See?" Mitch said.

***

The next morning's bright sunshine and clear sky indicated it would be another perfect day on the water.

"Want to go fishing? I promise I'll let you go home tonight. It looks like a beautiful day on the water. We shouldn't waste it."

Mitch was right; it was going to be a beautiful day to go out on the boat. Aimee consented, but he had to take her to Target first. She slept in a tee shirt of Mitch's and her dress from the night before. She ran in and got what she needed, a pair of black shorts, a t-shirt, sunscreen, and a hat. They went back to his place and got ready.

"All set." Aimee came out in her new clothes.

"You look perfect. You could wear a burlap sack and still look perfect. Let's go."

They left her car at his place, and he drove to the marina. He had a cooler and supplies. He loaded those first and reached out for her hand.

"Prepare to board," Mitch said as he helped her on. She sat, and he expertly handled the boat to a spot he said was good fishing. He dropped anchor and prepared the rods.

"So, Aimee, tell me what you know about fishing."

"Why?"

"You seem to have a grasp on pretty much everything, and I wondered what your skill level was as it pertained to fishing. I bet you once went deep sea fishing for marlin."

"I know how to tie a fish hook on the line, I can bait the hook with a worm, and I know you have to know how to set the hook once you have a nibble and the fish takes the bait."

"Worms don't bother you?"

"No. I know you're supposed to hook the fish in the mouth, and it's not fun getting the hook out if they swallow it. I'm not particularly eager to handle the fish, either. They're too slimy."

"Your dad taught you all that?"

"No, my Mom. We used to go to my Aunt's camp on the river, and the guys wouldn't let me go out on the boat. First, I was too little, then it was because I was a girl. My sister and my cousin used to ride bikes into town and hang out, so they weren't interested.

My Mom taught me, and we'd fish off the dock. Mostly sunfish and crappies. We would keep count and see who caught more. The girls always won. They were looking for big fish like lake trout or salmon. Every once in a while, I'd land a good-sized bass, and we'd save it to show the guys. I've never been deep sea fishing, though."

"You never cease to amaze me."

"Not having kids left a lot of time to pursue other interests."

"Are you sorry you never got married or had kids?"

"Not really. I just lived my life day by day, and nobody ever came along that offered the possibilities of such a life. I never sought one out, either, so it didn't happen. I don't think about it, but I would have been a great mom because my Mom was a great mom. She knew how to take care of a family."

"It's too bad she died so young. I would have liked to meet her. She sounds a lot like you. Hey! You've got a bite!"

Aimee took the pole. There was some action happening at the tip of her pole. She could feel the fish show interest in her lure, but nothing major. Aimee held the pole, watched the end of the rod as it bounced, and patiently waited. Suddenly, the pole jerked down, at which point Aimee pulled back and *bammed!* It was fish on! It was Aimee's job to wrestle it close enough so Mitch could bring it in onboard with the net.

That fish was not happy. It worked like hell to get away, and Aimee worked like hell to bring it in. It was a matter of who would tire out first. She finally got it close enough for Mitch to scoop it up in the net, still fighting like hell.

"Holy shit, Aimee! That's got to be a ten-, twelve-pound trout!"

"Here. Give the line to me and take a picture. I want to let it go."

Mitch took Aimee's picture holding the fish up, and since she hooked it clean through the mouth, it was a piece of cake to use a pair of pliers to set it free. Mitch let it go, and it disappeared into the dark water.

"Bye, fishy. Be more careful next time not to take the bait," Aimee told the fish as it swam away.

"I'm impressed. You handled that like a pro."

"Are you kidding? I'm exhausted."

"You mentioned you spent time at your aunt's camp. Do you know how to waterski?"

"Yes, but that was a long time ago. I'd have to use two skis now."

"You've skied with only one?"

"A long time ago," she emphasized.

"No wonder you never found a guy who measures up."

"No, I think it was more like having older brothers and sisters. I learned stuff earlier. Other kids were learning how to tie their shoes, and I was already on roller skates. I was first out of the gate and left everyone else in the dust."

He was sitting in the captain's chair and pulled her over so she was between his legs; he had his hands on her hips.

"Have you ever been in love, Aimee?"

"From waterskiing to love? That's quite a leap. Anyway, I don't think so. I'm in love with love for a living. Being in love recreationally seemed like overkill."

"What about that guy, Connor?"

"Will you leave him alone? I liked him a lot. Maybe even loved him a little bit. I don't know. It was years ago, and if it matters to you now, this right here"—Aimee gesturing between them—"is a waste of time."

"Sorry, he doesn't matter. How about now? Think about it. The sun on your face, the gentle rocking of the water, the sounds of the gulls. The smell of suntan lotion. My arms around you."

"I see what you did there, backdooring me into a serious conversation. Your arms around me feel very nice. The smell of sunblock. The squawk gulls, all of this. This would be a very nice place to fall in love."

"Why don't you fall in love with me? You know, research for one of your books," Mitch said.

"I could. It would have to be unrequited, though. I'd be the girl at the marina selling bait, and you'd be the wealthy playboy. Your boat would be filled with supermodels, and I'd smell like gas and fish guts."

"You paint quite a picture there. You could take a shower, and I could be a regular guy."

"That wouldn't sell. Why all the questions?"

"Because I might be interested in falling in love with you, but if you have no interest in falling in love with me, I'll stop thinking about you like that. We'd stay friends."

"You can do that? Turn it off like that? In my book, you'd fall in love with me despite not wanting to. You'd fight your feelings because I was unsuitable. You'd be in turmoil. Usually, you'd date someone else to try to make me jealous."

"This falling in love you write about seems very complicated."

"It's supposed to be. Actually, that's not true. When you fall in love with someone, it's like getting struck by lightning. You have no choice. It's the love interest that makes it complicated. You have to convince them they love you back; they just don't know it yet."

"I see. Well, what if the person comes right out and says, 'I love you,' what does the love interest do then?"

Aimee leaned back and looked at him. She knew he was doing a little fishing himself. He wanted to know how she felt about him.

"Look. I'm fifty years old and have never been in love before. Maybe when I was younger, I fell in love with parts of people, or superficially. Regardless, none of it lasted, so it must not have been real love. Writing filled the hole the absence of love created, or maybe I dug the hole and filled it with my books, so there deliberately was no room for love. I don't know. Perhaps I thought that all love was fleeting, not meant to last. I figured that's why the divorce rate was so high. It's kind of scary to think about.

"Now, I'm looking at the hole in my life. If I don't write so much, something has to fill it. Nature hates a vacuum. So, instead of love on paper, what about love in real life? I think I'm probably too old to run off to have a mad, passionate affair. This must be how becoming a crazy cat lady starts."

Mitch looked at Aimee, not sure what she was thinking or saying. *I guess I have to come right out with it.*

"Aimee, look at me. This is not a story. It's real life. I was struck by lightning. I love you. What about you? Do you feel the same way about me? By the way, this is a big deal for me. I'm taking a risk here—a big risk. Before I met you, I had absolutely no interest in women. I had things in my life I was happy with, I was content. Falling in love was not on the list, but I got struck by lightning, as I said. What do I do now?"

Aimee looked back at him and shrugged. "Kiss me?"

"No," Mitch said. "Tell me how you feel."

"How do I feel? Scared shitless. I have no idea how to be in love. Can you accept that I'm going to screw up and make mistakes? I'll probably act like an idiot middle schooler and say juvenile things."

"As long as you tell me you love me, I can accept anything."

"If you asked me about this last week, I would have said no because I would have been too scared to say yes. But seeing you on your home turf and with your kids makes me want to say yes. I want to be a part of your life. What I feel for you is way bigger than anything I've ever felt before, and it's real. It's not written on paper. I'm going to say, 'Mitch, I love you back,' and roll the dice."

"You won't be sorry. I promise I'll always find a way to make you happy. Now, I'll kiss you."

He grabbed her and smushed her to him and kissed her with such a fury of passion she felt like he was the iceberg and she was the Titanic. She was going down with the ship and took a swan dive off the deck into dark and uncertain waters; positive Mitch would be there on the other side to keep her from drowning.

They spent the rest of the afternoon fishing. Mitch caught one, but Aimee's was bigger. They flirted and made out and acted like two teenagers who'd been in the sun too long. They had sandwiches and bottled water for lunch. Mitch also had the cooler stocked with beer, but they were drunk on each other and needed no additional alcohol to make the other more attractive.

It was about four o'clock when they went back to his boat slip. Aimee was a capable first mate and very helpful in docking the boat. She put the fenders out and expertly tied the rope around the cleat without being told. He put the top on to put it away for the night. She helped him clean up; he took the cooler, and she took the trash.

Admitting how they felt about each other allowed them to relax and enjoy each other, each not wondering what was on the other's mind. They laughed and joked and kissed each other all the way back to his place. Mitch parked the car and gave Aimee the key to his apartment so she could run ahead to take a shower. He followed behind with the cooler. Mitch happened to glance over at her car and saw a flyer tucked under her wiper blade. He walked over and grabbed it, ready to crumple it and throw it out. Before he did, Mitch glanced at it and realized it wasn't a menu from some miscellaneous Chinese restaurant; it was a note. "Not My Kids," it said.

Aimee stayed another night and drove home on Sunday. When Aimee thought about it, she had spent the last twenty or so years devoid of much human contact outside of getting change back from a cashier or a hug from a friend. She had no family to interact with at home. She had her two trips into the city for business. Occasionally, Aimee would have dinner with a male author on the roster of her agent's clients. The last time, he was the bestselling holistic lifestyle guru. Apparently, soap was one of those chemically-filled household items that should be eschewed at all costs. Aimee politely declined any other offers.

***

Chapter 20

Aimee and Mitch still kept the same schedule; dinners during the week at one of their midpoint restaurants. The only difference was they saw each other more often on weekends, and occasionally, she went on a road trip to exchange cars. He still asked her to move to Rochester; she still said, "Not yet."

Mitch decided Aimee needed a new car. Her old car was fine for her old life, but now she was on the road more; she needed more reliable transportation.

"More reliable transportation? I don't think so. My car is just fine."

Mitch knew enough about Aimee that whatever she did was her own idea, and all those years of being responsible for herself proved her more than capable. Since she had no interest in a new car, Mitch needed to create it. One week, he met her driving a Lexus and the next, a Mercedes. He happened to show up in a '68 Ford Mustang and was surprised at how much she liked it.

"You like this car? I was going to bring it to a dealer in Westchester, but if you want it, we could work something out."

"No, this is the car Steve McQueen drove in the movie *Bullitt*. I like the pedigree. It's a cool car, but I can't drive around in a car like this. It would make people too interested in me, directly in conflict with my desire to be as unassuming as possible."

"I never thought about that. Guys would be interested in a car like this, and subsequently, you. You need to maintain as low a profile as possible. You're my undiscovered gem, nobody else's. We need to find you a nice, nondescript Chevy."

"Now, find me a '73 Firebird, and we can talk."

"I don't think so. I wonder if I can find a Yugo."

"A Yugo? Good luck."

***

Mitch invited Aimee to be his date at a wedding. One of his best salespeople, Serena, was getting married. She had been hired initially to answer phones, but after her first six months, she sold her first car right out from under the salesperson. He snuck out for a cigarette, and a couple came in looking for a car. Rather than waste time trying to hunt the guy down, Serena went out on the lot with the couple, the Feltons. She walked them around, discussing what they wanted versus what they needed. He wanted a truck. She wanted a sedan. They bought them both.

Aimee stayed at the hotel where the wedding was being held. She didn't want to get in Ryan's way; three of them were at Mitch's apartment, and getting ready at the same time would be difficult. Anyway, it was easier for her to spread her things out. Mitch decided to stay with her Friday night and go back to his place on Saturday morning to get dressed. He'd get her when she was ready and escort her downstairs.

Aimee made arrangements for a spray tan and a blowout. She wasn't the kind of person who liked to sunbathe. She'd be in the sun if she were doing something, so Aimee ended up with tan arms but a pale chest. Her dress had a deep V in the front, and she looked odd with the skin of her chest so white. Since she was at the wedding, they did her makeup and gave her a blowout. Aimee realized halfway through they thought she was with the bridal party, but the bride and her attendants were drinking champagne and getting their hair done in the next room. Aimee thanked her and gave her a twenty-dollar tip. The girl slipped it in her pocket, smiled, and wished Aimee a good time at the wedding.

Aimee slipped out of her robe and caught the elevator to her room. She was expecting Mitch to come at three, but since she had her make-up and hair done, she was ready by two-thirty. There was a knock on the door. She answered, and it was Mitch.

"Why are you here so early?" Aimee asked him. "You just left." She took a minute and looked at him. She had never seen him dressed any other way than casual, and here he was in what looked like a custom-tailored black suit, white shirt, and teal-colored tie. She whistled.

"Boy, you clean up nice. Interesting choice for the tie, though."

"It was a gift from the bride. She asked me to wear it, so I did. I'm early because I thought you might need help zipping up your dress."

"I'm all set. Maybe you can unzip it later."

"I've brought you a present, " he said as he handed her a box.

"Why? Whatever for?"

"Open it."

Aimee opened it. It was a pendant necklace. The pendant looked like it was a meteorite.

"Is this what I think it is?"

"Yes. Whenever you get remotely dressed up, you wear that cuff. I don't care that some guy gave it to you twenty-five years ago. You must like it; you still wear it. I found the one you can wear around your neck. This way, I'll be the one closest to your heart."

"You're such a cheese ball, but I love it. Here, could you put it on me?"

He did. It was the perfect length. Long enough to skim the top of her cleavage. It was on the larger side and immediately caused the eye to wander, perhaps down and into the valley of her breasts.

"There. You look stunning. Don't stand next to the bride. You'll ruin the pictures."

Aimee laughed. He was repeating what she told his daughter.

"That's lovely," Aimee said. "Thank you. Want to go downstairs?"

"No. We have a few minutes. I want to practice unzipping the dress."

"No need. Standard government issue zippers."

"The government has no standard. Ever deal with the IRS?

They took the elevator down to the lobby. There were guests already milling around the hall, waiting for the doors to open to the main ballroom. The bride was Mitch's star salesperson. Mitch said he had never met anyone like her; she sold a BMW and Escalade her first week. The lady who purchased the Beemer told her bridge club how wonderful Serena was; if it weren't for her, she'd be driving some big truck. Consequently, later that month, Serena sold a Mercedes and an Audi to two ladies from Mrs. Felton's bridge club, and she'd been on fire ever since. Her competitiveness even lit a fire under the other sales associate, Sam. He took the customer's loyalty for granted until Serena showed him how it worked.

He introduced her to so many people she doubted she'd remember anyone's name. He pulled her off to the side. "I forgot the envelope. It's in the car. Are you going to be okay if I leave you alone for a few minutes?"

"No. I plan on running off with the groom the first chance I get."

"Well, I better hurry. Be right back," Mitch said and walked away in the general direction of the exit.

Aimee leaned against the wall, out of the way of the foot traffic. An attractive blond woman approached her.

"Are you Aimee Dunsmore?" she asked.

"Yes, that would be me. Have we met before?"

"No, but I believe you know my husband quite well."

Aimee leaned back and took a good, hard look at her. *This must be Sandy.* She could see Ryan's resemblance in her. Aimee figured she needed to tread lightly.

"Yes, I know Mitch."

"You more than 'know' him."

"Is there anything I can help you with?" Aimee asked, trying to draw the conversation away from Mitch.

"Yes. For starters, you can stay away from my husband."

"From what I understand, your husband thinks he's been divorced from you for many years."

"Yes, we did divorce, but I think we've been able to work through our differences. We've gotten a lot closer, and I believe a reconciliation will be happening shortly."

"Does Mitch realize this? He's under the impression you're his ex-wife, and that's how things are going to stay."

Sandy laughed. "You poor girl. You believed Mitch when he said we were through. I think you're probably his last fling before he moves back in."

"I think you need to talk to Mitch about this. It's none of my business."

"You're right. It *is* none of your business. I think it would solve a lot of problems if you stayed away from my husband."

"Solve a lot of problems for who?" Aimee asked her.

"*You.* Stay away from Mitch."

"Look, Sandy, is it? You haven't been married to him for a long time. Like I said, talk to Mitch about it if you have any questions."

"Look, Aimee, is it?" Sandy repeated sarcastically. "Stay away from Mitch. I'm not going to tell you again. Stay away from my husband," she warned as she walked away.

Aimee didn't know what to make out of Sandy's appearance. She was pretty sure Mitch was done with her. Aimee knew in her heart Mitch was not interested in his ex-wife. *Sandy's trying to play head games with me,* Aimee thought. *Let her try all she likes. It won't do any good.*

She absent-mindedly fingered the pendant Mitch gave her as she waited. Aimee was lost in her thoughts when Mitch came back. She was unsure whether or not to tell him about Sandy but decided not to. He didn't need to stress out about his ex bothering her. Aimee chose to disregard Sandy and not worry about her. Sandy and Mitch were over, and that was that.

The ballroom was open for a cocktail hour so the guests could mix and speak to others who may not be seated nearby during dinner. There was a general hum of voices that rose and fell as the servers circulated with appetizers. When it was time, the drapes separated magically, the dinner tables were visible, and the party moved over to take their seats.

They sat at what could only be considered as the Raleigh Automotive table. Ryan and Cassie sat with them, as well as Sam and his wife. The woman whom Mitch hired to replace Serena and her date rounded out the table. They *oohed* and *awed* over the decorated room. It was a Renaissance theme, with lots of naked cherubs and statues. Serena's dress was influenced by this period but also was very modern. Same with her bridal party, only their dresses were a deep teal color, the same color as Mitch's tie. Everything was top shelf. A string quartet played during dinner, and there was a DJ afterward.

"Aimee, I need to tell you my ex-wife is here. She's friends with Serena's mother. I don't think she'll bother us. Ryan said she had a new doctor, and she was taking her meds," Mitch said.

"Is that right? Have you seen her?" Aimee asked, not mentioning her earlier contact with Sandy.

"No, and I don't want to."

Aimee thought about their prior conversation. Sandy said she considered Mitch her husband. The divorce wasn't going to last, yet here they were at the same function, and Sandy wasn't creeping around stalking Mitch. She was nowhere to be seen, so if they were genuinely reconciling, she would at least be circling Mitch. *Remember, she's got issues. You can't believe her,* Aimee thought to herself.

"Come on, Aimee. Dance with me."

"I don't know how to dance," Aimee confessed.

"What? I've discovered the one thing you don't know how to do?"

"I was too busy in the library when there was dancing in gym class."

"Come with me. Put your arms around my neck and sway back and forth. Glue your front to mine, and it will be fine."

He pulled her out onto the dance floor, and she hung off him as he said. It was nice; she had her face tucked in his neck, and he had his hand on the small of her back, pressing her against him. She started to feel the warmth spread throughout her, and it spilled out from deep down in her pelvis. Aimee sighed into his chest.

"You're doing fine. It feels good, doesn't it?"

"Yeah. I've never had a book centered around dance, but I think it could work. All this touching and moving is kind of romantic, you know?" She felt the hardness of his erection pressed up against her. "I should sign up for dance lessons. I might just do that for research."

"If you moved here, I'd do it with you."

"It's just research. A couple of dances. Maybe the Merengue."

"I'd like to learn the Merengue."

"I'll think about it later."

They slowed, danced one more number, and returned to the table. Sam, who was not totally dim-witted, observed Mitch with his girlfriend. Mitch's hand was never more than three inches from her at all times. His body language communicated he was so into her; Mitch had it *bad.* She smiled and touched his arm. Mitch looked incredibly happy.

Sandy watched the two of them for a minute and turned back to her table. She laughed at something somebody at her table said and stopped looking at them.

***

Mitch and Aimee went up to her room after they cut the cake. He was able to stream music to slow dance to, took Aimee into his arms, held her tight, and started to dance with her. Mitch liked the way her face fit into the space where his neck met his chest; it allowed him to place his cheek against the top of her head and smell her shampoo. Aimee felt so soft and lovely. He thought about how right it felt with her, how falling in love with her was as easy as breathing.

"I love you, Aimee. You're the best there is. I'm so lucky you chose to stay locked away in your room and write books about love instead of trying to find it. I would never have met you. How sad would that be?"

"I love you, too, Mitch. You opened up the world for me. I never realized what I was missing. My life was fine. Fine sucks. I want better. I want the best. I want it all with you."

"Whatever you want, I'll get it for you. I promise."

"I don't want anything but you. I don't need anything but you."

"Let's get out of these fancy clothes and get under the covers. Let me show you how much I love you."

"Let's. This slow dancing is very romantic. Show me how much you love me."

He let her go. "Turn around. I want to unzip your dress with my teeth."

Aimee laughed. He tried but needed his fingers, kissing each vertebra as he exposed them. Her dress fell to the floor, and soon, they were both naked, rolling around under the covers. Aimee felt safe and protected with Mitch; giving herself over to him was the easiest thing in the world for her to do.

"Fan belt. Timing chain. Dual exhaust. Barracuda. Road Runner. GTO."

"Talking dirty, are you?"

"Trying to. I'm running out of words."

"You can stop. I'm sufficiently aroused."

Aimee pushed her body against his, and he pushed back. "I can see that. Or feel it."

Mitch felt honored to be chosen by a woman of Aimee's caliber. She could have picked anyone, and she picked him. He wanted to be by her side in life as well as in bed. He loved the sigh that escaped from her lips as she entered her.

"Aimee. Look at me."

She opened her eyes. He saw trust as well as desire as she looked at him. He moved against her, and she moved back. Like rubbing two sticks together, the spark caught fire, and soon, they reached the point where they were smashing together like waves against rocks.

"Love me, Mitch," Aimee growled.

"I do, Aimee. I will." Mitch promised and took the dominant role between them.

She clung to him, and like a bomb exploding under the sheets, the two of them achieved something deeper than either of them expected. When he rolled off her, she rolled up against him to make the moment last. He held her as the embers of passion died, but it didn't matter. Mitch and Aimee belonged together, and it was no more complicated than that.

Chapter 21

Mitch wanted Aimee to come to the dealership before she went home. He had a car he wanted her to consider. He thought if she would be driving more, she needed to do it in a better car. Aimee decided she'd humor Mitch and look at the vehicle. She was pleasantly surprised. It was the white version of Mrs. Felton's car.

"This is a really nice car, Mitch."

"We had the exact model in black, and it sold in less than twenty-four hours. I thought I'd see if you wanted it before it went on the lot. I'm giving it to you for what we paid for it. I think you'd look awesome behind the wheel. Put on some big shades, and you'll look like Jackie O."

"I don't know, Mitch. I've never spent money like this. I feel like I'm saying, 'Guess what? I'm Rich, and you're not.'"

He reached out and held both her arms. "Aimee. You *are* rich. I bet you're sitting on a whole pile of cash. Unless you gamble or do drugs, I can't think of anything you've done with your money except use it to make more money. Your car is five years old. You live on a regular street, not in a gated community. You don't walk around dripping in diamonds. You've worked hard for the past twenty-five years. Shouldn't you treat yourself a little bit?"

"What's in it for you?"

"Me? I can drive it. Come on, take it out for a spin. See how you like it."

She was on the fence until she got on the highway. Mitch could see her smile get bigger the faster she went. Aimee drove it for about half an hour and returned to the dealership.

"I knew if I drove it, I'd want it. Now, I'll have to worry about when I park it somewhere. I think it is a good idea to upgrade the Honda, but there's no reason to get rid of it. It runs fine."

"There isn't a good reason why you can't have both. Keep the Honda and drive it when the weather's terrible, or you have to park somewhere sketchy."

"Okay. Write it up, and I'll have the bank transfer the money. I think you gave away your parking spot in my garage."

"Do I have to give the door opener back?"

"No, I can park the Honda outside."

"Thank you. Let's grab some coffee before you get on the road. Get in my car; I'll drive. I can drop you off to pick up your car later."

They ended up going to a drive-thru and sitting in his car.

"That was a nice wedding yesterday, wasn't it?" Mitch said.

"It was. It was beautiful. Your ex-wife's a pretty woman," Aimee said.

"Sandy? I guess so, but I don't look at her like that anymore. Why bring her up?"

"She came over to me and told me that you two are getting back together, and I needed to remove myself from the situation because I was in the way, preventing your reconciliation."

"When did this happen?" Mitch asked, rubbing his temples.

"When you went back to get the card, Sandy came over to tell me I was in the way of you two getting back together."

"How did she seem?" Mitch asked, afraid for Aimee.

"How did she seem? She seemed fine. She seemed calm. Rational. Like she was doing me a favor by telling me things were rocky, but you'd ultimately end up together, and I'd end up roadkill."

"What did you think?"

“What did *I* think? I think *I* wished this wedding was last month. Last month, things were casual. You told me there were no crazy exes. It’d be easy to say, ‘See ya.’ Now, things are different. It’s hard now, being emotionally invested in you and sad your ex-wife won’t let go. I believe you one hundred percent and the things you told me, but I won’t be moving to Rochester any time soon.”

“Aw, Aimee. I’m sorry. I had no idea she’d approach you. I don’t know why she acted like we were getting back together. If I knew you’d get caught up in this, I would’ve never called you. Speaking to you is the last thing I thought she’d do. If Sandy came up and told you how awful a human being I was, and you should run for the hills before I made you suffer, that I could believe. Telling you we were working things out is a new one. Are you okay? Do you want to stop seeing me? I don’t want you to, but I’d understand if you felt that way.”

“As I said, if this were a month ago, I’d spit in your face and run like hell. Now, I can’t. I love you, and I hope I’m not wrong in believing you. I think she was messing with my head, that’s all. I hope you understand why I don’t want to stay here.”

“I understand, but she’s not the only one who’s going to be fucking with people’s heads. I’ll tell Ryan that after what his mom said, you don’t want to ever see me again. It’s over between us, thanks to her. Let her think she’s won, and she’ll forget about you.”

“That sounds doable. There’s no reason why Sandy can’t believe she scared me away.”

“She didn’t, did she? Aimee, we’re good, right?” Mitch wanted to believe it. He was worried the more time Aimee had to think it over, the more likely she’d cut and run.

“We’re good. I’m just going to lay low over the next few weeks. We can still meet for dinner, and if you can’t live without me, you’re going to have to make the drive. I'm sorry, but I'm too old to fight over some guy. I'll go so deep in my gopher hole you won't see me until next February."

"Don't, Aimee. She gets fixated on things. That day, it was you. Out of sight, out of mind. She'll find something else to obsess over."

"Be careful, Mitch. If you're her default target, it's not going to help us. If Sandy figures out I'm still in the picture, and she got played, who knows what she'll do."

"Probably nothing. She didn't threaten you. She just said, 'Hands off my man.' You'll believe her and dump me. That's it. The end."

***

Chapter 22

Mitch took Aimee back to her car. He told her he would get the paperwork for her new vehicle ready, send it on to her financial advisor, and he'd be in touch. Don't worry about Sandy; he'll take care of it, he told her. He kissed her goodbye—a nice, long kiss. Mitch watched Aimee drive away. Once he was sure she was off, he took out his phone and called his son.

"Hey, Ryan. You up yet?"

"I am now. What's up?"

"I need to talk to your mother. She said a few things to Aimee, and I got dumped. Aimee said she was too old to fight over a guy, and Sandy could have me."

"That sucks. I imagine she's at Grandma's house."

"I'll try over there. Sorry to wake you. Bye," Mitch said and hung up.

Mitch drove over to Sandy's parents' house. He didn't want to cause a scene, but for her to believe it, he had to sell it hard. Mitch pulled into the driveway, parked, got out, and pounded on the back door.

"Sandy! Sandy! Answer the door! I know you're in there!" he yelled. Sandy's father, George, came to the door.

"Mitch. What's going on? Sandy's upstairs."

"I need to talk to Sandy. She's gone way too far this time. I want you to be here; it's better if you stay. I want you to hear this, too."

"I'll get her. Do you want to come in? Coffee?"

Mitch shook his head, and George went in to get his daughter. He came out a few minutes later with Sandy. He was pulling on her arm; she looked as if she wanted to go back inside and hide under the bed.

"You know what, Sandy?" Mitch said harshly. "You did it. You *really* did it this time. I can't tell you how many times you've let me know how you feel about me. I get it. You hate me. That's not a secret. You've told everyone.

"But Aimee? What did she ever do to you? I know why you did it. You did it to hurt me. I liked her. She liked me, but not anymore. She said, 'You aren't worth the drama. I never want to see you again.' *She never wants to see me again*," Mitch said, hard and firm. "I don't know why you feel the need to punish me over and over again. Well, you win. You can do whatever you want now, but not to me. You'll never see me again.

"George, you're a great guy. You and Linda should take a cruise around the world and get away from her. You're too old to deal with this bullshit. Leave Sandy here all by herself. She's driven away everyone who's ever loved her. She deserves to be alone. I'll never forgive you, Sandy. If you want to punish someone, try yourself. Everyone else is done with you." Mitch turned and looked at George.

"I love you and Linda like family. You deserve to be happy, too. The next time she goes off, call the cops. It's been years of this. She won't help herself; that's on her. Don't let her drag you down with her."

"That's all I have to say. Sandy, if you come near me again, I'm calling the cops. We're done. Take a vacation, George. You deserve it."

Mitch got in his car and drove to the marina. He wanted the peace and solitude he could only find on the water. Mitch spent the rest of the day fishing and tried not to think about Aimee. Just when he felt they reached a good place, Sandy had to ruin it. She's wrecked too much of his life ever to forgive her. He had loved her, cared about her, and tried to help her. Now, he was done with her.

***

Aimee met Mitch at their halfway point restaurant the following week. He wasn't happy. Mitch felt Aimee would slip away from him if he didn't see her. Mitch knew she said otherwise, but there was a panic in the back of his throat he couldn't dislodge. It was stuck, and only talking to Aimee seemed to quiet it down, but as soon as he hung up, it rose and threatened to choke him.

Aimee's hand was on the table. He covered her hand with his. "Aimee, I can't do this. I need to see you more than once a week."

"You can come to stay with me for a while. It's a hell of a commute, but you don't have to be there all week, do you? You're the boss. Take the weekdays off and cover weekends. Let Ryan get in some summer fun before it's over. You go fishing and check on the store. Maybe move a few cars around. In the beginning, spend half a day on a Saturday morning in your office, play some solitaire on your computer and leave. Stop by once in a while. As long as there's someone with the final say around, they'll be fine. The rest of the time, stay with me. Do any cars need a repo? Let's do that."

"That could work. I'd be here or on the boat. I told Sandy I never wanted to see her again; maybe this is how to do it. I do have to pick up a car in New Jersey. It's not quite the Jersey Shore, but it's someplace to go. You don't mind me staying with you?"

"As long as you take out the trash, stay as long as you want."

"I'm serious, Aimee. I want to be with you. Let's get married."

"NO. Absolutely not. Where did that come from? What's the point? Your kids are adults; my ovaries are like petrified wood. The whole concept of family is already flawed. We don't need the paper. We do what we want, when we want, for the most part. If we are supposed to be together, we will be. The paper means nothing."

"It might mean something later."

"We can talk about things later if that point is applicable. Right now, we play the rest of the summer like you're a lovesick heartbroken mess furious at Sandy for breaking us up, and I'm a real bitch for letting you go. That's how this goes down. You can stay with me whenever you want, but I'm not moving to Rochester any time soon."

***

The rest of July went smoothly. Sandy backed off. She didn't approach his apartment or stop by the dealership. Sandy stopped pumping Ryan for information. She asked Ryan about him one time.

"Look, Mom, he comes by, but if he's not here, he's on his boat. He's hurting pretty badly about losing Aimee, so I'm giving him some space."

Sandy didn't respond. Ryan thought she might be feeling a little guilty about causing Mitch so much damage. Her going after Aimee surprised Ryan. He thought the new medication was helping her, but now he wasn't so sure.

Good. Maybe I should go down to the marina and drill a few holes in his boat so he'd sink to the bottom of the lake, Sandy thought. *That wouldn't work. I don't want him dead; I want him miserable. Getting rid of his little cupcake wounded him.* That made her glad. Sandy couldn't let go of her need to punish Mitch. She couldn't articulate why exactly it was so important to her that Mitch suffered, only that he did.

Mitch and Aimee followed their plan; she stayed away from Rochester, and he stayed at her place during the week. She went to New Jersey a couple of times with him and saw some incredibly high-end automobiles. Mitch and Aimee stayed at the shore for a few days. They had a lot of fun together.

Unfortunately, Sandy decided to check on Aimee's house. Punishing Mitch wasn't enough. If he liked Aimee enough, he might try to get her back. She needed to make sure Aimee wanted nothing to do with Mitch.

Sandy used her mother's maroon SUV to spy on Aimee. Her silver sedan might be too obvious. Aimee's blue Honda was parked in her driveway. She put the BMW in the garage. Aimee left to go to the store, and Sandy followed her.

Once, while Aimee was inside the drugstore, Sandy used a penknife and poked a hole in her tire. She watched with glee as Aimee had to wait for roadside assistance and get the spare tire on so she could drive it to a gas station for a new tire. It took most of her afternoon for Aimee to get her tire fixed. Sandy found great satisfaction in Aimee's inconvenience.

Some of the rage she directed toward Mitch was now being focused on Aimee. Since Mitch told her he never wanted to see her again, he was true to his word. Sandy watched his apartment, but he was never there. Aimee, however, was easy to watch. She came and went, unaware she was on Sandy's radar.

It was pure luck. Sandy never saw Mitch. He usually left early in the morning and returned late in the afternoon. He had the door opener, and he drove different cars off the lot. Sandy stalked Aimee from around eleven to three. Some days, it was a complete waste of time, especially when Mitch and Aimee traveled. The longer between sightings, the angrier Sandy got. Once, she followed Aimee to the grocery store. After Aimee went inside, Sandy poured maple syrup on the driver's side door handle. Sandy watched Aimee's frustration after she tried to open the door with her hand covered in a sticky mess.

One day, when Aimee's car wasn't in the driveway, Sandy got the nerve to walk up to the side door and smashed the handle with a hammer so it couldn't open. If Aimee went inside a store, Sandy always shoved flyers and restaurant menus under her wiper blades.

As Aimee described these random incidents to Mitch, he got concerned for her. He didn't want to tell Aimee who he thought was responsible. Staying away on weekends was hard. He worried Sandy would confront Aimee when he wasn't there. Mitch had not seen Sandy since he told her he was finished with her. He feared that since he wasn't around, Sandy transferred her hatred for him onto Aimee.

Labor Day was coming up, and Mitch wanted to take Aimee away for the weekend. He didn't want her alone for an extended length of time. Mitch thought Sandy was getting worse. Why she went after Aimee was obvious. She was something he liked, and Sandy had made it her life's work to destroy every good thing Mitch had. Maybe he should break it off with Aimee and move, perhaps, to New Jersey. That was the only thing he could think of to get Sandy to stop harassing Aimee and give him a chance at an ordinary but lonely life.

Mitch had a friend who had a camp on the river. He was going out of town and offered it to Mitch for the weekend. Mitch wanted to be with Aimee without the tension of Sandy overshadowing them. He was sick of Sandy. Mitch was to the point where tying the anchor around her neck and throwing her overboard was starting to look more and more attractive.

***

They finished dinner and cleaned up the dishes when Mitch broached the idea of a long weekend. Surprisingly, she was for it. Aimee wanted to go away someplace they could be alone together. All this cloak-and-dagger stuff was draining. A long weekend out of Sandy's reach would be perfect. The minute he brought it up, she jumped on it.

"I would love to go somewhere where I can relax. This is hard, Mitch. I feel like Sandy's spying on me all the time. I only met Sandy that one time. I'm not sure I even remember her face, but I see her everywhere. A cabin in the woods sounds good, but that's where even more freaky stuff happens. I'd rather take my chances with a bear or an ex-murderer than your ex-wife."

"Thank you. I do think it would be great not to have to think about her. It's just you and me, the birds and the bees, and oh, bears. We could leave Friday afternoon and come back on Monday. Would that work? We'd have to pack all the food and everything. There's no store you can run to; you have to decide what you want to eat before."

"You mean plan out all our meals? I think I can handle that. Let's do this. Let's sneak off the grid for a while."

"Okay, I'll get you Friday afternoon and bring you home Sunday. Bring enough food for breakfast, sandwiches. And dinner. Yikes, that's a lot. Keep some fresh fruit around. We can split the cost. I'll go to the liquor store. It's only us two. It can't be that much. So what? Why am I worried? What do I care? Meet you here Friday at three p.m. sharp."

"See? We'll be gone before anyone notices."

"Love you. See you." He kissed her goodbye. "Miss you."

***

Chapter 23

Aimee and Mitch were on their way by three-thirty. They were settled at the camp by five. They could stay at the main house or above the boathouse. The boathouse sounded more romantic, and they chose to stay there. It was a big room broken into areas; dressers and bookcases created walls for closed-off sleeping areas, but it was like a dormitory. The kitchen was amazing. It had granite countertops with an island and stools, and the slab of granite had its own name. Mitch wasn't sure, but the place might have been featured in *Architectural Digest*.

"When you said the camp in the woods, I pictured moss on the roof and a sagging porch. But I think we're at somebody's investment property. This is a second home. It's too nice to be called a camp."

"He considers it his 'his place on the river,' or 'his camp,'" Mitch said. "Anyway, it's ours for the weekend. Are you disappointed? We can pitch a tent and sleep outside if you want."

"I do want to cook everything on an open fire. I didn't bring anything complicated because I thought we'd be roughing it."

"What's on the menu tonight?"

"When you camp, you start with the most perishable meal and finish up with hot dogs." Aimee looked in the cooler. "Huh. The other thing you do is freeze everything so it hasn't been sitting around too long before you eat it. The steaks are still frozen; they might be tomorrow's dinner. They haven't thawed out yet. I guess we'll start with the hot dogs. I bought some potato salad. That's perishable, so I think that's for tonight. Can you build a fire?" Aimee asked him.

"Can't you do it? You seem to know how to do everything else."

"Yeah, I do, but that's what the guys do. It's supposed to appeal to the caveman in you, but I cheated. I bought some fire starters. Now you have to go search for firewood and get this fire started."

"Aimee, you know there's a fully functional fridge and oven inside."

"Yeah, but that's cheating. Find some wood and get this thing started."

"Can we at least sleep inside?"

"It's not camping unless you sleep on an air mattress that has a hole in it, and you wake up miserable because you ended up sleeping on a rock or a root. I suppose we can cheat and sleep in the boathouse. Nobody has to know."

"If the mosquitoes are bad, can we go inside?" Mitch asked.

Aimee looked at him. "Everything I have is for camping. You were supposed to cover the sleeping bags and tent. I don't see them. You've been here before, haven't you? You knew we weren't camping."

"Yes, I've been here before. The word camping may mean different things to different people. You are a die-hard camper. I didn't realize how experienced a camper you are, once again leaving nothing for the dude to do. How about this? I'll start the fire, and we'll eat out here like you want. Out on the water tomorrow. That's our plan."

"That's the plan? Sounds good. This old-school style of camping I think I may have aged out of, " Aimee said, fixing her hair high up on her head in a bun. "That kind of camping is what my family used to do when we were kids. We had three tents—one for the boys, one for the girls, and one for my parents. We kids had a blast, and my poor mother did all the work. I don't think it was much of a vacation for her. The boathouse is looking better and better." Aimee sounded sad; thinking about her mom made Aimee miss her.

"We used to play cards at night in our tents by flashlight, and my dad would yell at us because we were using up the batteries. We'd sit around the campfire and listen to my dad tell ghost stories. Go fishing. We rented a boat, and my dad would hug the shoreline, and we'd see all kinds of nature, like egrets and lily pads. Then Eddie and my sister got older and had summer jobs. We went a few times without them, but we stopped. It wasn't the same."

"I used to go camping in college," Mitch said. "A bunch of guys, a lot of beer, and a campfire. We were loud and obnoxious and got kicked out more than once. It was a lot of fun. You're right about the rock. We'd pass out wherever, and when we woke up the following day, everyone would be complaining about sleeping on a rock they never noticed when they were hammered."

"Let's eat dinner and play some cards," Aimee suggested.

Mitch went to get some wood for the fire. He didn't have to go far; there was a pile of it stacked neatly against the house. He brought it back and used the fire starter to light it. Once he was sure it caught and wasn't going to go out, he went in search of two long sticks. Mitch had a pocket knife and cut two straight sticks. He brought them back and handed them to Aimee.

"For the weeny roast," he said.

She opened the cooler and handed him the hot dogs. "For your weeny, " she said and laughed. He put the hot dogs on sticks and gave her one. She had the rolls and condiments on top of the beverage cooler.

"We don't have anything to drink, " Mitch said. "You put everything on top of the drinks cooler."

"Here, hold my weeny," Aimee said and laughed again. She opened the cooler she sat upon and pulled out a bottle of wine.

"Here. Give me your weeny and get the corkscrew out of that box."

"I'll give you my weeny all right. After dinner."

"Grab two paper cups and a couple of forks."

Soon, they were ready to eat. They had hot dogs and potato salad. They ate the potato salad right out of the container and drank the wine out of Dixie cups. What little trash there was, they burned in the fire.

"There. No evidence of humans except ashes. Perfect," Aimee said.

"What about the empty wine bottle?"

"We take that back with us. Are you getting bit? I am."

"Let's go inside now. We need to bring the coolers and stuff in, too."

Once inside, they lay on all the beds to get comfortable. Much like Goldilocks, they evaluated each one until they found one just right. Mitch rolled onto her and started to kiss her. She had a bit of a buzz from the wine and relaxed into him. Mitch was strong and intelligent, he gave her a sense of security she never knew she had missed.

Being on her own for so long meant Aimee always had to be in charge; there was no one except her siblings she could depend on, and they were scattered everywhere. There was no one in her day-to-day life she could lean on. When she was with Mitch, she had someone she trusted, allowing her to just *be*. No decisions needed to be made; she could go with the flow and be part of a couple. Aimee decided she liked being a couple with Mitch.

Mitch wasn't thinking about Aimee that way. She was kind-hearted and sweet and had a spirit others lacked. When an opportunity presented itself, she went for it and thought about the wisdom of it afterward.

In bed with her was the surprise of his life. Maybe that's why people needed bifocals as they aged. It was God's way of softening the fact you were old and in bed with another old person. Up close, things were blurry, like a soft-focus lens. Some things shouldn't be seen up close, like wrinkles and enlarged pores. This way, the blow of growing old didn't strike quite so hard.

To Mitch, having Aimee next to him was God's greatest gift. He slogged through a lot of shit in his life, and if being with Aimee was his reward, he'd slog through it all over again. She was so soft, so willing to love him that Mitch could not believe his luck. Years of bitterness and venom Sandy directed at him hurt and left him scarred. She wounded him a little more each time. As much as Mitch tried to tell himself she couldn't help it, she was sick; over time, it gradually seeped into his soul. He couldn't help internalizing it. Mitch thought he was polluted and stained. He stopped looking for love. It was too much for his bruised ego to think someone would want a man as damaged as he was, and then he met Aimee. She was as normal as they come, and she wasn't interested in his scars. Aimee loved him anyway.

Mitch enveloped Aimee in his heart and his arms, and she returned the embrace with one of her own. He took his time exploring Aimee, and she just laid back and let him. She was so beautiful; Mitch thought she glowed. Aimee welcomed him and, with each move of her hips, invited him in further until they were joined as one. They moved together, breathed together, and came together. They even sighed with contentment together.

Mitch rolled off her, inwardly congratulating himself that he could bring that smile to her face. She smiled that way only for him. Mitch knew it wasn't fair to use her to validate him, but she did. Aimee was a healing balm for his soul. He felt invincible with her at his side. Mitch wondered if she felt the same way.

"Aimee, I want to ask you a question. No pressure, just a point to ponder. You say you love me. How deep does it go?"

"Huh. Let me ponder, how deep does my love go? Isn't that a song by the Bee Gees? The disco era? That's going way back." She rolled over and looked at him with her almond-shaped eyes and smiled. *Poor Mitch,* she thought. *His ego has been stuck in the spin cycle for too long. He feels anything of value he possessed had been wrung out years ago, leaving him high and dry.*

"I'll tell you. I never much believed in love, even though my books tell a different story. Maybe all those forces working against true love my characters have to go through to be together made me think, 'Who needs it?' I bet all those lovers in my books five years into the future are bitching about taking out the trash or leaving the cap off the toothpaste.

"But you? Loving you is the easiest thing I've ever done, and you bring enough drama for both of us. I mean, Sandy's tough. She's unpredictable. Volatile. She's like a hurricane raining bombs. Or maybe landmines. You pretty much know what's going to happen, but you don't know *when.*

"Despite it all, she doesn't matter. You are important enough to deal with her now, but let's create an exit strategy. What do you want? Where do you want to go? I live where I live because it was the easiest choice at the time. It wouldn't be that hard to leave; there's no family left, so I have no reason to stay. If you want to go, retire early, and let Ryan take over, let's do it. I've got enough money to buy myself a cruise ship and take you around the world. You in?"

"Am I in? Yes and no. Yes, let's leave. Not forever, but for a change of scenery. I have my own money. Maybe not as much as you, but my expenses have been low. The kids didn't need child support, but I helped them with college. Sandy got the house and half my 401K, but that was years ago. Right now, I'm pretty flush. I may be crazy to blow it on the first pretty girl I meet, but she's way out of my league, and I doubt I'd ever come across anyone close. She won't marry me, but who cares? It's such a luxury to fall in love at my age, but I did. The miracle of it all is she loves me back."

"She does," Aimee said. "What if my karmic retribution for not taking off that day wasn't an atonement for a past sin but a reward? A miracle for both of us. I think we deserve one."

"It could be. Or the stars aligned. Whatever it was, it was a blessing from the universe. Do you want to go outside and look at the stars? It's dark enough, and there's no light pollution," Mitch asked her.

"Absolutely. This may sound dumb, but I like to think the energy that was my parents has been absorbed into the stars. Energy doesn't disappear; it just changes form. So, the universe embraced them. I don't know. It just gives me a sense of peace to think that they're up there somewhere."

They got dressed; Mitch grabbed a quilt off the back of the couch and headed outside. He went first and used the flashlight to make sure Aimee didn't trip over a root or rock. He found a good spot and spread the quilt out.

They lay down and looked to the sky. It was a beautiful night; anything outside the halo of the flashlight disappeared into the inky darkness. The moon had yet to rise; the stars had no competition to dim their brightness. Mitch and Aimee lay silently and marveled at the vastness of space. After a bit, he identified some constellations, easy ones like the Big Dipper or Orion's Belt.

Aimee took out her phone and pointed it at the sky. She had an app that identified the stars in the night sky.

"Hey, that's cheating," Mitch said. "I was an Eagle Scout and spent years memorizing the stars. Look. We can see the Milky Way since the moon isn't up yet."

"Technology replaces ingenuity again."

"Give me that phone. I'm going to throw it in the lake. Technology ruins the mood once again," Mitch said and pretended to make a move to grab it.

***

They spent the next day on the boat. He took her to a place where people tended to drop anchor and swim. Mitch had an inflatable tube they both hung off of when they tired of swimming. He hung off one side, Aimee the other. She used her feet to keep touching his legs, saying, “That wasn’t me. It was a fish.” Mitch and Aimee decided to get out of the water and eat lunch.

Lunch was sandwiches and bottled water. Mitch applied sunscreen to Aimee. He slathered it on her like he was frosting a cake. She did the same to him, and they hugged their slippery bodies together and laughed. Mitch picked her up and threw her overboard, tossed the tube into the water, and dove in after her. They spent the rest of the afternoon in the water, hanging off the tube and laughing.

They returned to the house by late afternoon. Aimee took a shower to rinse off the sunscreen and wash her hair. After Mitch took his shower, they sat outside and watched the traffic on the river go by. Every once in a while, someone water skiing or riding on a tube would have a spectacular wipeout. Both of them would groan in sympathy and laugh.

“Ow,” Mitch said. “That had to hurt.”

***

The next day, they decided to take a long boat ride. Mitch hugged the shore, and they checked out other camps. Both had enough of the sun the day before and were more than happy to stay dry. He found a shady cove and just let the boat drift. Aimee went over and started to kiss Mitch. Each kiss led to another, and soon, Aimee dropped her shorts and underwear.

“What are you doing?” Mitch said, shocked.

“Preparing to come aboard, Captain. Or maybe preparing to come.”

“Here?”

Aimee snuggled up to him. “You’ve never had sex on this boat before?”

"Uh, no," he said, "I've never had a female here. This is my sanctuary. I come here to get away from women. You're the first, and that's only because you could fish."

"Putting a worm on a hook excites you?" she asked as she straddled him, pressing herself onto his bare leg, gently rocking herself back and forth.

"What about putting the worm somewhere else?"

"You are a wicked, wicked woman," he said and pushed his thigh up against her. She slowly rode his leg up and down.

"You want it, don't you?" she said, grinding against him.

He brought his mouth down on hers and said, "You want it more." He pulled her to him, took possession of her with his kiss, and didn't stop kissing her until she had to push herself away to breathe.

He grabbed her butt cheeks with both hands and pressed her firmly against his leg. She giggled and said his leg hair tickled.

"I'm going to tickle you into oblivion," he said and moved her up and down his leg. Mitch felt his thigh grow wet at her response, and her body moved as if unconnected to her brain. He held her firmly and let her body run the show, and soon, she was making little noises that sounded like a moan low in her throat, at which point he pressed her firmly against his leg, and she started to twitch and make sounds he only heard when she orgasmed. He held her fast so she had no place to go but to use his leg as an instrument of pleasure. After the last ripple escaped her, Aimee collapsed in his arms.

"Was it good for you, too?" she said facetiously.

"Aimee, the only thing that ever humped my leg was a husky named Niko, but feel free anytime the mood possesses you. The fact that I can get a hot girl off just using my leg elevates my status from a regular guy to an elite player."

"Oh, God," she said, two bright red spots on her cheeks. "I tried to seduce you, but I guess I started without you and didn't give you a chance to catch up. Sorry about that."

"Are you kidding? I'm never going to wash my leg again."

She bent over and grabbed her clothes. She put them back on and smiled at him. "Maybe next time."

"Look, Aimee, I know you've been in a drought for the last twenty years, but not all that much has changed. Men are usually pigs, but all of us have egos. Women are sweet and lovely and way more mature. Guys do not appreciate how delicate they are.

"However, if he comes across the right girl, a girl who gives him a real shot to the ego, he'll do whatever stupid thing she wants to keep her. You give me way more than I give you. You make me feel good about being a man.

"I haven't felt that way in years. Sandy was water torture to my psyche. Over time, things piled up, and other things eroded. There wasn't much left of me. I didn't feel like I could do anything other than move, but I couldn't leave Ryan. So I stayed. But you, Aimee, make me feel like the world's a better place because I'm in it. You love me. I have to be something special if an incredible girl like you wants me."

Aimee wrapped her arms around him and hugged him tightly. She didn't say anything; his sharing his state of mind and how he felt was a big deal for him. Mitch had a huge heart that had been battered and bruised, but now he had hope. He had Aimee.

"You done?" he asked her. "Want to hump my other leg?"

Aimee laughed. "Maybe tomorrow."

Tomorrow, Mitch thought. *It's nice to have a tomorrow to think about.*

They spent the next couple of days as a repeat like the others, minus the leg humping. Aimee and Mitch got a lot of color, even with layers of sunblock. Before they headed for the marina, they took a long cruise around, taking in the sights one last time.

***

Ryan's phone rang. He looked at the caller ID; it was his mother. He planned on spending his day off with friends; he hoped his mother didn't ruin it. He heard about Mitch's last stand concerning his mom and wondered if he could do the same thing.

Sandy was a consumer. She consumed other people's time and attention. When someone stopped over to say hi, she was a verbal consumer, dominating her visitors' time with the laundry list of her complaints. She talked so much that her guests never got a word in past, "Hi."

The flip side was she aurally assaulted people. People could only listen to so much, but at that point, Sandy was only getting started. She dominated the air space and ear space. Any contact with her left people exhausted. It was terrible if you casually ran into her; it was ten times worse if she sought you out.

"Hey, Mom, what's up?"

"I'm looking for Mitch." She stopped calling him their father or dad years ago.

"He took a few days off to go fishing."

"With whom?"

"Some worms?"

"Ha. Ha. Very funny."

"I wish I could help you, Mom, but I can't. Look, James is picking me up soon, and I'm not ready. I have to go. Love you." Ryan hung up. *That wasn't so hard*, he thought.

Ryan just got out of the shower and heard someone banging on the door. He wrapped a towel around his waist and answered the door with water dripping off his hair.

"Hey. James, you're not—"

"It's me," Sandy said as she pushed her way through the door.

"Mom, I don't have time for this."

"It won't take long. What do you know about Mitch?"

"I already told you. He went fishing."

"Where?"

"Somewhere on the river. He didn't say anything specific about exactly where."

"Was he alone?"

"I already told you I don't know. Mom, James is coming, and I have to get ready." Ryan turned and walked into his bedroom, Sandy right behind him. When Ryan turned to shut the door, he couldn't; Sandy was right there blocking the doorway.

"Jesus! Mom, I told you I don't know anything about Dad, now please leave. You're making me late." Ryan ushered her out of his room and shut the door.

Ryan should have ushered her out of the apartment. Once he shut the bedroom door, Sandy went into Mitch's room, looking for proof he was involved with another woman. She opened the drawers and looked through his things, searching for anything feminine. She found a twenty-dollar bill and shoved it in her pocket.

Sandy went into Mitch's bathroom, hunting for evidence of him having a romantic interest. There was no Tampax or makeup. No forgotten jewelry a woman might take off before taking a shower. She looked in the shower and checked the various products like shampoo and body wash, looking for items marketed for women. No special razors or face cream. She pulled the shower curtain back but didn't bother to close it all the way and went back into his bedroom.

Sandy opened his closet, looking for any clues. A dress, a pair of heels, a woman's-sized sneaker, anything, but she came up empty. She went through his jacket pockets and found another twenty, which she stuck in her pocket, but nothing incriminating. She went to his desk and rifled through his papers. She looked through the drawers but found nothing. Sandy was pissed. Something was going on, and she would get to the bottom of it. She left Mitch's room and ran into Ryan.

"Geez, Mom! I thought you had left! What were you doing in Dad's room?"

"Nothing. Is there any bottled water in there?" Sandy asked, pointing to the refrigerator. She didn't wait for an answer and opened the door. She knocked a magnet off that held up a piece of paper. She bent over and picked up the magnet and paper to affix it back on thc fridgc door.

"Fuck," she said, crumpling the paper in her hand. It was a post-it note. It read "A" with her new phone number. She stomped out the door without saying goodbye.

***

Chapter 24

Sandy sped out of the apartment complex and headed to the marina. Mitch had his choice of vehicles from the inventory at the dealership, so Sandy wasn't sure what car he was driving, but she knew where his slip was located. She hoped they were still there. She pulled into the parking lot, spewing gravel that left more than one car with tiny pits in the paint finish. Sandy slammed her car door and went on a rampage, looking for Mitch.

Mitch and Aimee returned to the marina and parked the boat in its slip. They made a trip to the car with the coolers, beach bags, and wet towels. They walked back down the dock to put the boat away. Aimee stood on the pier with a canvas bag to pack miscellaneous items. Mitch was in the boat handing Aimee things like sunscreen and half-filled water bottles when they heard yelling and cursing.

They looked to the source of the commotion and saw Sandy storming down the pier, screaming out Mitch's name. Aimee looked at Mitch and said, "Uh-oh."

Sandy stopped when she reached Mitch. She screamed and swore at Mitch. He was below her in the boat. He calmly pulled out his phone and punched 911.

"Leave now, Sandy. Leave now, or I press send," he said with steel in his voice. "Leave."

Sandy, her face bright red and sweaty, screamed. "You want to call 911, Mitch? Well, I'll give you a good reason!" She turned to Aimee and, with both hands, shoved Aimee hard off the dock. Aimee flew off, hit her head on the back of Mitch's boat, and sank silently into the filthy, disgusting, polluted water of the marina.

Mitch looked at Sandy with disbelief on his face as he scrambled to the stern.

"Call 911!" he yelled as loud as he could and dropped his phone. "Call 911! She's drowning!" He was half out of the boat, searching for Aimee in the murky water. He struggled but was finally able to grab the neck of her shirt and pull her up. He knew he had to keep her face out of the water, but if she had water in her lungs, she could drown anyway.

Two young guys came running and helped pull her out. They each took an armpit and hauled her out, holding her upside down to get the water out of her lungs. She gagged and choked as her body tried to clear her lungs.

After that, she puked her guts up on each of their boat shoes. She is wretched as Mitch handles part of her in the boat while the two men hoist Aimee out and place her on the dock. She threw up again, nasty, foul water from between the boats, but because she was on her side, it went through planks and not into her lungs.

Since Mitch was still in the boat, he was at eye level with her.

"Aimee," he said and shook her shoulder. "Aimee. Aimee! Wake up!"

"Awk," she said in response, "eyes. Burning. Eyes."

Mitch had a gallon jug of water he always kept onboard. He passed it up to the men who stood next to her.

"Wash out her eyes! She must have gotten gas in her eyes!"

They did as they were told and used the whole gallon.

"She's bleeding. There's blood near her head," the taller one said.

"There's blood down here, too," said the guy by her feet.

"Where's the ambulance?" Mitch asked. He had held things together until the mention of blood. Panic started flooding his nervous system.

A crowd started to gather around, drawn in by the commotion. Sandy disappeared as soon as Aimee hit the water. The realization of what she did and the price she might have to pay for doing it caused her to flee the scene. Mitch was so concerned about Aimee that he didn't think about Sandy at all.

"Where's that fucking ambulance?" Mitch said to nobody, the panic now evident in his voice. He heard yelling from the parking lot. The EMTs arrived and hurried down the dock, but people had their phones out and didn't want to miss a viral moment on the off chance they became Insta-famous.

The EMTs didn't give a crap about someone becoming an Insta-celebrity and ordered, "Get out of the way or go in the water," as they made their way down the dock.

"It's okay, Aimee, help is here," Mitch said from the boat. He was leaning over and kept the hair off her face. She was ungodly pale and looked like Neptune's ugly stepsister. She had seaweed stuck in her hair, and he was gently pulling pieces off her head, worried he caused the cut on her head to bleed more. He felt helpless, and it was the only thing he could think to do to help her. People scattered, and the EMTs came through with a bodyboard.

They asked several questions and looked at her head and calf. They asked her name and kept telling her what they were doing. They said even though she was not responding now, it wasn't so big a concern because she spoke earlier. The cut on her calf was deep and would need stitches. They fixed her to the board and prepared to carry her to the ambulance that finally arrived. Aimee's eyes fluttered open, and said, "Mitch."

He climbed out of the boat and followed behind her, elbows out to prevent any gawkers from impeding his progress.

"Hey, buddy. You the husband?" one of the medical people asked him.

"Yes," Mitch said.

"Get in here quick," Mitch hopped in the back of the ambulance. The EMT guy kept calling out numbers which was meaningless to Mitch.

"Is she going to be okay? Is she? She's going to be alright, isn't she?" Mitch kept saying.

"She's stable for now," was all he was told.

They brought her into the ER and put her in an exam room. The security guard showed him the waiting area and told him to have a seat and that somebody would be with him shortly.

A woman approached him. Mitch stood up.

"Aimee. Is she okay? Can I see her now?"

"No, sir, I'm sorry. I have no update for you at this time. I'm from the Admissions Department. I was hoping we could get the paperwork out of the way while she's being evaluated."

"Paperwork? What paperwork?"

"Name, address, insurance."

"You gotta be fucking kidding me. Insurance? Now?" Mitch asked.

"It's better to get it out of the way. The sooner we finish it, the sooner you can see her," the woman said gently.

"You're holding her hostage until I give you her insurance information? Are you kidding me?" The rest of the waiting room perked up and watched Mitch behave like they wanted to. "You got to be fucking kidding me! It's all in the car! I'll be right back."

Mitch patted down his pockets and realized he left his phone on the boat. The woman was nice enough to offer to use her phone. His mind went blank. The only number he could recall was Ryan's.

Ryan answered after a couple of rings. "Hey, Dad, what's up?"

"Long story. Are you nearby?"

"No. About two hours away. What'd you need?"

"Aimee's purse. It's under the front seat of the car at the marina. I need someone to get it and bring it to the hospital."

"The hospital? Is everything alright?"

"Like I said, long story. Who else has keys to the store?"

"Serena does."

"Could you give me her number? I left my phone in the boat."

"What car do you have?"

"Blue Tahoe."

"What number can she call to get a hold of you?"

Mitch told him and said her purse was under the front seat. Ryan hung up, and Mitch sat off to the side and waited. The woman was more than patient; she allowed him to sit although others were waiting for service. She took them to another admissions desk. The phone rang, and she motioned to Mitch he could pick it up.

"Hey Mitch," Serena said. "The blue Tahoe? I'm on my way to the marina now. What hospital? Okay, hang tight. Be right there."

He asked to use the phone again. The clerk nodded. He dialed Ryan and told him not to worry. Serena was on her way. When Ryan asked why Mitch was at the hospital, he said Aimee fell and hurt her head but didn't elaborate.

Mitch saw a few police officers come in and talk to the security guard, who pointed Mitch out. The officers neared Mitch and motioned him off to the side.

They introduced themselves and asked Mitch who he was.

"Mitchell Raleigh. Why?"

The shorter, heavier cop said they were investigating an incident at the marina and understood he was involved.

"Involved? Yes, you could say I was involved. What questions do you have for me? Can you make it quick? I'm waiting for some insurance information, and I need to see my wife."

"We were called to answer the report of an altercation at the marina, and a woman was hurt and brought here by ambulance. We're interested in what you saw."

"What I saw? I saw my ex-wife causing a scene, and when I got my phone out to call 911, she pushed Aimee off the dock. Aimee hit her head on the boat and sank like a stone. We were able to get her out, but she ingested quite a bit of the marina water. I don't know how much of it got in her lungs. She threw up on the dock but was unconscious most of the time. The ambulance people said she was 'stable for now.'" He saw Serena and her husband Jeff come through the pneumatic doors and look for him. "Please. I have to go now."

"One more question, your contact information. Name and phone number?" Mitch hurried and answered. He pushed them aside and met Serena. She handed him Aimee's purse and gave him Aimee's wallet.

"Mitch, is she okay?"

"Serena. Jeff. Sorry to interrupt your holiday, but thank you. They won't let me see her until they get her insurance information, the vultures. I don't have my phone; I think I dropped it in the boat when Aimee went into the water. I have to take care of this now, or else I'd explain."

"Here." She handed him his phone. "Ryan told me to check your boat. Good luck. Keep me posted," Serena said as she and Jeff headed to the exit.

Mitch looked at the woman who he spoke to earlier. She was waving him over. "I'll have Ryan fill you in later, " he said over his shoulder as he moved toward the desk.

The woman took her insurance cards and quickly entered Aimee's data. "I'll check on your wife, Mr. Dunsmore. Have a seat in the waiting area, and somebody will be out to talk with you soon." Mitch went back and sat down.

***

Chapter 25

Mitch sat there, his leg bouncing up and down in agitation. He looked at the other people waiting like him. Some had been triaged down a step due to Aimee's true emergency. Mitch wondered if they were silently cursing him, but he didn't care. He noticed a little girl sitting on her mother's lap, sucking her thumb quietly. She was too ill to cause trouble like her two brothers, jumping and running around enough to get a warning from the guard. Mitch felt bad for what he assumed was a single mom; he figured she'd leave the boys with their dad if she had a choice. She quietly told them to knock it off, except she said they better cut that shit out.

Someone dressed in scrubs came into the waiting room.

"Mr. Dunsmore?" he called.

Mitch jumped up. "That's me. How is Aimee? Is she going to be alright?"

"This way, please."

Mitch followed him into the back. He stopped in front of an exam room.

"I didn't want to have this conversation in the waiting room. I'm Dr. Price. I want to update you on your wife's condition. First of all, we sewed up her head. Our initial clinical exam shows no loss of neurological function, which is excellent news, but we do need to do an MRI to make sure there's not something we overlooked. She's going to have a bald spot from shaving her hair to stitch her up. If that's her biggest worry, that's good.

"She had quite a deep cut on her calf; we stitched that up as well. It wasn't a clean cut, but we were able to get it closed. She'll have a gnarly scar, but it looks worse than it is.

"Now, her lungs are another story. She did have water from the marina enter her lungs, and when you tried to remove it at the scene, that was smart. However, the water itself is the issue. There was gas, oil, wastewater, bacteria, and all sorts of contamination. We are monitoring her blood gases to check a number of things, but I think we are going to lavage her lungs. That's a fancy word for rinsing them out. We are very concerned about her getting pneumonia; as much of that gunk we can get out, the more we decrease her chance of a lung infection.

"Right now, we need to get the staff together to schedule the procedures. There may be some delay, it being Labor Day weekend and all. I will tell you she will need to be in isolation on heavy-duty antibiotics for at least a week. We're not going to wait for the lab to tell us exactly what germs we need to treat; we're starting with the big guns, and we can fine-tune things once we obtain more information.

"You can go in and wait with her until we bring her upstairs. She's in here." He pointed to the room. Mitch followed him in. "Mrs. Dunsmore, your husband is here." The doctor turned to Mitch. "We put ointment in her eyes to avoid the chance of infection or scarring from anything in the water. That's why they're bandaged, but that's mostly a preventative measure."

Mitch's eyes voiced his unsaid concern.

"Once again, we felt we had to get ahead of possible complications. There's no evidence of damage, but the water quality was so poor we don't want to take any chances. Don't be alarmed by her eyes being bandaged like I said. Once we have an ophthalmologist check them over, we'll know more, but for now, we're erring on the side of caution."

The doctor moved to the bedside, and he placed his hand on her shoulder. "Mrs. Dunsmore, your husband's here."

"My husband?"

"Yes, it's me, baby. Mitch." Mitch pulled a chair over to the bedside. He touched Aimee's arm, the one without the IV and nodded at the doctor. The doctor left her room.

"How hard did I smack my head? I don't remember getting married."

"Well, you did. I took your last name. I'm now Mr. Aimee Dunsmore. They assumed, and I didn't correct."

"I can't talk, Mitch. I feel like I'm going to vomit."

"Then vomit. Get as much of that shit out as possible." He placed a plastic kidney-shaped bowl in her hand. "Don't talk. I'll be here. I'm not going anywhere." He curled his fingers and brushed her cheek.

"I can't see, Mitch."

"You're not supposed to. They put ointment in your eyes. Now hush, Aimee—rest. You're going to go upstairs in a little bit and have some tests, but don't worry. I'll be waiting."

"Tests? For what?" Aimee's voice wavered.

"To get your head examined."

"Why? What's wrong?"

"You married me, didn't you? They're looking for rocks."

"Am I going to be all right? I'm scared."

"All these tests are to make sure you're good. That water was pretty dirty. They sewed up your head and your leg. Now, they'll check everything else out. So stop talking and settle down. I'll be here. I won't leave. Try to relax."

"Mitch—"

"Don't talk to me. I won't answer." They sat in silence until the orderly came to take her up for her MRI. "I'm right here, Aimee. Don't worry. I have to talk to somebody out front; as soon as I'm done, I'll be outside in the hall. I love you, Aimee. Don't worry."

"I love you, too, Mitch. Don't leave."

"Time to take a ride, Mrs. Dunsmore. We have a waiting room; your husband will be right there when you're done." He pushed the stretcher out to the elevator. The doors closed, and off she went.

Mitch went to the front desk; the seat in front of the initial lady's desk was empty, so he sat there. He wanted to know how it would work after the MRI, when she would go for her lungs to be washed out, and where.

He got the standard, "We don't know, depends on the availability of staff and procedure room." The MRI suite was on five; he could wait up there. The coffee was better, the woman, her name tag read "Frances," told him.

Mitch sat in the waiting room, trying to clear his head before he went upstairs. Frances came over and sat next to him.

"A young lady brought this for you." She gave him a zip-lock bag full of rice. He looked puzzled. "To dry out your phone. It must have gotten wet."

God bless Serena. The reason she was so valuable was she thought two steps ahead of everything.

"Also, the police stopped by and wanted to speak to you again. He gave me his card to pass on to you and asked if you could call him as soon as you could. Go upstairs to be with your wife. Call him later when your phone dries out. Good luck, Mr. Dunsmore," Frances said and went back to her desk.

He pinned on the visitor badge and took the elevator to the fifth floor. He followed the color-coded lines to the Imaging Department. The person sitting at the desk told him he was in the right spot and she was still getting her MRI. Mrs. Dunsmore should be out shortly and to take a seat.

Mitch thought about notifying her siblings but figured he'd wait until he had some news to tell them. He had her phone; it was in the purse Serena brought him. He didn't know her code to get in. When she came out, he could use her finger if he needed to unlock it.

"Mr. Dunsmore?" the receptionist called. He approached the desk.

"Your wife is finished, and they'll be bringing her out and right on up to the procedure lab. You'll have a minute to see her. Don't tell them I told you this, but stay with the stretcher and escort her up to the lab. They won't think about the fact you shouldn't be there. Act as if nobody told you couldn't. Stand in the hall so you catch them, and good luck, Mr. Dunsmore."

Mitch thanked her and went to wait for the double doors to open. The lady at the desk was right. The doors opened, and Aimee came out, escorted by two people in scrubs. Mitch fell in step with them and was able to speak to her in the elevator.

"Aimee, how'd it go?" he asked her.

"I can't see, Mitch."

"They put medicine in your eyes and bandaged them to keep it in. It'll be okay. How are you feeling? Hanging in there, okay?"

"Yeah, I think so. I'm still here, right? I can't see any bright lights, so I don't think I'm crossing over."

"No, you're still here on Earth. You're getting your lungs checked out."

"When I heard your voice, I thought I was in hell for sure."

"Very funny, Aimee," Mitch said, although he didn't think it was funny at all. "Can't you give her something and knock her out? At least keep her quiet?"

The elevator opened, and they pushed the stretcher down a long hall to a set of double doors that said: *No Admittance Medical Personnel Only*. They opened automatically, Aimee went through, and they closed, leaving Mitch alone, staring at the closed doors.

He wasn't sure what he was supposed to do next. Nobody was around to direct him to a waiting room. He took the elevator back down to the ER and hoped Frances was free. Mitch was at a complete loss.

Two people were ahead of him with the usual summertime injuries, a ten-year-old boy with a bad case of road rash and a broken arm from skateboarding, and a couple with a bad case of food poisoning from potato salad left too long in the hot sun. Frances waved him over.

"What can I help you with, Mr. Dunsmore?"

"Is it okay if I sit? I don't want to cut ahead of anyone." Frances pointed at the chair, so Mitch sat.

"I don't know what to do next," he confessed. "She had the MRI and now, I guess, is getting her lungs washed out. What happens next? Who's the doctor in charge? When will we find out the results?"

"Let me look." Her fingers flew over the keyboard, click-clacking away. "The doctor is the same one you talked to earlier, Dr. Price. He has orders she's to be admitted 'for observation and isolation in a single room, and IV antibiotics per infection control protocol.' She's going to be in room 4140. Once he gets the results, he'll discuss a treatment plan.

"Right now, to get to her room, it's the second bank of elevators up to the fourth floor. The even numbers are to the left. If you're hungry, the cafeteria is downstairs. You might want to grab a sandwich or two and bring them upstairs. Your wife might be hungry, and it being a holiday weekend, getting something sent up from the cafeteria might be slow."

“Thank you, Frances. I think I was running on nervous energy, and now I’m crashing. I’ll get some sandwiches and wait for her upstairs. I don’t know how I would have managed all this without you.”

“That’s what I’m here for. They’ll send you a survey about your experience here. Make sure you write, ‘Frances in admitting is a Rock Star.’”

“I sure will. Thanks again,” Mitch said as he headed towards the elevators. He went into the cafeteria and bought a couple of pre-packed sandwiches to bring back upstairs. Mitch found the room with no problem at all. He sat in a chair outside in the hall and ate his sandwich while he waited.

While he sat, he watched the hospital traffic pass by, people in green scrubs and white lab coats. Clothes so ubiquitous you couldn’t tell a janitor from the chief of staff. A tall guy stopped and stuck his head in Aimee’s room but found it empty. Mitch realized this was his moment.

“Pardon me, Dr. Price? Do you have a minute? I’ll buy you dinner,” he said.

The doctor looked at him and the outstretched hand holding the sandwich. He accepted the sandwich. “Thanks,” he said as he opened the triangle, took out half, and took a large bite.

“You admitted my wife, Aimee Dunsmore. I was hoping you could give me an update. Did the tests show anything?”

“The MRI showed no swelling or leaking blood vessels; the worst it could be is a concussion. The lungs are clear, but she is still going to be here for the next five days or so on antibiotics and supplemental oxygen. I am going to keep the bandages on her eyes until we can get an ophthalmologist consult. It’s mostly to keep the antibiotic ointment in her eyes and give them a rest, but a specialist should look at them to be sure. All in all, things could have been so much worse. I’m worried mainly about her lungs. That water was funky.

"Her blood gases look good, but we'll keep her on oxygen so her lungs don't have to work so hard. All in all, I'm pleased. I think she'll be fine."

"Thank you, Dr. Price."

"Thanks for dinner. I'll see you soon." The doctor left, on to his next patient.

Aimee came back, asleep from the medication. Mitch stayed until the next morning so she didn't wake up alone and confused.

***

Sandy flew home in a rage. *If that stupid girl wasn't here, none of this would be happening,* she thought. Sandy's rage began to dissipate and was replaced by fear. When Sandy saw things in black and white, good or bad, it was easy to justify her red rage. Once the fuel of her anger burned out, she was forced to think about her behavior and any damage she caused. If only Mitch stayed away from her, Sandy felt she was okay. He shouldn't piss her off, and everything would be fine. Mitch should have known that.

Sometimes, when Sandy had a period where her moods weren't driving her behavior, she would have moments of clarity. The things she destroyed when she was raging would flash across her mind. Those images were burned in her brain. Sandy had bouts of sanity where she felt shame and guilt regarding her actions, and these drove her in the opposite direction. She felt horrible, then worthless, and would disappear down her rabbit hole into depression. Sandy locked herself in her room and did not leave, not to eat or shower, for days at a time.

That's where she was headed now. Sandy felt sadness drop down on her like bricks. She was an awful person and did awful things. Mitch was right, that bastard. She did terrible things to the people who loved her. Soon, her parents would give up on her. Bella already did. She moved hours away to get away from her. Ryan was sick of her, too. He avoided her calls. She arrived home, parked the car, snuck into the house, and locked herself in her room. Sandy got in bed and started to cry. It might be days before she stopped.

~~.~~

Mitch stayed the night in Aimee's room, trying to sleep in a chair, but he was unable to get much rest. The whole day had been draining. Once he found out Aimee should be all right, the last bit of tension eased. He felt like a balloon with no air, no longer able to hold its shape; he was tired and, most of all, guilty.

Mitch felt he put Aimee in jeopardy by including her in his life. He knew Sandy was nuts, but he couldn't believe she went as far as she did. Aimee could have gotten severely injured. She still could suffer long-term problems with her lungs; she wasn't out of the woods yet. The way she looked with her eyes bandaged up made him sick to his stomach. Mitch needed to leave. He needed to talk to George and the police. Sandy had gone off the deep end, and something needed to be done with her.

"Hello? Is anybody here?" Aimee was awake.

The day shift started, and the hospital was waking up, too. Carts rolled up and down the hall; the murmurs of the staff changing shifts and giving orders grew louder. Mops clanged against buckets, and doctors started their rounds, followed by medical students who barely had a whole month under their belts.

"Aimee, it's Mitch. I'm still here."

Before she could answer him, there was a knock on the door.

"Good morning, Mrs. Dunsmore, how are you doing today? I'm Dr. Byatt, and these are some of our medical students."

How the fuck should we know how she's doing? Mitch thought.

"Dr. Byatt, you tell us how she's doing. We have no idea how she's doing or even how she's supposed to be doing. We don't even know who her doctor is," Mitch said.

The doctor shuffled through some papers and ignored Mitch. "She had an MRI that looked good, her blood gases are okay. They could be better, but that will come with time. We're keeping her on oxygen to help her breathe. Later today, she'll have another chest X-ray to check her lungs, more blood work to keep track of her blood gas levels, and a visit from the ophthalmologist. The team will decide if she's on the right antibiotics once we gather the results. We'll know more this afternoon. Don't worry, Mrs. Dunsmore. So far, things look good."

He turned and ushered his flock of newbie doctors out into the hall, peppering them with questions about blood gases and antibiotics.

"Mitch? What did you think about all that?"

"I think so far, so good."

An aide came in, wished them a good morning, and set down Aimee's breakfast. Oatmeal, sliced strawberries, wheat toast, and coffee.

"Are you hungry? I can feed you if you want."

"Mitch. Have you been here all night?"

"Yes."

"Well, go home and get some sleep. I'm not going anywhere."

"I will. I'll go after you eat. I'll help you with the oatmeal." He grabbed a spoon and stuck it in the oatmeal. "Open wide," he said, and deliberately missed her mouth and stuck it on her chin.

"Very funny. Fix me a cup of coffee, show me the toast and leave. I'm not sure I'll be able to eat anything. I'm not hungry. Go home. Take a shower, grab a nap, and come back later. Go."

"I'm not even going to argue. I didn't sleep at all sitting in that chair." He took her hand and put the coffee cup in it, he put a slice of toast in the other. He wrapped the call button around the arm of her bed rail, within her reach should she need help.

"I'll be back soon. Try to take a nap," Mitch said, kissed the top of her head, and left. She smelled like the marina. Her hair smelled of gasoline and dead fish. He probably smelled just as bad, he was wearing the same clothes as yesterday.

He stopped by the nursing station on his way out, looking for the nurse in charge of Aimee. She was on the phone. He watched her as she was on hold, ignoring him. He waited, but after five minutes, he took the receiver out of her hand and hung it up. He heard a few people laugh under their breath, and the unit secretary laughed out loud.

"Excuse me. I'm sure if you call them back, they'll be happy to put you on hold. I, however, am right here in front of you and need a minute. The patient in 4140, Aimee Dunsmore, fell into a cesspool filled with gas, oil and sewage yesterday. She needs a shower. Desperately. I'm going to leave and come back later today. If she hasn't showered, I'll give her one myself, and we can take it up with your supervisor. Thank you." Mitch turned and left.

He went to the front exit and out into the sunshine. He called the policeman and George to ask them to meet him at the Double Shot diner in an hour. He called an Uber to take him back to his place. He took a shower, changed, and went to the diner. The officer, Detective Owens, was already there. They sat in a booth and waited for George. Once all three were there, Mitch spoke.

"George Rhett, Detective Owens. The detective wanted to talk to me about an incident at the marina, and Sandy was involved, unfortunately. Detective, why don't you start," Mitch said.

Detective Owens flipped through his notebook. "Yesterday, about three p.m., we got a call of a disturbance at the marina. A woman was screaming and yelling and knocked another woman off the dock. The two guys who helped pull the second woman out said she was bleeding from her head and leg and had been underwater. The man in the boat helped get her head above water, that was you, Mr. Mitchell Raleigh, the owner of the boat. A 911 call came in, and she was taken by ambulance to Holy Ghost Hospital, and from what I understand, was admitted and is still there."

"Detective Owens, George is the first woman's father. She is also my ex-wife. We haven't been married for many years, but Sandy, Sandy's sick. She has a mental illness. She swings from one extreme to the other. Sandy believes I am the source of all her unhappiness and has harassed me for years. I couldn't take it anymore. I told her I was done, that she didn't want help, and that I wasn't the reason for all her misery. She's had success in controlling herself with medication, but she refuses to take it.

"I told her if I ever saw her again, I'd call 911. If she wouldn't let the doctors help her, that wasn't on me. Or George. It's killing him to see his daughter like this.

"But Aimee, the one who went in the water, she's an innocent bystander. Her only crime was she liked me. Now, she's in the hospital. The marina water is full of biohazards. When Sandy pushed her off the dock, she hit her head, got knocked out, and went underwater. Aimee needed stitches on her head and also on her leg. I think she hit the propeller.

"She went under, and that water got in her lungs and stomach and her eyes. They think she'll be all right, but she could get pneumonia from the contaminated water in her lungs. She could be blind, but they don't think so because the first thing we did was flush out her eyes. There are so many reasons she's lucky this time.

"But George, nothing is going to get better unless we force her. I think she should get arrested and charged for assault. Have the police assess her mental competence. Maybe they can make a deal to have her go to an inpatient facility instead of jail. I loved Sandy once, and I don't want to punish her, but now she's a danger to herself and others.

"I think it's more than you can handle, George. She's getting worse. I left her because she slapped me, and I didn't want my kids to grow up in a home that normalized violence. Now, she lashed out at a complete stranger. I know it's breaking your heart, George, but she needs help. Professional help you aren't qualified to give her."

George looked at Mitch, his eyes, after all this time, still held unshed tears. Sandy was his only daughter, and he grieved for the girl she used to be. He retired from his job as a mason, only to become Sandy's buffer between her illness and the world around them. He felt awful when his grandson called for help. Sandy held Mitch responsible all these years as the sole cause of her behavior. She blamed him for almost everything, from making her lose her temper to poisoning her kids against her.

George also knew Mitch had put up with her for far too long, in part to shield the kids from their mother's moods and to help him contain her. Mitch stayed and allowed Sandy to dump her bitterness onto his shoulders so George didn't have to carry the full weight. Perhaps Mitch was right.

Sandy *was* getting worse. Her attack on the girl at the marina was more than enough proof. Maybe the legal system could do what they couldn't—force her into treatment. They had enabled her long enough. Maybe she behaved like she did because she didn't have to change. This might provide a big enough incentive for her to get a grip on herself and take ownership of *her* problems. They tried everything else. Let the legal system try to enforce upon her the need for her to get her shit together.

"Mitch, as much as I hate to say this, you're right. I'm not enough. I can't fix her. It's hard to admit you've failed your child. The only thing we haven't tried is jail," George said, sadness clouding his eyes.

"Look, George, the last thing you did was fail Sandy. You have tried everything you possibly could, but you've run out of options. Unfortunately, this is the only option left. It doesn't have anything to do with you. It's Sandy's last option. Maybe this will motivate her. You can't help her anymore. She has to help herself."

George slowly nodded his head in agreement.

"So, Detective Owens, I think Sandy needs to be arrested for assault or whatever the charges are. After all, her actions put a woman in the hospital. If I know anything about Aimee, she won't press charges. We need to get Sandy in front of somebody with authority to get her help. Nobody wants to punish her, we want her to get help.

"Her kids miss her. I know she's not happy the way things are. I don't know how these things work. Can she turn herself in, and if she doesn't, you'll issue a warrant for her arrest? I think if George and Ryan talk to her, they might be able to persuade her how important it is to take care of this."

That was the plan. Tomorrow, her father and her son will beg her to turn herself in. Mitch picked up the tab and asked George for a ride to the marina to get his car. He went back to the hospital to see if Aimee got her shower.

***

Chapter 26

Mitch returned to Aimee's bedside later that afternoon, pleased she managed a shower. He kissed her head to make sure. She had, but there was a whiff of marina every so often. He was going to soak her in the tub as soon as possible. Mitch figured they avoided her sutures and didn't shampoo that part of her hair.

Before he went into her room, he stopped by the nurse's station to see if there was anything new in her chart. The nurse assigned to her case checked the computer. He saw the updated notes. The ophthalmologist had checked her eyes and deemed them as healing nicely. The hospitalist said the stitches were not showing any signs of infection, and the neurologist discharged her from his service; the MRI was clean. All that was missing was an update about her lungs. Mitch asked to have the hospitalist paged to her room. He figured that guy would have more pull getting a hold of the lung doctor than a patient. He walked away and went to Aimee's room.

"Good morning, sunshine. How are you feeling today?"

"Oh, Mitch, I'm so glad you're back. People must think because I have bandages on my eyes, I can't hear. They come here and discuss me like I'm a side of beef."

"I find that hard to believe. A side of beef has nothing on you. I think all the interns are new; they look at you more from a clinical perspective. They haven't taught bedside manners yet. I've asked the hospital doctor to come in and discuss discharging you. Your head looks good, both inside and out. Your eyes are good. We need to see how your lungs are doing and figure out a plan."

"A plan? What kind of plan?"

"Getting you out of this place, for one."

"What's 'for two'?"

"You don't miss a trick, do you? Do you remember what happened at the marina? Why were you in the water in the first place?"

"Yes. Your ex-wife pushed me off the dock."

"Right. Sandy pushed you off the dock, you hit your head on the boat, you sliced open your leg, and you disappeared under the water."

"All that?"

"There's more. Sandy is going to get arrested."

"Really? I mean, what's that going to do to her? Mentally."

"Here's the deal. She's going to go before the judge today. I told her dad that if she went to an inpatient facility and got help, you wouldn't press charges. She desperately needs help. Pushing you off the dock was the last straw. Sandy doesn't need to go to jail; she needs to get herself right in the head. For lack of a better phrase, she needs an extended vacation in the nuthouse."

"I wouldn't press charges. She's sick."

"I know that, but we need to use it as leverage to make her go somewhere she can't voluntarily discharge herself. Court ordered. Instead of you being in court, I'd like to record your statement on my phone."

"Is that even legal?"

"I don't know, but she's not safe to be around." Mitch pulled out his phone. Just repeat what you said to me. You don't want to punish her; you want her someplace she can get the help she needs, and if she doesn't comply, you'll press charges, and she'll have to go to jail. That's all."

"Are you going to tape me like this?"

"It's an excellent visual, your eyes bandaged up, you in your hospital bed."

"I want her to get better. My Mom died so young; her kids have got to miss her. I miss my Mom every day. They need a healthy parent—two healthy parents."

"Her dad is finding a place for her right now. Once he finds one, he'll tell the cop she's ready. They're going to give her twenty-four hours to turn herself in, or they issue a warrant for her arrest. Hopefully, the judge will listen to your statement and offer her help rather than jail. So, get ready for your close-up."

Mitch took her statement, and she ad-libbed at the end; she'd help pay for it.

"Why did you say that? That wasn't what we discussed."

"A couple of reasons. Her kids. They deserve a mom they can rely on. I miss my Mom every day. Sandy's here. If she gets better, she can be there for her kids. It's not too late for her. For her dad. I don't know how much longer he can keep pushing this boulder uphill and for you. You deserve some peace of mind. You can't keep protecting Ryan. I think Bella knows the score, as much as you try not to tell her. And the last reason is because I can. If I can help Sandy get better, that would be the best investment I could ever make."

Mitch didn't tell her he had left his phone on. He would call George and tell him of Aimee's generous offer. He knew Aimee was sincere. If there was a wrong she could right, she'd do it without being asked. That's why she didn't leave the grocery store that day. She was a sunflower in a field of weeds.

***

George went to talk to Linda, his wife and told her the plan. Linda was the one who managed Sandy for many years. When Sandy started having mood swings in high school, Linda was right on top of her, taking her to counselors and therapists making sure she took her medication as needed. In her junior year of college, she stopped taking her medication, thinking she was all better. She wasn't. Sandy dropped out of college, and that's when her emotions started to rule her. To her, her mania was passion. When she loved, she loved so hard that she lost a lot of boyfriends. They couldn't handle the intensity of her feelings. Sandy couldn't either.

Sandy was bereft at the loss of her love object and would take to her bed, her mood black and depressed. Linda would start over and get Sandy on track, and things would be good.

It was during one of Sandy's highs she eloped in Las Vegas. She immediately got pregnant and wouldn't take her medication. Pregnancy must have agreed with her; it was when she was at her happiest. The postpartum depression that followed was way deeper than her mother had ever experienced or could even imagine.

Linda didn't think it was possible to be on the edge of despair like Sandy. It was how she'd cycle through it. Linda would get Sandy and start all over. Jim, Sandy's husband, helped as much as he could with Bella. Linda finally got Sandy all settled, and she got pregnant again. Again, she stopped her meds, but the pregnancy hormones carried her through. The inevitable crash followed, and Jim had his hands full with two little kids and no help from their mother. Even with help from her parents, it became too much for Jim, and he left.

Sandy and the kids moved back in with Linda and George. Linda again took her to the appropriate doctors and got her well enough to take some enjoyment out of being with her kids. She was a good mom; she cared and provided them with plenty of love during the good times.

She met Mitch, who loved her and the kids. They married, bought a house and settled into domestic tranquility. He adopted the kids. Sandy stayed on her meds, and other than one episode when Bella was ten, Sandy was the girl Mitch fell in love with.

Then puberty hit Bella, and as she developed into a woman, Sandy grew into a middle-aged woman. It caused Sandy to go off the rails. She viewed Bella as her rival. Mitch spent Bella's high school years referring between the two women.

Mitch helped Bella get accepted to the university of her choice, which is located four hours away. Sandy was furious that Bella was attending college so far from home and accused Mitch of deliberately driving Bella away from her mother. Sandy thought Mitch wanted the kids to hate her so he could be the favored parent.

Mitch was always on the opposite side of Sandy at every turn. In her mind, he was always plotting against her, trying to take her kids away. Then, the fight where she slapped him occurred. He moved out and gave Bella a car. They each had their own rooms and anything they needed. He made sure Ryan saw a therapist to help him understand his mother's behavior, and it wasn't his fault when she lost it.

Mitch helped Ryan with college, and his first semester was when Mitch divorced Sandy. She wore him out. He was content to live out the rest of his life as a bachelor, spending his free time fishing. That's what Mitch did until Ryan graduated and stepped into a leadership role in the family business, and Mitch opened West Lake Luxury Motors. He split his time between the two, relocating a Tesla when he stopped at Wegman's to use the restroom and grab a bite to eat. He fortuitously met Aimee Dunsmore in the grocery store parking lot.

***

Chapter 27

Sandy was locked in her room. Her parents always gave her a wide berth when she swung into her depression. Once again, it was mostly due to the fact they couldn't relate to the depth of her depression, but it reached a point where she had evolved into violence. The reasons why were no longer useful, and they had to address her behavior.

"Sandy. I need to talk to you. Let me in, or I'll take the door off the hinges if I have to," George said.

"Please, Sandy. This is important," her mother echoed.

Their request met with silence. Linda took a hairpin and pushed it into lock, jiggled it, and it opened. Her parents entered the room, and Linda opened the curtains to let in the light. George sat on the bed and spoke to his daughter.

"Sandy. You're in some big trouble and need to pay attention." No answer. "The gloves are off, Sandy. No longer are your mother and I going to cover for you. Here is your situation. You assaulted a woman at the marina. She's still in the hospital. The police have given you twenty-four hours to turn yourself in. If you do that, instead of going to jail, they'll order you to a mandatory psychiatric facility for thirty days to allow you to get help, and the woman you assaulted will not press charges.

"If you don't, the cops are going to take you out of here in cuffs, and you lose all control. You will go to jail, and we aren't going to bail you out. You'll be charged. You'll have no choice if they deem you mentally incompetent and have no say as to where they place you. This is it. Your mom and I are tired and have helped you as much as we can. Now, you have to decide. Either get up and get dressed, or stay in bed and roll the dice with the legal system." He stood up.

"Linda, it's time to go," he said, and they exited the room. Linda held herself together and did not dissolve into tears. What George said was true. They were tired. Linda was even too tired to cry.

***

Sandy's parents said their piece and went about their day. Mitch called George, and then he called Detective Owens. He talked to the DA; the offer on the table was good only for the day. If Sandy chose not to take it, she would be arrested, and that would be that.

Two hours later, Sandy came out of her room. Not exactly contrite, but more like resigned, she approached her dad. He was sitting at the dining room table sorting through the mail.

"Daddy?"

"Wait for your mother. Linda, come on in. Sandy's here." Linda came in from the kitchen, drying her hands on a dish towel. Neither parent responded, the success of the plan resided in Sandy's heart and mind. They were done. It was up to Sandy to choose her future.

"Mommy, Daddy, I can't live like this. I blame everybody else, I can't help thinking it's their fault. I know it damages everyone around me. Ryan, Bella, you guys, even Mitch. I can't help what I think, what I feel. I know it's wrong. I can't believe what I did at the marina to Mitch's friend. I'm not that kind of person, but I am. I did that. I put a woman in the hospital." Sandy started to get weepy. "I need help. A hospital, medications, a shrink. Whatever I have to do. I'll go away, I'll go wherever you think I have the best chance to get better. It has to happen now. I love my kids. I love you. I don't want to lose anyone. Help me."

George called Mitch and said to meet him at the precinct, he would have the Detective and the ADA ready.

They were escorted to a conference room. Mitch was not there. He got there earlier, had the cop record what Aimee said on tape and left. He did what he could but let George and Sandy decide her path. She looked at the floor. The detective played the whole tape, including her offer to help Sandy. Sandy cried.

"Why would she do that? Why would she do that for me?"

"Sandy, she's a nice person," George explained. "There are a lot of nice people in the world. You are so busy being angry that you push people away and miss out on a lot of good things and good people. Take this help. Otherwise, you'll go to jail, and your chance to build something with your kids will be gone," George said, trying not to put any hope in his voice.

"I will. I'll try my hardest to do my best."

"This is the information about where you'll be going. Unfortunately, you need to be brought in by the police, and there is no contact for the first two weeks." Detective Owens said, sliding some pamphlets across the table. "Sandy, as a warning: If you leave early, a warrant will be issued for your arrest, and you will become part of the criminal justice system. No second chances. You'll go directly to jail."

"I'll go. I'm not going to make any promises because you won't believe me, but I will show you. I understand now that the problem is me. I have to own it, and nobody can fix it but me." Sandy stood up. "I'm ready."

"Unfortunately, we'll have to go through booking and put you in cuffs for transport," Detective Owens said. "You can say goodbye here and spare your parents the visual. It's just a formality, but still, it's better for your parents, trust me."

This time, Sandy said goodbye to her parents without the weeping and histrionics of her past attempts. They heard something different in her voice; commitment. Her mother was the one in tears. She hugged her parents tight.

“Thank you, Mom. Thank you, Dad. You held me together, waiting for me to get to this point. It’s here. I’m no longer putting the burden on your shoulders. I can solve this problem. I *will* solve it. It’s time for you to go and let me get started.”

George and Linda said goodbye, and Sandy was escorted out a back door. George held his wife. He didn’t know if she was praying if he was holding her up, or both.

***

Mitch heard from George that Sandy cooperated with going to a residential psychiatric facility. He also wanted to thank Aimee for her surprisingly generous gift. The recording of why Aimee wanted to help her made Sandy cry. Sandy decided there was much more to life than the misery and anguish tar pit she found herself mired in, and she wanted good. Sandy wanted to experience the good things life had to offer. If it meant medication, a residential facility for an extended stay, therapy, or whatever, she was committed to making it work.

Mitch was happy to hear Sandy’s desire to fix things but guardedly optimistic about the outcome. He was pleased she wanted to repair things with the kids, with that as her objective, she maybe would follow through. As far as Mitch, thank him for being there for the kids when she wasn’t, and let him go. Wish him well, and let him go.

***

He was going to visit Aimee. This was her last day of antibiotics, and hopefully, she could go home. He brought her a present. The bandages on her eyes were no longer needed, but she had to wear those cheap plastic glasses eye surgery patients were given.

She was sitting up in bed, getting antsy. "Hello, Mitch. Welcome to the Dunsmore wing of Holy Moly Home for Passive-Aggressive Patients. Get me the fuck out of here."

"Here. I got you a present."

She opened the bag and pulled out a pair of Ray-Ban sunglasses. "Thank you!" She pulled the hospital-grade eye protection off and replaced them with the ones he gifted her with. "How do I look?"

"Like a million bucks." She was able to take a shower herself and scrubbed that last bit of marina stench off her. "You smell like a million bucks, too."

"What's that supposed to mean?"

"It means you smelled like gasoline and dead fish."

"Oh, I guess I just got used to it. I didn't notice."

"You had other things to think about. Any idea when you'll be released?"

"I think it's up to whether or not my lungs are clear. They want to make sure there are no residual pockets of gunk where germs can germinate. I have a chest X-ray scheduled today. Hopefully soon. I've got to get out of here, or I will get sick. This place is crawling with germs."

"Yes, I can see that. Where do you want to go when you get released?"

"Home," Aimee said.

"Where is home? Are you moving to Rochester? You don't have to answer that. I already know." Mitch said with an exaggerated sigh.

"I've decided to go home and rehab. After that, I'm going to call a realtor and put the house on the market. I think I'm ready to make a move."

"A move? Where?"

"Rochester. Buy a condo in a development where they take care of the maintenance. The question is how big a place I should get. Are you planning on moving in with me?"

"I'd love to. Are you asking me to?" He said, frowning, wondering if that conk on the head loosened a few screws.

"I believe I am. You can help me pick one out."

"I can't believe I'm going to be Mr. Dunsmore for real," Mitch said, sounding rather pleased. "You didn't give me a ring. If you want it, put a ring on it." He waved his hand in front of her face, making it so close he bumped her nose.

One of the attendants came into the room and laughed. "Ms. Dunsmore, pardon me, but you can do better." They all laughed.

"You might be right," Aimee said. "Although he's incredibly rich and extremely handsome."

"Then put a ring on it, quick! Can't let that pass you by. Time for your X-ray. You ready to take a ride?"

"I am. Mitch, while I'm gone, find me a condo," Aimee said as she got in the wheelchair.

***

Aimee was discharged later that day. Mitch drove her home and helped her recover. A friend of Aimee's from high school sold real estate. She was given the listing and sold it within a month.

Aimee moved into a three-bedroom condo Mitch found for her. He let Ryan have the apartment. Sandy came home and worked on repairing the relationships with the most important people in her life. She found it a hard and long process, but she was willing to put in the work and showed no sign of quitting.

"Are you sure? Isn't it kind of big?" Aimee asked about the condo.

"For our grandchildren, if we ever have any. Or we each get our own office."

"Mitch, I want to take a vacation. After all this change, I need a vacation. Do you need to move any cars to New Jersey anytime soon?

"I can always find a car to relocate to New Jersey. I can't believe you could go anywhere on vacation, and you want to go to New Jersey."

"Not New Jersey. Someplace special. Only the best place on Earth."

Aimee called Ione to see if the upper cottage was free. Ione said she would have it opened for her to use whenever she wanted.

Aimee took Mitch there, and he was suitably impressed. Aimee took him down to the beach to watch the sunset. Dolores didn't disappoint and graced them with a spectacular display; the red-orange disc of the sun sunk below the horizon.

"Isn't this place magic? Isn't it the most romantic place in the world?"

Mitch hugged her and agreed. "It is magic. It's paradise."

"No. It's Paradise Point," Aimee told him.

The End

Acknowledgment

A special thanks to my friend and beta reader, Judy Hentges. I cannot express enough thanks to Moira King, a professional writer and advisor, and Monica King for being totally awesome human beings.

About the Author

Cynthia A. King is a debut author, and this is her first novel. She is retired from her professional life and an extensive career of volunteerism to focus on writing. She lives in upstate NY with an empty nest of two adult daughters. One husband, a dog and one cat remain behind.

www.ingramcontent.com/pod-product-compliance
Lightning Source LLC
Chambersburg PA
CBHW070636310726
48982CB00001B/295
9798893240696